# Assassin's War

A Novel

by

Gregg Vann

ISBN: 1482343800
ISBN-13: 978-1482343809

Silver Rocket Press

Author Website: Greggvann.com

For my father,

James Benjamin Vann

# CONTENTS

We never stray far from the beast.

No matter how elaborate the trappings of our technology—the improbable enlightenment we claim to possess—man is no better than even the most feral of creatures. And often, we are far, far worse.

Where the beast kills out of necessity, or a primal compunction to do so, we kill for power...for greed...sport and pleasure. Treating life as a mere commodity, a pliable impediment to be removed as needed.

Just another avenue to manifest our most base desires.

We view life as currency to be spent—as long as we can do so without invoking the wrath of someone stronger than ourselves. And in that statement lies the truth of it: the only real restraint placed on man and his ilk—the arguably intelligent species of the galaxy—is the fear of retribution.

Was it any wonder, then, that this day would eventually come? The ascendancy of another creature...one far more powerful. An animal whose views closely mirrored our own on the cruel, yet necessary dictates of life.

So why were we so surprised when *that* beast set out to destroy us all?

**From the collected writings of Brother Augustus Dyson.**
**Buddhist Master of Bodhi Prime**

# CHAPTER ONE

I grabbed the back of his head with one hand, using the other to drive the needleblade deep into his eye socket—plunging it far back into the brain. There was a slight bump in the handle as the blade expanded inside his skull, pushing spikes out from its hollow core and into the surrounding tissue. The response was immediate; the guard's body seized up taunt, then began to slowly collapse to the ground. I used my firm grip on his head to quietly lower the lifeless form to the dirt.

*One down, several hundred to go.*

I depressed a button at the base of the handle and the spikes retracted, allowing me to pull the blade out and slide it back into a sheath on my wrist. Then I grabbed the corpse by its clothing and dragged it behind a half-wall attached to the side of the remote sentry outpost.

I walked back around and stepped inside the squat structure, quickly finding the communications console and attaching an intelligent responder to it. The device would locate the guard's schedule and all recorded transmissions, then use that information to mimic his voice—reporting in as required. The device was also capable of communicating independently if the outpost was contacted unexpectedly—

extrapolating the necessary responses based on what it found in the normal com traffic between the outpost and the base's security command.

With this precaution in place, I walked back outside and toggled my infra-lens to scan the horizon. The eyepiece cut through the deep blackness of night, creating a faux vista that exposed more detail than even Nilot's bright daylight typically revealed. Panning down to the valley below, I was forced to admire the completeness of the security grid. Multi layered and robust, it was renowned for its ability to keep prisoners in, and would-be rescuers out. And in its twenty year history of housing the Udek Confederation's greatest enemies, this installation had been never been successfully breached.

*Until tonight*, I thought. *Tonight, that reputation falls. Tonight...we will both be free.*

I reactivated my darksuit and left the outpost behind, melding back into the night as I followed the craggy, rock trail that stretched further up the side of the mountain. I moved quickly yet silently, just in case there were audio monitors. My suit kept me invisible to video scanners, but it was up to me to mask my sound trail. And I did so with practiced moves—shaped by years of operational experience. In an occupation where the slightest sound could alert your enemy and cost you your life, you learned to exist in a nether-state—there, but *not* there. You mastered silent movement.

Or you died.

I peered out over the rock ledge as I moved, watching through the hazy atmosphere as the lights dotting the plain below flickered in and out. Each one indicating a military structure that ranged in size from simple guard posts, like the one I'd just left, to heavily fortified bunkers, manned by dozens of highly trained commandos. All part of a lethal web designed to repel large assaults from without...or quell violent uprisings from within. But they hadn't anticipated my actions—a clandestine infiltration by one man—at least, I hoped they hadn't.

The most prominent feature across the landscape below was a pair of bright red lines, running adjacent to one another through the center of the plain. They marked the main road leading to the prison's entrance; a direct and infamous route to death or permanent disappearance. But I had another access point in mind that would help me avoid either of those fates; a much more circuitous route that *should* allow me to get inside undetected.

For the next half hour, I moved briskly up the trail, jogging parallel to the red lines of death far below. I watched carefully as I got closer to the prison proper. At first, I could only make out buildings and large vehicles, but eventually, I got close enough to see individual people as they moved about on their assigned duties. I slowed down accordingly to better mask my own movements.

The well-worn path finally ended at a wooden barrier—a crossbar barricade with a glaring, fluorescent warning sign attached. On the other side of it, I saw that the trail was gone, leaving only a small ledge where the path used to be. From my research for this mission, I knew that the footpath had broken off and collapsed into the canyon, long ago. The remaining ledge was a mere six inches wide, just enough for a passable, if perilous footing.

I stepped behind the garish barricade and placed my back against the rock wall—my feet side-to-side—then began inching my way forward to get around a jagged outcropping. As I came around the corner—emerging on the other side of the mountain—I saw the end of the ledge just ahead. From this tiny perch, I didn't need to lean out to see the prison below; it was so close now that light spilling out from the buildings merged with pivoting searchlights to cast an eerie glow...one that threatened my concealment.

I increased the magnification on my lenses and watched as the armed patrols moved through the compound below me—following the usual pattern, just as expected. The crisscrossing patrol routes were stringent and unchanging—designed for maximum efficiency—but their regularity was an unusual weakness in an otherwise impressive display of security. One of the very few I found to exploit.

Pushing away from the wall slightly, I pulled a self-boring eyebolt from my backpack and pressed it into the rock face directly above my head. Four tiny legs popped out of the cylinder to steady it, then the round, center insert began to rotate, effortlessly boring into the rock.

As the bolt set about its work, I removed my rifle from the vertical sling next to my backpack and zoomed in on the force field surrounding the prison below. I measured out the exact trajectory I would need to land on the correct roof, and then estimated the smallest aperture required to breach the shield with minimal disruption. Timing would be critical. The hole had to last long enough for me to glide through without touching the edges, but not so long as to set off the intrusion alarms.

It was *not* an easy thing to do.

My lenses calculated and displayed an optimized glide path, and then I lined up my shot accordingly. I leaned back against the rock to steady myself and then slowly pulled the trigger, watching through the scope as the tiny disrupt-projectile flew toward its target. The result was anticlimactic, but satisfying; a small hole appeared in the shield and then began to incrementally grow larger. If you weren't looking for it, it would never become apparent. But I was watching the breach unfold in real time, and saw the creeping hole produce subtle changes in the color and shade of the force field. The view through the gap was darker and more detailed than the surrounding area.

I placed a lockdart on the tip of the rifle, and then tied it to a spool of microfilament on my belt. Once again I raised the gun to fire, but this time had to make allowances for the unique wind conditions on both sides of the force field. Outside, the wind was from the west and sporadic. But inside the compound, the environmental controls pushed a steady stream of air in the opposite direction. My lenses read all of these variables and provided a continuously updated line of fire through the scope. The path changed rapidly as I watched, displayed as a curved white line that shifted up or down—and side to side—as the conditions changed.

I concentrated closely on the flow of information and fired.

I held my breath as the black carbon dart flew through the air—sailing through the newly opened hole in the shield. I finally exhaled when the dart hit home and the scope's telemetry confirmed its position. It had ended up perfectly placed in an upright stanchion, with just the right amount of elevation for my descent.

Reaching back over my shoulder, I dropped the rifle into its sling—with luck, I wouldn't need it anymore—then I attached the microfilament to the eyebolt, now firmly lodged in the rock overhead. I gave it a tug to test the connection, then pulled a glide tube out of my backpack and locked my gloves together around it—snapping it over the microfilament via a tiny slit that ran down its length.

*Now I wait,* I thought.

Watching the guards make their rounds below actually comforted me. As long as they did what they were expected to do, I could make this happen. But any variation at all in their routine would disrupt my timing, and rob me of this one chance to infiltrate the base.

*Keep going...that's it...two more meters...*

I leapt.

A trio of guards walked around the rear corner of the building, starting the clock on a precise series of events that I'd planned for meticulously. Flying down the line, the crisp night air and adrenaline worked together to heighten my senses; I used that clarity to visibly scan the structures on this side of the prison complex. *One person at one window...* That's all it would take to end this mission right now. But it didn't happen. I compressed my gloves and the binders activated, slowing my drop to a gentle slide. I landed on the roof with barely a bump.

In one motion, I hit the release on the dart and pulled it from the pillar—the microfilament broke down and dissipated into the wind. No trace remaining. Looking back, I was gratified to see the small window I'd sailed through closing up tightly behind me, erasing all evidence of my passage.

I'd done it. I'd broken into one of the most heavily protected sites in the entire galaxy.

Now all I had to do was complete my mission.

And get back out again.

# CHAPTER TWO

By the time the patrol had rounded the building for a third time, I'd worked my way down from the roof and to the bottom floor—using darkened window sills and exterior piping as climbing structures. I lightly dropped the last few feet to the ground, then quickly bypassed the security lock—entering the building before the patrol made their way back around front. The door opened into a short, brightly lit hallway, dead-ending at a desk with a single, surprised occupant.

"Who the hell are yo—?"

His question was cut short by the thrown blade slicing through his larynx.

The guard frantically grabbed at the knife—splattering blood across the desk and nearby walls as he twisted his body madly. Somehow, he managed to grasp the small dagger with his blood-drenched fingers and yanked it out of his neck. He looked down at the blade in disbelief, and then back over at me before collapsing. His body bounced off the desk and then fell to the floor. I ran over and retrieved my knife—still clenched in his hand—then searched the security station thoroughly until I found the release switch. I triggered it and a large door behind the desk slid aside, disappearing into the wall.

Through the opening, I saw a large cellblock with a central, common area that lay open all the way up to the roof. Confinement cells lined the outside walls of each of the five levels, all linked together by metal stairs and walkways. The Nilot prison complex was huge, and there were hundreds of prisoners in this one block alone, but I was only concerned with one of them.

*Dasi.*

*My wife.*

I knew exactly where she was being held and started walking briskly—then jogging—until finally, I broke into a run. I bolted up the first set of stairs that led to the second floor. But even in my haste, I made sure my footfalls remained silent—just as I had been trained to do. I'd chosen the middle of the night for many reasons, striking when everyone was asleep was chief among them.

I hit the top of the steps and started reading cell numbers. 226...227...228.

*Here.*

Manipulating the same cypherpick I'd used to get into the building, I bypassed the simple lock and flung the door open. Knife in hand, I darted inside. A disheveled figure that had been hidden under the covers sat up in bed.

"Who are you?" he croaked.

"Shhhh. Where is she? Where is Dasi?"

He stood up with difficulty and gave me a strange look; I did a quick threat assessment and found none. He was a badly injured Blenej Red—his two lower arms amputated roughly at the elbows. It was obvious to me that he'd been beaten and tortured.

"An Udek woman," I whispered harshly. "This woman." I showed him the holo-image that I always carried with me.

"Who are you?" he asked again. The effort to speak caused him to start coughing loudly.

"Quiet!" I admonished him. "I'm her husband."

His eyes widened and some of the color bled from his face. "You are too late, Udek. They killed her. They killed her yesterday in the middle of this block."

*No! It can't be!*

"You may be one of *them*, but I pity you, Udek. No one should have to endure what they did to her." He shook his head slowly and his face grew sympathetic. "They terrified and humiliated her in front of the entire block—yelling at her—kicking and punching her in the stomach. She cried the whole time, calling for someone named Tien. They laughed at her...spit on her...told her *he* was the reason she was being put to death."

He sat back down on the bed and looked up at me compassionately; I stood there dumbfounded, frozen in disbelief.

"They recorded it all," he continued. "They said it was a lesson for all enemies of the Udek. And they made us watch...the entire block. They made us all... I am a soldier, Udek. I have seen death—caused it myself on many occasions—so believe me when I tell you that this was as depraved and sadistic as anything I've ever seen...even in war. In the end, the guards stripped her naked, taking turns cutting long strips of flesh off her body while she wailed."

The prisoner took a breath and fought the impulse to cough again. He looked down at the floor of the dingy cell and placed his head in his two remaining hands. "She screamed...cried for help...pleading for someone to save her life. She begged for Tien to come. She just knew he would. She really *believed* that. But this is Nilot; she had to know it was impossible. When the pain became overwhelming and she couldn't remain conscious any longer for their amusement, they garroted her."

He looked up to meet my eyes again. "The guards left her

body in view for hours before finally dragging her away by the hair."

*No. It can't be. She can't be...*

I couldn't breathe.

The room closed in on me—an oppressive weight, crushing in from every side, getting heavier and heavier. This cell was so small, and dark...so very, very dark.

My only thought was to leave—to get out of there. To get away from...*this*. I started backing up, through the door and out of the cell. If I wasn't here...if I didn't know...then it wouldn't be true.

*It couldn't be true.*

"Stop! Don't move!"

I froze, listening to the sound of dozens of footsteps clanking up the stairways. I slowly turned my head from left to right and saw guards coming at me from both sides of the walkway, leveling their guns at me. More were crossing the common area below and heading toward the stairs to join them. In all, there had to be twenty guards in the cellblock now. And only one of me.

But *I* would be enough.

Especially now.

My two middle fingers closed slowly onto my palm. The guards weren't close enough yet to see the movement, or if they were, they didn't recognize the significance of it. I depressed the control pad at the base of my glove three times—releasing a concussion-smoke capsule from my belt. When it hit the platform at my feet, a wall of sound and light exploded, followed by the rapid expulsion of dark smoke.

My earpieces—designed to augment my hearing as well as for communication—automatically shut out the explosion. And my lenses compensated for the blinding flash. The guards closest to me weren't so well equipped and fell down, clutching helplessly at their eyes and ears. Those further away lost sight of me as a black cloud expanded out from the capsule.

I spun around and grabbed the railing, using it to leap over the edge and swing down to the first floor. I tucked myself into a rolling ball as I hit the ground—to minimize the impact of the fall. But it still hurt. As I jumped up to my feet, I pulled my rifle out of its sling and shot the two guards closest to me. Ducking behind a large service cart used to feed the inmates, I pulled two more smoke capsules from my belt and threw them out into the center of the room. The combination of all three devices quickly reduced the visibility to zero in the entire block. The inmates were waking now, and the sound of their voices mixed with the confused and conflicting orders from the guards.

"Everyone down on the first floor," one of the guards yelled out.

"No," another barked. "Get up higher and try to spot him."

With my lenses, I could read the heat signatures from everyone in the building. I calmly...methodically...began shooting those that weren't in cells.

*They killed her!* My mind screamed. *The animals killed her!*

But my hands remained steady. The rifle growing hot as I fired; up, down, left and right. Stationary, running...even injured and crawling. I shot them all. Always the same, always the head; there would be no survivors. They all died in darkness, never knowing where the shots came from.

Never seeing the face of the man who killed them.

When I was certain that every heat signature was cooling, I moved to the door and out of the block—back into the hallway where I'd knifed the desk guard. I wasn't naïve; I knew that the entire base would be on alert—that I probably wouldn't get out of here alive—but I didn't plan on leaving now anyway. I intended to visit the warden first and learn why Dasi was murdered.

I was going to find out who was responsible. And then I was going to kill them.

# CHAPTER THREE

I pushed the door open a crack and threw out two flash grenades timed to explode five seconds apart. After the second telltale pop, I darted outside and started scaling the wall of the building, making my way back up to the roof. I no longer needed to remain silent and climbed quickly, glancing back only long enough to see several disoriented guards struggle to their feet. A loud klaxon pierced the night air, and I saw the bright lights of approaching vehicles—speeding in from other parts of the base.

After pulling myself over a disused drainage gutter that framed the top of the building, I vaulted onto the roof, drawing my rifle and ducking behind a large electrical box. I leaned out to check the mostly open space and saw that it was still deserted...for now anyway. I knew that I only had a few precious minutes to act, so I quickly accessed the stolen prison schematics stored in my lens array to locate the warden's office. Normally, he wouldn't be there at this time of night, but the building also doubled as the prison's action station; he should be headed there now to lead the search for me. The office was only a short distance from this cellblock, but I needed to make them think I was headed in the opposite direction if I was going to have any chance of getting there alive.

I peeked out over the edge to see three personnel carriers stop in front of the building. Udek commandos began to pour out of them as I watched—elite troops that were battle-hardened and very capable. They fanned out to surround the cellblock, and I saw several of them begin to scan the rooftops with helmet lenses and rifle-mounted scopes.

I had only seconds to devise a plan.

I aimed the rifle at a large patch of open air, just to the side of a distant building, and fired two disrupt shells—spacing the shots three meters apart. As they ate away at the shield, they merged to form a large hole in the force field. Other alarms then began to sound, eclipsing the roar of the original klaxon.

Many of the commandos started to move toward the breach, believing I was trying to escape through it. It was an easy assumption, and the logical thing for me to do, but I wasn't concerned with logic now; I was motivated by revenge.

I ran across the roof and stabbed a lockdart into the same upright stanchion I'd used to land on the building. Then I put another one on the rifle, attached the microfilament to it, and fired at the ledge of the building across from me. I clamped down on the wire and swung over the edge.

The trip was short and fast, and I hit the side of the structure hard, compressing my legs to reduce the shock. I reached up and pulled myself onto the roof, then ran to the opposite edge and jumped over to the next building, landing roughly. As I worked my way to the center of the compound like this, the buildings got closer and closer together. And after several, much easier jumps, I checked my position to find I was already close to the target. I lodged a lockdart between two sturdy pipes, and then played out some microfilament from its housing and tied it to the dart. I tested the setup with a sharp tug, and then used it to lower myself back down to the ground.

Looking around, I saw that I'd dropped in close to an abandoned sentry post, evidence of how completely they'd bought my escape charade. I ducked into a darkened alley created by the close proximity of the buildings, and then ran toward my destination—still maybe fifty meters away. My darksuit rendered me almost invisible in the shadows, and I kept to them for the final stretch.

Before emerging from the alley, I peeked around the corner—spotting the building that housed the warden's office. Two guards were posted outside it, but they were too distracted to notice me. I could hear the pair excitedly discussing the current situation, rather than scanning the area for hostile forces, as they should have been.

*This prison's reputation has made them complacent,* I thought.

I knew I needed to drop them both before they had a chance to sound an alarm; it was imperative that the commandos didn't know I was in this part of the compound. I spun the ammo dial on the side of the rifle to Silent Projectile, then focused in on their movements and mannerisms—their personal ticks and gestures.

Timing would be critical.

The guards were spaced approximately a meter apart; one constantly shifted his weight from foot to foot, while the other had a habit of turning sideways to face his companion as he spoke. I moved the rifle barrel from guard to guard and slowed my breathing. Watching, waiting...there. One turned in to speak as the other shifted his weight in the same direction. I fired—pulling the trigger twice without pause—and both of the guards collapsed. Each hit by a single shot that sliced through their throats—silencing them, and severing their spines at the base of the skull.

They had no choice but to fall silently to the ground and die.

I sprinted out from cover and moved past the two bodies; there was no use trying to conceal them, their absence would be just as noticeable as their corpses, then I jumped up the three steps leading into the exterior foyer of the squat building. The door wasn't even locked—a further testament to their hubris. It opened with a gentle push, and I moved stealthily through the opening, finding myself in a short hall with two doors on either side. Set between the left pair of doors, I saw a stairwell descending to an underground level. The sign above the opening identified it as the Situation Room. I crossed the hall and began descending the stairs slowly, keeping off to one side and planting my feet gently.

Other than the small, glowing strips that marked each step, the staircase was dark. The only real source of illumination was light spilling in from the brightly lit room below. I heard three distinct voices rising up through the air.

"It has to be Tien! Who else could possibly do it?"

"But he was seen on Rilen less than two days ago...looking for her. He couldn't have gotten here so quickly."

"I'll say it again. Who else is capable? Or *this* motivated."

"Enough! Both of you," a third voice thundered, silencing the two men.

"Apologies, Warden Cullz."

"Yes. Apologies."

"It *is* Tien," Cullz continued, "of that I'm certain. What I can't fathom is how he found out we were holding her here in the first place. I should have told the general, no. I despise having anything to do with the Special Corp and their operatives."

"Yet here we are, Warden. Regardless, he won't get past my commandos, Special Corp or not."

I reached the bottom of the stairs and ducked down low to

peer around the corner. There were only three people in the small room, the warden, and two men on either side of him—their insignia identifying them as a guard supervisor and commando captain. Without hesitation, I leaned out and shot them both through the chest.

Before their bodies hit the ground, I fired again, striking the astonished warden in both knees. He feebly grabbed at what was left of his legs and rolled down onto on the floor.

I stepped out of cover and calmly walked over to him.

"Why?" I asked, ignoring his screams. My tone was level and detached. "Why did you kill her?"

"I didn't...it wasn't—" I cut off his denials by shooting him in the arm.

"*Why*?" I repeated.

"Wait! It wasn't m... General Queltz! It was General Queltz! He didn't tell me why...I swear! He just sent the order to have her killed. You have to believe me!"

"Was it also his idea to torture her first? Or did you decide that yourself?"

His eyes went wide in fear. "No! No! It was the guards! I had nothing to do with that! I swear to you!"

I shot him in the other arm at the elbow, rendering the last of his limbs useless. Then I pulled out the needleblade and he started sobbing. I leaned over and lifted his head up by the hair.

"Please don't...don't kill me...it's Queltz you want. It was him!" Tears were streaming down his face now, and I could smell that he'd lost control of his bowels.

"Don't worry, *Warden*. I'll deal with him soon enough."

I slit his throat, and then dropped his head down hard on the floor. Let him spend his last few moments in terror while his life bled away.

*Just as Dasi had.*

I heard a choked cough and looked down to find the

commando still alive. *I'd been careless!* He hit a communications device on his wrist and barely got out a whisper. "Situation Room...he's in the—"

I stomped his head down, but it was too late—they were coming. I quickly shortened the stock on my rifle to a close-combat configuration and ran back up the stairs. But as soon as I reached the top, I saw three commandos coming through the front door.

And they saw me.

I ducked back behind the wall and we exchanged fire. I managed to take two of them down quickly, but as I stepped out to shoot again, the third one got off a round, striking me in the leg. I returned fire, hitting him in the head twice—the second shot just barely piercing his armor. As he fell, glass shattered out of a large window above the front door and projectiles slammed into the wall next me, missing my chest by millimeters.

*Snipers.*

I awkwardly stumbled back into the stairwell for cover; there was no feeling in my right leg and I looked down and saw why. The commando had used an explosive round, and what remained after the impact was a tangled mass of flesh and exposed bone...barely holding me up. I was reaching down to spool off some microfilament to use as a tourniquet when a concussive round sailed past my head; it bounced off the wall behind me and detonated.

My optic and hearing apparatus did their best to compensate, but the explosion was too large and shorted out all of my electronics. I pulled the lenses off and yanked out the earplugs, throwing them all back down the stairs behind me. My vision was blurry and I could taste blood in my mouth. I looked back out into the hall just as the front door blew off its hinges, exploding into fragments that sailed through the smoky air.

Commandos came rushing in and I fired indiscriminately. My vision was useless, but I laid down a withering barrage of mixed munitions fire that certainly killed many of them. Then a sharp sting hit my left eye and my head flew back; I staggered forward into the open, taking multiple hits to the chest…so hard to breathe.

I kept firing until they hit the rifle itself and it blew apart in my hands…*with my hand*s. As I looked down with my remaining eye at the shredded gore that had once been my arms, a commando stepped forward and struck me in the head with the butt of his rifle.

And blackness overtook me.

"Stop!" I heard someone call out. "I want him alive!"

But I already knew that wasn't going to happen.

It was my final thought before I died.

# CHAPTER FOUR

The large ship thundered through the atmosphere, a conical trail dissipating in its wake as it leveled out for the approach to the research facility. Unlike most spacecraft that strove for elegant design and aesthetic perfection, this ship was all business.

The business of war.

Brother Dyson looked up at the vessel as it came into view and sighed. He'd told them not to come—that it was no use—but they didn't listen.

*Ha,* he reflected amusedly, *do they ever?*

Of all the races that contracted with the Bodhi to resurrect their dead, the Udek had always been the most problematic. They were remarkably ambivalent about the consciousness transfer process itself, the procedure in which a perfect clone was imbued with the mind of the deceased—complete with all of their memories up until the last cerebral mapping, but they detested the monk's religious dictates. Specifically, the one requiring that before anyone could be *reborn,* they had to cleanse their karma by undergoing a penance ritual. Without exception, all clients had to seek atonement for their prior sins.

Brother Dyson viewed the Udek protests a gross overreaction, born from their distrust of all religion. Besides, the actual person themselves didn't have to perform the cleansing ritual—the journey to make amends for misdeeds from their previous life. A cyborg monk was crafted to look like the deceased, and *that* construct went about dispensing restitution to the wronged. All while a new, perfect clone grew to full size back on Bodhi Prime.

The dead client's consciousness made the journey as well, installed inside a 'soul chamber' deep within the cyborg's chest cavity—the deceased's mind kept fully aware of what was going on so they could reflect on the harm they'd done. But they did not, *could not*, control the cybernetic monk. It was programmed by the Bodhi to accomplish its mission to *their* requirements, and they'd taken extreme measures to make sure their cybernetic creations couldn't be tampered with.

The Bodhi protected their secrets well.

When the penance tasks were complete, the consciousness was then transferred from the cyborg into the newly cloned body—the person ready to resume their normal lives as if they'd never died; the entire experience a small side-trip on their long journey through life.

Most clients were grateful for the extremely expensive service—penance requirements and all—but not the Udek. *Never the Udek.* Dyson suspected that it wasn't the actual atonement that angered them, as much as it was the Bodhi forcing them to do something against their will; they were always such a difficult race. And certainly, the old monk knew, not one to be trifled with.

Dyson watched as the big ship came to a rest on the commercial sized landing pad, just outside the main laboratory. As the desert sand kicked up by the landing cleared, he noticed the deep, black scorching and impact damage. It was obvious that the Udek had fought their way here through the Brenin lines; a desperate bid for his approval for some reckless plan of theirs.

*That desperation will make them even more dangerous,* he mused.

Colorful wisps of gas accompanied a loud popping sound as the airlock opened on the side of the ship; methane, and other more exotic compounds, escaped from the craft and drifted off into the oxygen-rich atmosphere of Bodhi Prime. The old monk watched as a ramp noisily extended from the airlock and down to the ground, digging into the runway slightly as it reached its full length.

Dyson braced himself as the Udek emerged—four in all—each fully armed and armored. And even though their faces were hidden, their mannerisms and brisk movements conveyed a militant purpose that left little doubt as to what nature of beings they were. Their fierce reputation was indeed warranted; the Udek were a severe and determined people.

As the group approached, one of the large creatures reached up to turn on his external communicator. "Brother Dyson, it is time. We need him. Now."

"As I told you when you first contacted me, General Queltz...as I've have told you *several* times since, it doesn't work like that."

The Udek closed the short distance between them and leaned over the much shorter man. To his credit, Dyson held his ground, even if he did lean back perceptibly.

"I will tell you one last time, *monk*, Tien is coming with us."

"It's just not possible, General. His clone isn't fully-grown yet, and his penance hasn't even begun. He is simply not ready."

There was a tinge of fear in the old monk's voice, but also the ring of truth. Queltz heard both.

"Then just give me the cyborg. Certainly *it's* active by

now."

"What? Impossible! We just began programming him. Tien is set to begin the cleansing ritual in a day or two. Come back in a month. I promise, everything will be ready then."

The Udek pulled his hand back to strike the monk, but then leveled his arm out in front of him instead, pointing at Dyson's face. "In another month, this war will be over you old fool! And this planet will be destroyed or subjugated, just like every other one the Brenin have attacked."

Dyson's back stiffened, and conviction colored his voice. "I would rather face that than betray my faith, General. One month...it's the best I can do."

Queltz lowered his voice, meeting the monk's defiant eyes with his own cold, black orbs. "*You* don't have a month."

He gestured behind himself to the damaged spacecraft. "The fleet that did that to my ship is eight days away from here—the Brenin are coming to Bodhi Prime much earlier than anticipated. I can leave with Tien, gather my forces and fight them. Or I can leave without him, and watch your planet burn from a safe distance. The choice is yours."

*Eight days.*

The old monk was stunned. Most projections had the Brenin heading in another direction altogether, but he could see that Queltz was telling the truth. Dyson looked at the general's face and weighed the possibilities. Would the Udek really allow Bodhi Prime to be destroyed? While it was true that they despised the Bodhi and their religious ways, surely they wouldn't rob themselves of the monk's services. They would lose access to the transference technology that guaranteed them immortality. Was this one man *that* important to them? As he watched the work crews start filing out of the damaged ship to make repairs, the old monk found his answer; the Udek had already risked their lives greatly just to get here. They were determined to get Tien, and they would abandon this planet to the Brenin if they didn't get their way.

Queltz *would* let Bodhi fall.

"Perhaps we should talk in my office," Dyson said tiredly.

"Perhaps we should, monk." Queltz turned to one of his subordinates. "Tell them to bring it."

The other Udek barked some orders into her com system and then nodded to Queltz. "It's on the way."

Dyson looked at them quizzically for a moment before the five set off together, walking silently toward a small collection of administrative offices sitting adjacent to the landing area. Even though Dyson kept an office here, most of the rooms in the complex were very simple—usually employed to prepare or debrief atonement monks, or occasionally to meet with off-worlders seeking the monk's services. Now they would host a negotiation that could determine the future of The Order of Buddha's Light itself...possibly deciding if there was even going to *be* a future.

*How will I get myself out of this one?* Dyson asked himself as they walked.

*How will I save us all?*

# CHAPTER FIVE

Queltz and his aide—a colonel if Dyson read the insignia properly—joined the monk in his office while the other two Udek waited in the hall, guarding the mysterious cargo container delivered from the Udek ship. Brother Dyson dropped into a thickly padded chair, set behind a large, wooden desk, and exhaled heavily. He gestured to some empty chairs. "Please, have a seat."

The Udek remained standing. The monk wasn't the least bit surprised.

This whole situation was beginning to remind him of the first time he'd dealt with the Udek, when they, like the other races of the galaxy, initially found out about the monk's discovery of the transference process. The Bodhi developed the method as a way to speed enlightenment; the belief being that if you could remember your sins from your past life, you wouldn't repeat them in the next. But even more importantly, going into your next life with your present "mind" allowed you to take specific steps to cleanse your karma for each *individual* offense committed against the fabric of life. With the transference process perfected, the aged monks began planting their own consciousnesses into perfect clones just before they died—crossing a technological bridge back to their youth with their accumulated wisdom intact. It was a direct path to Nirvana.

Or so the monks believed.

But the other races saw it as an avenue for immortality—the same mind, but in a new, younger cloned body. And many of them were bent on seizing the process for themselves, a few violently so. Brother Dyson had seen the danger and hastily negotiated non-interference treaties, using the technology itself as a bargaining chip. He agreed to provide the services to all who could afford it, and in doing so, secured a deterrent against the more violent species, the Udek in particular. None of the races would allow others to interfere with the Bodhi—securing the procedure for all who wanted it. Not even the Udek could stand up to *everyone*.

Now Dyson was bargaining again, under a new threat, but this time the danger was even more certain. The Brenin made the Udek look like schoolyard bullies by comparison, especially as they stood in front of him now...staring impatiently like children.

"What is so important about this one man, General?" Dyson asked.

"I don't expect you to understand, monk, but Tien is one of a kind. Even within our elite fighting units, he is renowned for his ability to infiltrate and eliminate targets—to improvise his way through or around any situation. He is as lethal a creature as has ever walked *any* planet—even managing to break into one of our most highly secure facilities undetected. And when he *was* finally discovered, he killed over two dozen heavily armed commandos, in addition to the guards he dispatched along the way. He is a relentless killing machine, monk, and he doesn't quit...ever. Did you see what was left of his body when we shipped it here?"

Dyson made a disgusted face. "I did. All of the pieces you'd bothered to gather up anyway. We had to sift through them to find the monitor you'd implanted. I'd never seen one of those devices before."

"All of our Special Corp operatives have them; they constantly scan and record their brain patterns. If we're able to retrieve the body after an agent dies on a mission, we can bring them back with their memories intact—right up until the moment of death; it's insurance against losing any valuable intelligence. But I admit, I was worried that you wouldn't be able to locate it in what remained after the firefight." Queltz leaned forward and placed both hands flat on the desk, drawing Dyson's full attention. "Tien wasn't caught in an explosion, monk, he was blown apart, piece-by-piece with weapons fire. They only managed to stop him by shooting his hands off—one of his legs had already been destroyed. If he'd had any limbs left, they'd probably still be trying to kill him. He doesn't know *how* to quit, monk. He is the most unrelenting, brutal killer we have ever trained."

Queltz seemed very proud of his assassin's remorseless ability to take life, but that made him the worst of the worst as far as Dyson was concerned. "How exactly does that help us *now*?" he asked.

"Because we have a plan to insert him into the Brenin fleet; to have him gather vital intelligence and strike at their leadership. This one man can turn the tide of this war, monk, before it's too late."

Dyson sat up straight. "How in Buddha's name will you get him into the fleet undiscovered? What reports I've seen makes it appear impossible to get anywhere near them without being decimated."

Queltz gestured to the hall. "With a special piece of cargo we've brought along."

"I don't understand, General."

"Bring me Tien and you will."

The aged monk gave the general a confused look.

"Tien," Queltz repeated. "Now."

Dyson shrugged. "Very well."

He hit the communications panel on the desk and called the laboratory.

"This is Brother Dyson. Have Kiro Tien and his programmer sent to my office immediately."

*"Of course, Brother. Right away."*

"Your people have discipline," Queltz said. "At least there's that."

"My people believe in our work, General. *That* is their motivation."

The general and his aide shared a dismissive glance.

"Your devotion to alien and outmoded concepts of morality is most amusing, monk. And if your belief is that strong, then why must you charge so much for the process? Your redemption is *costly*, human."

"We have expenses. The penance process—"

"That process is ridiculous," Queltz interrupted. "With luck, this war will free my people from you and your *faith."*

"Without repentance, General, there can be no rebirth."

"We shall see, monk. We shall see... This war is bringing change across the galaxy. The Bodhi may find themselves on the other side of dependency very soon, if not today, even."

The two glared at one another as the door opened and Kiro Tien entered with his assigned programmer, Brother Kiva. Dyson bade them both to sit and made introductions.

"...and this is General Queltz."

"Queltz?" Tien asked, suddenly alert.

"Yes," the general confirmed. "I'm the one who sent you here to be *reborn* after that disastrous rescue attempt of yours on Nilot. Believe me, if I didn't need you, you would still be dead."

"Of course," Tien replied calmly. "And was it also you who

ordered my wife's abduction?"

"It was, spy. You Special Corp assassins think you are above command decisions. You think you can operate with impunity. You cannot. After you refused your mission on Gil and disappeared, I had to take other measures to control you."

"My *mission*, as you call it, was to kill the child of some bureaucrat's political rival. I refused."

"Silence! You will not discuss our internal matters in front of outsiders. You don't get to pick and choose what orders you will accept, spy. Regardless, it's far too late for you to develop a conscience now. I've seen your files and I *know* the things you've done. I can't imagine how long a list this cursed monk came up with to include all of *your* sins. But then again, so much of it is classified; I doubt even he knows how many atrocities you've committed." Queltz shook his head before continuing, struggling to control his anger. "But don't worry, spy, this time your new found morality shouldn't give you any qualms; I'm ordering you on an important war mission that even *you* can approve of."

Tien ignored the general's diatribe and continued to stare at his face. "One last question, *Queltz*. Are you the one that ordered my wife's execution?"

"Yes, you impudent... We took her as leverage when you went renegade. And when you refused to surrender, she became a lesson to the other spies: follow orders, or *your* families will suffer the same fate."

"I see," Tien replied. He turned to his programmer. "Kiva, how much current goes through this cyborg construct?"

"I...I don't know exactly."

"Brother Dyson, surely you have some idea."

"Well...yes," the monk said, surprised. "But I don't understand your need to know."

"Humor me, please."

"Around 500 mA, more or less."

"Thank you, Brother Dyson."

Tien raised his right hand and stuck two fingers in his mouth, biting down hard. Blood splattered onto Kiva's face, and the young monk jumped up and away, staggering backward against the wall.

Everyone in the room stared in shocked silence as Tien used his teeth to rake the skin off the fingers, exposing the metal framework underneath. Then he stood up, spitting out the faux flesh and twisting some of the wiring from the two fingers together.

"Queltz stepped forward to confront him. "What the hell are you doing?"

Tien responded by leaping on the general and driving the two fingers into the back of his neck, just between the armored collar and helmet. Queltz started shuddering uncontrollably and his thrashing almost threw Tien off, but the spy held on tightly, continuing to pump current into the general.

The colonel came to her senses and leveled her pistol at Tien, just as the two soldiers in the hall came rushing in—drawn by the commotion. Shots rang out and Tien flinched, but held on tightly; his sturdy cyborg body withstanding more punishment than any organic life form ever could. But the Udek kept firing, and eventually, even its reinforced skeleton succumbed to the impacts. Tien fell away from Queltz and they both collapsed.

The Udek stopped firing and Dyson ran over to check the two. Queltz was dead; Tien had electrocuted him using the general's spine as a conduit. Dyson knew that his neural network would be fried as well. There would be no rebirth for *this* Queltz. If there was an earlier copy of his mind on file, the Udek may want him revived, but after what Dyson heard about the murder of Tien's wife, the monk was in no hurry to investigate. Tien was miraculously still alive, but the cyborg body was damaged beyond repair.

"What the hell are we going to do now?" the colonel barked.

Tien reached up and grabbed Dyson's robe, pulling him down; the monk's ear coming to rest just inches from the dying assassin's lips.

"I know why they came here, monk, what they wanted from me. I will save your planet. I will stop the Brenin. Bring me back...and I will win this war. One condition. One condition only..."

"But how?" Dyson asked, exasperated. "There is no time to build another cyborg body, and your clone isn't ready!"

"You will find a way, monk...you must."

Dyson mind raced, but there was no solution. No possible way to resurrect him before the Brenin arrived. Tien jerked his collar again.

"My condition, monk."

"Yes? What is it, Tien?"

"I want my wife back." Tien coughed hard, and a grey fluid bubbled up from his throat to stain his lips. "I know the prison has the genetic and neural information you need...bring her back."

"I can't possibly get that—"

"She can!" Tien weakly pointed at Queltz's aide with his other hand. "Do it...or we all perish. And then I'll join Dasi again anyway...in death."

Tien coughed once more, splattering the sticky, grey substance across his chin. Then he stopped moving altogether and his hand fell away from Dyson's collar.

The old monk rose from the floor and looked at the programmer. "Bother Kiva, have him taken to the lab and extract the soul chamber while I figure out what to do next."

"I'm sorry, Brother Dyson, there was no time to activate the Shepherd Personality, we couldn't control—"

"It's not your fault, Brother Kiva. Now do as I say."

The other monk nodded and went over to the desk to call for help.

"Colonel...?"

"Eraz."

"Can you do what he says, Colonel Eraz?"

"Tien was right; they keep the prisoner's complete brain patterns on record, just in case they die during interrogation and require further...questioning. The prison should also have the necessary medical records."

"So we *can* get his cooperation. But how can we get him into a body...so he can complete the mission before the Brenin fleet arrives?"

"Dyson...I don't pretend to know how you monks bring people back to life, or how you create the cyborgs that look *just* like them, but I have something to show you. Come with me."

Eraz stepped over Queltz's body and walked out into the hall. Dyson and the two soldiers followed her out of the office.

The container from the Udek ship—a silver ovoid nearly three meters long—floated motionlessly up against the wall. Eraz stepped up to it and keyed in a security code. The top portion slid aside and Brother Dyson walked over to look inside.

His jaw dropped.

"What the...what *is* that?"

"This," she replied, "is what the Brenin *look* like."

# CHAPTER SIX

*Why is everything so blurry?*

*Wait...not blurry... It's not out of focus; it's multiplied. There are four distinct images of everything I see—slightly offset, and each a different color—but four of everything...all in the same view.*

*Why are there four?*

"Tien? How do you feel?" The voice was familiar, but not overly so.

*Where am I? And what's wrong with my eyes?*

"Who are you?" I asked the non-distinct apparition. "Why can't I see?"

"I'm Brother Dyson. Do you remember me? Do you remember who *you* are?"

"Kiro Tien, Udek Special Corp. I remember everything, monk. So you did it. You managed to transfer me into another body after all. "

"Not exactly."

I squinted hard, trying to clear my vision...*what the hell?* I felt a second pair of eyelids close, right after the first slid shut.

"Open your eyes slowly, Tien. Don't squint or try to focus. Relax your eyes and let them work naturally."

I did as he said, and the colors and multiple images coalesced into a single vision. It was the most defined view of the world imaginable, crisp and clear beyond description. Looking to my left, I saw Dyson shutting down some machinery. I was in the lab, seated upright in an operating chair, wearing a dark blue uniform. I reached up to feel my eyes and stopped abruptly when I saw my hand; it was a monochrome, black and white...and partially translucent. It was thin but not fragile, and had six fingers.

*Udek had five.*

"What have you done to me, monk?" I demanded.

"What you asked, Tien. And I will keep our bargain. Will you?"

"*What* did you do?"

"What was necessary, but I fear I may have corrupted my own karma irreparably. You are in a Brenin body; Queltz killed the creature on his way here and put the body in stasis. We installed the soul chamber inside it, and did our level-best to integrate everything properly, but the physiology is so strange; I fear what the end result may be."

"You put me in a Brenin corpse!"

"Only temporarily. We can transfer you to your clone when you return. If you return."

*My vision...the hand...it all made sense now.*

"My senses are in revolt, monk. This *air* tastes bizarre."

I shifted forward in the chair and stood up awkwardly. I wasn't as tall as I'd been, yet still towered over the monk. I took a few steps forward and marveled at the mechanism of my legs. The gait was long and fast.

Dyson noticed my surprise. "It's called digitigrade. Very common in some Earth species of animals, but I've never seen it in a sentient race. Until now."

I stumbled to the side and was forced to correct myself. "It will take some getting used to."

"You have until tomorrow. Colonel Eraz is leaving then. And you are going with her."

"Where is she?" I asked.

"Just outside the door. I thought we should talk first, especially after what happened between you and Queltz."

"Talk about what?"

"About *our* arrangement, Tien. They explained to me what you are—what you are capable of. I want you to save Bodhi Prime. I don't care about the Udek plans, and I suspect you don't either, but if you can sabotage the Brenin fleet and give the Udek a chance defeat them, I promise to restore you and your wife. Eraz is having her information sent to me now, and we will begin growing her clone as soon as it arrives."

"And why are we having this conversation in private, monk?"

"Because I wanted to personally promise you this: no matter what the Udek want done with you two after this is all over, I will see that you are set free. And also make sure you have a ship and money enough to live out your lives somewhere away from these animals."

"These *animals* are my people," I replied testily. "And if you insist on judging us with your misguided sense of morality, you should know that I am far from innocent myself. In fact, even among the amoral Udek, my actions are often viewed as *immoral*. You don't know anything about me, monk."

"Oh, I do know about you, Tien. More than you think. Possibly even more than you know about yourself. I have counseled many over the years, seen acts of depravity that make yours seem tame in comparison. I will grant you this, though, I've never before met such a proficient killer."

"Killing is what I do best, monk. I've never met my equal if he exists. But don't pretend to understand my mind, it is beyond you."

"Really?" Dyson replied. "Tell me, Tien, why didn't you kill that child when they ordered you to? You've never abandoned a mission before...so why now? You've set explosive traps in public places that killed hundreds—innocents as well as your intended targets. You even blew up an entire starship full of people once to kill a single passenger onboard."

*How did he know about that?*

"And I *know* that you've expressly murdered children before," he continued. "That's probably why they chose you for this mission in the first place. Why was this child different? What was so special about him? Of all of the thousands of lives you've taken over the years, what was so exceptional about *this* one boy?"

"Nothing. As you say, I've killed children before."

"Ah...so you see my point, then. If there was nothing unique about the target, then maybe the difference was with *you*. You've changed, Tien, whether you realize it or not. And I believe you are on the cusp of redemption."

"Ha! Oh, that's very entertaining, monk, but save your baseless suppositions for someone else. Spend those efforts on someone you at least have a *chance* of convincing. They are wasted on me."

"Are they? You like to think of yourself as a remorseless killer, Tien, but if you are so devoid of all emotion—have no empathy whatsoever—then why entertain our bargain at all? You are in *that* body, prepared to undergo a mission we both know will probably end in your death, all for the love of one person...Dasi. And yes, Tien, make no mistake, it is *love* that drives you."

*Enough!*

"Silence, monk!" I snapped. "Other than bringing her back to me, Dasi is not your concern. Drop this ridiculous attempt to analyze me now before I show you just how *remorseless* I can be. Now... What about our agreement?"

The old monk shrugged, conceding the argument, but not his sentiments. "Believe as you will, Tien, but I know I'm right. And I will keep our bargain: freedom for you and Dasi, regardless of what the Udek want. You and I both know they will never let you be."

The blasted monk had a point. They wouldn't just let a member of the Special Corp go free. Hell, they'd imprisoned Dasi just to control me. This Brother Dyson seemed to know a great deal about how the Udek Confederation operated, and I was beginning to think I may have underestimated him entirely.

"How do I know I can trust you, monk?"

"Because the fate of my world is in your hands. I should think that would be enough."

"For now, maybe. And afterward, assuming I can even do this, how do I know you will keep your word?"

"You will have to trust me, Tien. I have no other assurances."

*Trust?*

Was he serious?

But what other choice did I really have? Especially in *this* body. Dyson controlled my clone, and the means to transfer me into it; I was completely at his mercy to regain my own body. And mercy was an unfamiliar concept with which I'd had little experience. But there was a much less complicated truth as well: Dyson and I needed each other, and we both had too much to lose if we failed to cooperate.

"We have an arrangement, monk, with one further condition; regardless what happens to me, even if I'm killed in this attempt, you will revive Dasi and set her free."

"Agreed, Tien. But I'd never hand her back over to the Udek regardless. I heard how she died in that prison."

I searched his face for any signs of deception, just as I'd been trained to do. And with the Brenin's superior vision, I was able to be even more accurate than usual. He exhibited no nervous behavior—his pupils were fixed and steady. Even the small thump from the carotid arteries in his neck remained placid. He was telling the truth.

"Very well, monk. Call in Eraz; I need to find out what she knows."

I watched as he moved to the door, marveling at the detail of it all. I could hear a slight scraping sound with each step as his sandals lifted from the floor. And when they met the ground again, it reverberated like a drum beat. I could even hear the air displaced by the footfalls, and determined that Dyson favored his right leg. My hearing was as equally enhanced as my vision, and I felt swallowed up by the amount of stimuli flooding in from every direction. I noted a faint hiss as the door slid open.

"It's about time, monk," Eraz said, storming angrily into the room. She was followed closely by the two soldiers, both of whom leveled their guns at me as soon as they cleared the doorway.

"Just look at it," one of them remarked.

"Shut up, and watch it closely," Eraz commanded. Then she turned her attention to me. "Is that really you in there, Tien?"

"It is, Colonel. Tell your men to lower their weapons and leave if you expect any cooperation from me."

Anger flashed across her face, followed quickly by a look of resignation. She nodded to the soldiers, and they reluctantly withdrew back into the hallway.

"Happy now, spy?"

"No. What was your plan, Eraz? What did Queltz have up his sleeve to deal with the Brenin?"

She started to speak, but then paused to stare at me. "I can't believe you are in that body. This is so...bizarre. And how can I understand you? The movements of your mouth don't match your words."

Dyson spoke up. "He's speaking Brenin. The soul chamber bridges his words through to the Brenin brain, where it's translated automatically into their language. He should be able to communicate with them flawlessly. I have synched the chamber's communications stream to this console, and it's broadcasting his *actual* speech. Without it, it would all be gibberish to us."

"What was Queltz's plan, Colonel?" I asked again, but more brusquely this time.

She took a few steps toward me before speaking, her eyes assessing me in fascination. "He didn't have one, actually."

*"What?"*

"It's true. After you infiltrated Nilot, he became convinced that you could get through the Brenin defenses and make your way onboard one of their ships. He didn't know exactly how you'd do it, but he knew you'd find a way."

"And once I got onboard, then what?"

Eraz became more animated. "The Brenin fleet is comprised of a mixture of cultural and military groups called clans. From what we've been able to uncover, it seems that they are naturally wary of one another. In fact, our intelligence points to large schisms throughout the Brenin ranks. It's a wonder they can work together at all."

"Yes. I know all this. I've seen those same reports."

"Of course... Queltz wanted you to assassinate the leader of this particular armada and implicate another Brenin faction in the murder. If we can place the blame on one of the other clans, we can take advantage of the chaos and retribution that follows." She cleared her throat noisily. "It would also be *very* helpful if you could find a way through that damnable shield they use to protect their fleets—it would be nice to level the playing field for a change."

"Is that all?" I scoffed.

But I knew that she was right...about everything. Not that it made what she was asking any easier. The Udek hadn't been very successful meeting the Brenin head-on in battle; that much was certain. For every one ship of theirs we managed to destroy, we lost ten of ours. If there *was* a way to make them fight each other, it would be an excellent start at turning this war around. And finding a way past their nearly impervious shielding might even prove more beneficial.

"What else?" I asked.

"What do you mean?"

"You are hiding something. What is it?"

I noticed a slight elevation in perspiration—the guarded tone of her voice—hesitation as she chose her words carefully, trying not to reveal...something.

She looked up at the ceiling, then back down at me, placing her hands on her hips. "This is classified, Tien. After what happened at Nilot, Queltz didn't want you to have access to any sensitive information. To be frank, I don't think he trusted anyone in Special Corp." She rubbed her chin and then blew out a hard breath. I saw the filters on her mask dilate and then shrink back to their original size in response.

"But Queltz is gone now, and these *are* desperate times. We've captured one of their ships," she announced. "We finally have a tangible piece of Brenin technology. On the way to Bodhi Prime to get you, we encountered a small Brenin craft shadowing the main fleet. At first, we thought it was an advance scout, but its movements didn't make sense. It was hiding *from* the Brenin fleet, staying just outside their sensor range. But not ours. We attacked and disabled it, finding that body you're wearing on board. It was the sole occupant. The Brenin corpse gave the general an idea. Queltz hoped that the monks could alter your clone, or even the cyborg, to look like that *thing* you're in now—so you could operate in their midst undetected. He never imagined *this* outcome, but if he'd known it was possible, he wouldn't have hesitated either. With or without your assent."

"We can change the atonement monk's appearances," Dyson chimed in. "We strive to make each look just like the client. But something at this level...it never would have worked. The research branch would have to work on the problem for months to overcome the issues...to make something indistinguishable from the rest of the Brenin. The locomotion alone—"

I waved them both to silence. "I understand the situation. Where is that ship now?"

"It's in our cargo hold. We are taking it back to the Confederation for study. We can learn so much...from Brenin ship fabrication, to whatever information we can glean from the databases on board— it's an intelligence goldmine."

"Yes it is, Colonel. Tell me, why should I risk *my* life for this mission? What will happen to me should I make it back?"

"A full pardon," she said assuredly. "That's what Queltz was going to offer you."

*Oh, I'm sure. And then one day, a few weeks or months later, I would mysteriously vanish. But I will play the game...for now anyway. Dyson is offering me what I want, and I need the colonel's cooperation to fulfill my end of the bargain with him.*

"We have an understanding, Eraz. With a few stipulations, of course."

She stiffened and eyed me suspiciously. "Such as?"

"I need that captured ship to infiltrate the Brenin fleet. It's my best chance."

"But we—"

"Relax, Colonel. We still have a couple of days until we meet up with the Brenin—plenty of time to study the ship. In fact, I'd *like* for you to rip it apart and take samples of everything. Just make sure it stays space-worthy...even if just barely. I want it to look like it's been through hell and back, and in desperate need of rescue."

"What else?" she sighed.

"I want Queltz dead."

"He is. *You* killed him."

"No, Colonel. I want every medical record and neural scan wiped. Each cerebral mapping ferreted out and destroyed. Every trace of that bastard disappeared from our records."

I watched her eyes widen behind the mask, then turned to Dyson. "And I want *your* pledge that that animal will never be resurrected, monk."

Dyson didn't hesitate. "You have it."

Eraz stomped hard on the ground before spitting out, "You are one vindictive bastard, Tien."

"Yes I am, Colonel."

"Remember that..."

# CHAPTER SEVEN

Early the next morning, I started practicing with my new body in an enclosed exercise space near the landing port. In spite of Bodhi Prime's reputation as a mostly arid wasteland, the air was surprisingly humid, and condensed moisture glistened on the glass windows overlooking the courtyard where I ran.

And *how* I could run.

But it was more than just simple speed, I was incredibly agile as well, abruptly switching direction at will and leaping with alarming distance and precision. I quickly grew into the new form. The brain and body were already used to working together flawlessly, it was more of a case of me learning what my new capabilities *were*, rather than how to use them.

I sprinted toward one of the block walls, ran up it, and then flipped over backward to land upright on the ground. It was a maneuver I'd practiced often with my Udek body, but in this form, I subconsciously made two complete revolutions before landing solidly on my feet. I'd always prided myself on my overall fitness and training regimen; I knew that my life depended on it. But this was on a whole different level. *This* was exhilarating.

My excitement waned rapidly when I jumped up on a

platform and tried to grasp some exercise rings, placed sequentially along a pole about five meters long. I fell repeatedly as I tried to swing from ring to ring—unable to grab them with enough strength to support my body. The extra fingers did nothing to improve my grip. It wasn't that the body was heavy, the hands were simply too weak, and lifting it was a chore. With a great deal of concentration, I was able to grab and hold on to one of the rings, but when I swung forward to grasp the next one, my grip failed and I dropped to the ground.

I finally gave up and walked over to a storage bin sitting in one corner of the courtyard. Rifling through the exercise equipment inside, I found a pair of small metal balls and placed one in each hand. I spun them around and through my fingers—on the inside and *outside* of my hands. They might not be strong, but these hands possessed tremendous dexterity.

"Tien!" someone shouted from behind me.

I turned around to see Eraz entering the courtyard, and even from this distance I noticed the tension on her face—the breathing mask did nothing to hide it. She'd inherited a great deal of responsibility when I killed Queltz and was bearing it poorly.

"It's time to go," she said. "The ship is as ready as we have time to make it; it'll have to do."

I walked over to join her at the entryway. "Kris sseak hunjeth. Gorasssshethel?"

"What the..." Eraz held up one hand. "Hold on." She removed a small, round object from her armor and held it out. "Try again."

"How are things going with the Brenin ship?" I heard my own words translated into Standard.

"We're almost done stripping off materials for study and diagramming the construction techniques, but we are having some real problems with the computer systems. They are…different."

"I imagine so," I replied, looking down at my new body. If our physical forms were so disparate, I could only imagine the differences in the mental processes. "And what is *that* device?" I said, pointing at the disk.

"A portable translator, given to me by Brother Dyson. By studying how that chamber inside you interacts with the Brenin brain, he devised a program that can provide ambient, real-time translation."

"Clever," I replied.

My ears picked up the whine of powerful engines spinning up in the distance, but I couldn't identify the particular sound. It certainly wasn't the Udek warship; it was too high pitched for that. As the noise grew louder, Eraz heard it as well. We both looked up as a maroon and gold burst-shuttle soared off into the sky, ascending quickly into the upper atmosphere and out of view.

"Whoever it is," I said, "they are certainly in a hurry."

"Brother Dyson," Eraz stated. "He said he had some important business to attend to." She shook her head and looked back down from the sky. "You would think that with the Brenin bearing down on Bodhi Prime his focus would be here."

I started to speak but she stopped me. "Don't worry. I gave him your wife's information last night and saw him order the creation of her clone. I don't like these monks, Tien, but they do seem to be honest."

She turned to leave and I followed her out of the courtyard, stopping just long enough to take another look at the empty sky. I saw the last of the vapor trail disappear in the growing wind.

*Where are you going Dyson? And what the hell are you up to?*

After a short walk to the landing platform, I saw the Udek

warship for the first time. As we got closer to the vessel, I could barely make out its name through the scorch marks and deep pitting across the hull. The Udek assigned names and numbers to ships for identification purposes only, not with the special care that other races used in labeling craft like this. There were never any symbolic phrases, or names of honored personages; it was just a simple, functional, assignation. And this ship's was the Ral 97M.

"Wait," Eraz called out as we walked up the ramp. "You are going to need this."

She tossed me an oxygen respirator and I stretched it across my face. "Of course," I replied.

I should've known that; I *did* know that, and I realized then that my concentration was off...my mind drifting. But there was no more time for wallowing in regret about Dasi and my failure to save her. I didn't even have the *luxury* of coming to terms with being trapped inside an alien body—I needed to get myself ready for this mission. I *needed* to be disciplined and focused.

Or I would surely fail.

We stepped into the airlock and the oxygen was blown out—replaced with a methane mixture that allowed Eraz to pull off her mask and take a deep breath.

"That's better," she said with satisfaction.

The inner door opened soon after, exposing the interior of the ship. Panels had been removed from this section and were lined up against the wall, as technicians repaired and replaced electronic modules and wiring. Even through the oxygen mask, I could smell the telltale odors of welding and strong adhesives.

I saw Udek crewman moving briskly in every direction as they rushed to fix the vessel, preparing it for another encounter with the Brenin. One of them saw us and walked over—the others parting to give him a wide berth.

"Lov," Eraz said. "Get us in the air at once. Set a course for the last known position of the Brenin fleet."

"Yes, of course. And where are we going to lock that *thing* up?"

I answered for her. "This *thing* will kill you if you try."

Eraz had mounted the translator on the front of her armor, and my words came out just as menacingly as I'd meant them to. Lov pivoted in my direction and stepped up closer to me, standing slightly sideways—shifting the majority of his weight to his back leg. He was thoroughly trained—his stance suggested as much—but there was a slight hesitation on his left side. A prior injury perhaps? I plotted my first strike in that area, eager to exploit the weakness.

"Stop!" Eraz barked. "Both of you. Lov, get to the bridge. We have more important things to do." He hesitated, looking at me contemptuously for a moment before storming off.

"And *he's* in the command structure," Eraz sighed. "How will I ever control the simple soldiers? We need to confine you to quarters. But first, I have a couple of things to show you."

We walked down the corridor to a large, nearby cargo bay, and as soon as we stepped through the heavily guarded door, I knew why she'd brought me here. The captured Brenin ship was parked right next to an exterior bay door, ready to take off as per my instructions. It looked like it had fallen from orbit, crashed, and was then pummeled with boulders.

"Nice work, Eraz. Will it fly?"

"Barely...just as requested."

"Excellent. I'll need you to hit it with a few, well-placed ion blasts once I'm far enough away from the ship. And make it look good, Colonel...without actually killing me, of course."

"Of course," she replied. "Now let's go inside, there are some other things you need to see."

I consciously restricted my gait, falling into step with her as we crossed the bay. I noticed that the bottom hatch was open on the small ship, and the door was hanging down and visible. We ducked underneath the fuselage and walked up a narrow ramp to go inside.

The interior was little more than a flight deck; there was a single console with two metal chairs in front of it. Looking around, I quickly realized that *everything* was bare metal. Curved, support spars lined the interior walls, with tubing and wires going through and around them. The Brenin hadn't skinned the inside of the ship, and all of the mechanical features normally hidden behind bulkheads and wall panels were on full display.

Eraz saw my reaction and explained. "This is how it was when we found it. The Brenin appear to be minimalists."

"So it seems. Or maybe it was stripped down for some other reason."

"I suppose that's possible. Regardless, the flight systems and instrumentation are all intact so you shouldn't have any trouble flying it. The controls are even similar to our own, forward, reverse, pitch, yaw etc..."

I took a seat in one of the flight chairs and glanced down at the panel; she was right, it *was* familiar. I could even read the text on the console; my dead, Brenin brain—pushed into service by the soul chamber—was still working as intended...somewhat.

I noticed a small, black obelisk marked *Research* jutting out from the panel. Curious, I reached over and attempted to activate it by spinning it left and right—but it wouldn't budge. Then I tried pulling at it instead, and the object slid out from the console almost an inch and started glowing brightly. I let go and it dropped out of sight, swallowed up completely by the control panel.

A partially transparent image appeared in the air in front of me; I could see right through it and out into the bay beyond via the front cockpit window. It was the depiction of a planet.

A familiar planet...

"It's Obas," I declared.

"The water planet? But why? There's nothing there. What do the Brenin want with Obas?"

"I'm not sure. Maybe it was simply their next target."

"Serves them right if it is. The Obas have chosen to sit this war out so far. Let's see how they feel when the Brenin are on *their* doorstep."

"What do you expect them to do, Eraz? It's a small civilization; there can't be more than five million Obas total. And they certainly don't have many ships."

"Well, maybe if they weren't such isolationist, and at least *tried* to interact with other races, they would be in a stronger position now."

"Maybe," I replied.

"I have another mystery for you as well," she said.

Eraz pulled open a pocket flap and reached inside, withdrawing a shiny, square object. She turned it over and I saw the picture of a Brenin mounted on the face of it. But this one was different from the form I now inhabited–it was smaller, more slender. Instinctively or deductively, I wasn't sure which, but *somehow* I knew it was female.

"Who is it?" I asked.

"We have no idea." Eraz let the object drop out of her hand and dangle, a thin, black string kept it from hitting the ground.

"A necklace?"

"It is. It was around his neck when we found him."

I studied the face as Eraz handed it over to me. Whoever it was, she was important to him. And that made her important to *me*. Everything I could discover about this body would help me blend in better once I made it onto a Brenin ship.

"I'm going to the bridge," Eraz said, motioning through the front window to summon two of the guards over. "Those two will escort you to your quarters when you're ready. We will make best speed to the Brenin fleet, and since we are converging on one another, we should meet up in a little over two day's time." She gave me a hard look. "Whatever plan you come up with, spy, it had better work."

"Colonel Eraz," I replied. "You'll be the second one to know if it doesn't."

# CHAPTER EIGHT

For the next two days, I familiarized myself with the Brenin ship, using my built-in translation abilities to access and read the information stored in its data banks. Much to Eraz's delight, I found some valuable intelligence, including the name of my target, Marshal Toz. I also uncovered a great deal of Brenin scouting information—mostly pertaining to our inhabited worlds. The files detailed the relative military strength of each populated planet, along with their defensive capabilities and possible weaknesses.

I quickly realized that this ship had some impressive scanning capabilities, and speculated that the Brenin had sent many just like it ahead of their fleet—to gather information before attacking. Unlike the Brenin armada, these small scout ships could move around undetected—gathering what they needed—and then return to the fleet with the accumulated data. The strategy was sound, and unfortunately, very productive; the Brenin seemed to know everything there was to know about us.

But there was information here about them as well.

There were *extensive* scans of the Brenin contingent we were moving to intercept. If I interpreted the information correctly, each ship had been mapped out thoroughly, looking for a particular biological pattern. This Brenin pilot was searching for someone specific in that fleet, and it was becoming increasingly apparent that he wasn't part of it at all—he was *studying* it. But why? And what did that mean for my plan to fly right into their formation? My instincts told me that there was a potential problem here...possibly a serious one. But despite this revelation, my plan still had to proceed—simply because there was no other way through their defenses.

During my search through the data, I also discovered a host of internal Brenin communications, indicating a high level of distrust between the different clans. Every order between them was questioned and torn apart—counter-proposals submitted and denied. Queltz's information had been correct; this *was* a fractious bunch. But by the way they coordinated their attacks against us, you'd never know it.

I was in the middle of reading a particularly nasty communiqué when Eraz popped up through the hatch. "It's time to launch," she said. "We will hit their sensor range in less than an hour."

"Excellent. I was starting to feel a little cooped up."

"Well...with any luck, you will soon be surrounded by new, Brenin friends," she smiled. "Have you come up with a plan yet?"

"Other than kill Marshall Toz, implicate another clan in his murder, and find a way to sabotage the shield array? No. But what more *plan* do I need?"

She gave me an exasperated look. "Getting in...getting back *out* again. Finding your target... You know, specifics."

"Ah...the details. I'll be the first to admit that I usually plan out every mission to the minute, if not the second. But over the years, I've found myself in many situations where things didn't go as planned—where I've been forced to think on the run. Nilot is one example. I'll just have to see how things develop and adapt. Stay flexible."

"I see," she said doubtfully. "Just don't forget that you *died* on Nilot." Her tone became more serious. "I'll spare you a speech about how important this is to the Udek people, or the galaxy in general, I doubt you'd be moved anyway."

"You're right about that, Colonel. But you needn't worry; I have ample motivation for success. And this mission is no different than any other I've been sent on. I'm being tasked with killing someone—something I'm highly skilled at. This situation is just a little more unique than most."

Eraz smirked. "It is at that." She pulled the translator off her armor and threw it to me. "Take this," she said. "On the off chance that you actually survive and need to call someone to pick you up."

I took the device and tucked it into my clothing. "Make it look good, Colonel."

"Oh, you don't have to worry about that, spy. I'll make it a point to knock you out of that chair."

"You're welcome to try," I replied.

She ducked back out of the ship and I started powering up the flight systems. Even though I'd used the vessel's database to study the controls and basic operation, I wasn't entirely convinced that I could fly the scout with enough proficiency to play my part in this charade. Reading about something, and actually doing it, often turned out to be two entirely different experiences—sometimes disastrously so. But I was comforted by the notion that any apparent ineptitude on my part would probably be attributed to the damage the ship had taken.

I watched through the front window as the guards left the cargo bay, then the large metal docking door slid aside—all that separated the ship from the vacuum of space was an imperceptible, semipermeable force field. I tapped on the control surface twice and the ship rose a meter off the deck. Then I slid a single finger sideways and the vessel lurched hard to the left, spinning up until it was almost perpendicular to the deck. I quickly reversed the motion with a little more care and the ship righted itself horizontally.

*Touchy.*

I suppose when your form is this dexterous, it only makes sense to build your machinery to reflect it. But my mind and reactions were still Udek, and graceful movements weren't in our nature. I cautiously lined the ship up with the force field and then powered through it, shooting out into the blackness of space.

Almost at once, I felt at ease. *This* was my normal—alone in a ship, embarking on a secretive and dangerous mission. And like so many other times in the past, my goal was to infiltrate, to sabotage...and to kill. Where many would feel fear or apprehension—terror because of the danger and uncertainty of it all—I relaxed. Yes...this was my home, the environment where I thrived.

Off to kill again.

*My* normal.

Eraz's voice blared through the speaker. *"Alright, Tien. Ready for the show?"*

"I am. I'll go full throttle and open up a lead. Stay close enough to make your attack convincing, but leave yourself enough room to escape."

*"We know what to do, spy,"* she replied testily.

I set the engines to maximum thrust and pointed the small ship at the approaching Brenin fleet, just now coming into sensor range.

As we sped toward the enemy armada, I looked down at the necklace again, trying to figure out who she was and what made her so special. The ship's data banks provided no clue to the identity of its pilot—no information *whatsoever*. In fact, the only thing that differentiated this Brenin body I wore from the rest of his species was this single piece of jewelry, and his relationship to the woman portrayed on it.

Who was she?

A wife? Did the Brenin even bond in that manner? Maybe she was the creature's mother, but there seemed to be no difference in age. Then again, we knew absolutely nothing about their biology or how the Brenin body matured over time. And did they even *have* mothers? There was simply not enough information to conclude anything; this female could be related to the pilot in any number of ways, or not at all for that matter.

All of this speculation made me think of my own family...of Dasi. Of how she'd been taken hostage and killed because of my actions. The irony of those events hadn't escaped me either. Families of Special Corp operatives were closely guarded, protected almost as diligently as the Corp kept its secrets. An agent's work could lead to reprisals, so their family's identities were well hidden, and they were always shadowed by discreet bodyguards. But those *protectors* were the ones who had taken Dasi. She'd been betrayed and murdered by her own government.

I should have realized...I should have known they would stoop to that level—done anything to rein me in. I should have gotten to Dasi faster. This was my fault, and I *will* fix it.

My thoughts were broken apart by the sound of weapons fire hitting the small ship—right on schedule. I grabbed the console to steady myself against the rocking motion caused by the impacts. Looking down at the ship's readout, I watched as the mild strikes knocked the craft sideways, slightly off its course, but nothing more significant was happening. *This isn't very convincing,* I thought. Then a massive blow struck the ship and I went flying out of my chair—smacking my head against a bulkhead before ending up on the floor.

*Nice work, Eraz.*

That sentiment evaporated when an alarm went off and

the atmosphere started noisily venting out of the ship. As the hull began to contort itself out of shape, the sound of twisting metal rose above the incessant hiss. But then, as quickly as it started, the leak was gone and everything went silent. *A self-sealing hull,* I reasoned.

I jumped back up and fell into the pilot's chair; the whole console was now powerless and the ship clearly adrift. Without sensors, I was reduced to looking out of the front window to find out what was happening. I saw the Udek warship firing—but not at me—their shots were ranging out past of my field of vision. It had to be the Brenin, but how had we miscalculated so badly? We shouldn't have reached them yet; Eraz's 'attack' was supposed to last a few minutes, to draw their attention from a distance.

I watched as the Udek warship shuddered, suffering through an intense barrage of energy fire, then it returned an impressive salvo of its own. My ship was struck again, and I hugged the console tightly to keep from being thrown back down to the floor. When I looked up again, I saw a ship slightly larger than my own speed past the window. It was flat and perfectly round, with brilliant colors flecked across the surface. I'd seen those marking before in an intelligence report.

It was an Obas fighter.

*What the hell is it doing out here? And why is it attacking us?*

As I tried to make sense of it all, my ship was hit again and the sound of hissing air returned. But this time, the vessel's emergency system didn't seem able to stop the leak. The lights flickered out and smoke began pouring out of a ventilation port overhead. Then the overpowering din of tearing metal filled the craft. I looked out the window just in time to see the Udek warship speed away.

Eraz had called a retreat.

A powerful flash erupted outside, forcing me to squint as

my ship lurched upward. Then a piece of metal bearing Obas markings bounced off the window and I realized that the fighter had just been destroyed. As more debris pinged off my dying ship, a teal colored hull began to fill my view. A massive Brenin vessel was moving in toward me. The immense ship practically glowed, filling my craft with ambient light.

The illumination allowed me to look around my ship, and I noticed a pale, blue liquid covering the console. It ran over the edge and down onto the floor in a steady drip. That same fluid was also flowing freely over my left eye, and I reached up to discover that I was bleeding profusely from my head. I became dizzy, and placed my other hand down on the console—to brace myself against the encroaching blackness. But my hand landed in a pool of blood and slipped off. I fell out of the chair and lay motionless on the deck, struggling to remain conscious. In my receding awareness, I heard the sound of torches cutting through metal, and strange, yet intelligible voices on the other side of the wall.

My enemy was coming to rescue me.

# CHAPTER NINE

I heard the voices again.

No...different ones now. I kept my eyes shut—my instincts telling me to hold still and pretend to sleep. They'd kept me alive this long and I heeded the warning. A female voice rose up from the fog of unfamiliar sounds.

"Marshal Toz? I'm surprised to see you in the infirmary at this time of day."

*Toz?* My target?

"Yes, Doctor Uli," he responded, his tone harsh and condescending. "I'm sure you are. But this situation requires my special attention."

"Of course," she said. I heard footsteps as the two approached where I lay.

"What can you tell me about him, doctor?"

"They just brought him in, so not much. But look at this."

I felt her grab my arm and resisted the impulse to pull away. She turned my hand over and tapped my wrist; there was a slight pinch as something broke through the skin, then retracted back into my forearm.

*What the hell?*

"Yano!" Toz exclaimed. "One of your clan, doctor. What is

he doing here?"

"I don't know, Marshal."

There was a loud crack and I felt her pull away sharply, dropping my hand back onto the gurney. I heard a stumbling impact, like a body slamming into something, and then the harsh clang of dozens of metallic things hitting the ground. The doctor cried out in pain.

"Find out. Now!" Toz yelled. "Revive him as soon as possible. I don't care if it kills him. I want to know what the hell he is doing here."

"Yes...yes sir," she sputtered.

The sound of doors sliding open broke the tension; it was followed by the wobble of wheels rolling across a hard surface.

The marshal's voice became animated. "Good...good. Get that set up immediately."

"It's so...*strange*," I heard Uli say, her voice returning to normal.

"Just another of the local animals, doctor. I wouldn't get too excited about it; they won't be with us much longer anyway. Speaking of which, the formula has already been transferred to your database; you may begin the testing at once. I want the results soon—and don't kill it, just in case the bio-weapons team comes up with alternatives and need to test other formulations."

"Yes, Marshal Toz."

"I have other matters to attend to," he said dismissively. "Answers, doctor. I want them. I want them *soon*. And clean up this mess."

"Of course, sir."

I heard footsteps as he walked away, trailed by at least two other Brenin, then a door slid open and closed again behind them. I slowly cracked open one eye and flitted a glance around the room.

The walls were constructed out of highly polished metal,

and glinted in the abundant illumination—provided by a glowing white ceiling overhead. In stark contrast, the floor was matte black, and absorbed every trace of light that touched it like a black hole. I counted three other people in the room with me.

Two, armed Brenin stood guard at the entryway to the room, while the female doctor was at the foot of my gurney, gathering up equipment that had been strewn about the floor when the marshal knocked her into a cabinet. Directly across from me, I saw a coffin-sized cylinder full of liquid—a shadowy figure motionless inside it. The doctor began to turn around and I quickly lowered my eyelid. She walked up to me and placed a disk on my chest, twisting it a half turn to seat it tightly against my skin. The device then started to vibrate, emitting a low-pitched hum.

"What's this now?" she said, confusion in her voice.

*She must be scanning me,* I realized...she'd found the soul chamber.

"What is it, doctor?" one of the guards asked.

"I *really* don't know. But I'm going to find out, right now."

I felt her breath on my chest as she leaned down closer to manipulate the scanner.

**{Decompress-Reset-OVERRIDE}**

*What the hell? Where is tha—?*

*Pain!*

My back arched up from the table and my eyes flew open. There was no pretense of sleep now...only unimaginable agony.

*Searing...like acid...burning a hole through my mind!*

It was unbearable, like someone cutting open my skull while I watched helplessly—savagely ripping my brain apart into chunks of useless flesh. But it wasn't anything the doctor had done; she'd backed away in shock.

And she looked *terrified.*

"Gahhhhhhhh!" I yelled, clawing at my head furiously with both hands. But I couldn't find the source; I couldn't make it stop.

**{Decompress-Reset-OVERRIDE/OVERRIDE...REPEAT COMMAND...FAIL!}**

*That voice...where was it coming from? Why does it hurt so much when it speaks?*

I started hyperventilating. I couldn't get any air. The *pain*...it was too much. I fought to stay conscious, and through the torment, I felt the guards grab me on both sides and push me back down to the gurney—pinning me to it with their own bodies. I heard them screaming at each other—and at me—but I couldn't understand the words. I couldn't understand anything but the pain.

**{Operational Matrix=Corruption detected. Shepherd Personality=Improper configuration...}**

"Stop it!" I screamed. "Make it stop! NOW!"

**{Emergency Pathway established—initiating OS base communication subsystem...}**

**{Say I'pra, Udek}**

*The voice... It was inside my head.*

**{Say I'pra, Udek. Say it now, or we will both surely die. Say it, and the pain will stop}**

"I'pra!" I screamed, repeating it again even louder. "I'pra!"

Almost immediately, the intolerable pain began to subside—becoming a manageable ache instead. I heard the outside voices once again, but now I could understand them.

"*What* did you just say?" Doctor Uli exclaimed. She walked over and stood beside me.

"I'pra," I spat out, then dropped my head down hard on the gurney.

"What's wrong with him, doctor?" one of the guards asked.

"I'm not sure," she replied. "Tie him to the table."

They did as she instructed using straps built into the gurney, while she retrieved the scanning disk from the floor where it had been thrown during my outburst. Uli looked me in the eyes as she passed it over my body, and I saw confusion cloud her features. I watched the deliberations play out across her face as questions flowed through her mind. Then something changed in the doctor's demeanor and I knew that she'd reached a decision. About what, I hadn't a clue.

"Get away from him," she yelled at the guards.

"Why? What is it, doctor?"

"Do as I say. Now! He may be contagious."

They both stepped back quickly, and she went over to where they'd retreated, methodically running the scanner over them in slow, sweeping motions.

"You two are fine," she said, and they relaxed somewhat. "But I need you to remain outside and make sure no one else comes in here. In fact, you should probably station yourselves away from the infirmary altogether. Cordon off this section on both sides of the corridor, and keep *everyone* out until I know what we're dealing with."

Neither guard protested, and they both stepped through the door hurriedly, sealing it shut behind them. The doctor checked that it was locked before running over to my side.

"Who are you?" she demanded. "I'm Yano. You can trust me."

Her face...it was familiar. I knew I'd seen it before. But where?

*Yes...that's it! She's the girl from the necklace.*

**{Seeris. Tell her your name is Seeris. Say it now if you want to survive}**

The voice in my head was back...loud and irrepressible.

**{DO IT!}**

"I am Seeris," I said, too weak to struggle against the voice any longer.

"Liar!" she snapped. "Seeris is my brother. And he's dead."

*Who the hell is Seeris?* I thought to myself, not really expecting an answer.

But I got one nonetheless.

**{I am Seeris}** the voice inside my head thundered.

**{What are you doing inside MY body, Udek?}**

# CHAPTER TEN

*His body?*

What the hell was he talking about? And where was *he*? The overpowering voice had filled my mind—coming from everywhere at once—yet nowhere in particular. Doctor Uli continued to look at me impatiently, waiting for answers.

"Who are you, really? A spy for the Yano?"

"I am Seeris," I repeated again, wary of the pain returning.

"I already told you," she said in frustration. "Seeris is dead."

**{Tell her there is carving of I'pra in the Kish tree where we played as children}**

I relayed the message verbatim.

"I'pra was my pet," she breathed out in disbelief. "But how could you know that?"

**{Tell her it is really me...Seeris. That I disguised myself so I could come and rescue her}**

*You are the corpse,* I thought to myself, *the body where Dyson put my chamber. You were dead!*

**{No. Not dead. Almost... Give her my message and I will explain}**

*Very well.*

Uli looked at me skeptically as I explained to her that Seeris had altered his appearance, but then she changed some settings on the scanner and waved it over me again. "Like Seeris, your juc sack has been removed on the right side, and...there *are* traces of reconstructive surgery to your face. And you are most *definitely* Yano... Is that really you Seeris?"

**{Yes}**

She stared at me...waiting for a response.

**{Tell her I said yes!}**

*You don't command me, Brenin.*

And then the pain returned and I started convulsing uncontrollably. Uli leaned away as I twisted violently against the straps, trying to get away from it. But the pain was everywhere; there was no escape. Just before I blacked out, the agony abruptly stopped and I fought to steady my breathing.

*Pain is not control,* I thought to myself, knowing he would hear me. *And I have no reason to cooperate with you.*

**{I know your mission, Udek. And I can help you. We can help each other}**

*Why would you want to help me?*

**{Because I don't care about this war or its outcome anymore; I only wish to escape it with my sister. And because neither you nor I really have a choice...do we?}**

It was clear that he could create debilitating pain throughout this body—rendering me helpless at will, and stopping me in my tracks. But without *my* cooperation, he wasn't going anywhere either.

Stalemate...for now anyway. I had little choice but to play it out and see what happened.

I looked at Uli and relayed his message. "He says, yes. It's him. Seeris is in here with me."

"In there with... Then who are *you*?"

"Kiro Tien. Udek Special Corp."

"Udek! But how?"

"That chamber you found in my chest...Seeris' chest...contains my consciousness. The Bodhi placed it in this body so I could disguise myself and infiltrate the fleet."

"How could they do *that*? I don't understand any of this," she replied.

"Then that makes three of us, doctor."

**{Give her your communications device, Udek. Tell her to scan the chamber the Bodhi installed and find the broadcast signal. She can then route my speech through her scanner}**

I instructed the doctor to reach into my tunic and pull out the translator disk Eraz had given me. Uli turned the little machine over in her hands, examining both sides of it as I explained Seeris' idea to her. She nodded, and then set about syncing her scanner with the internal signal coming from the chamber.

"I think I've found it," she announced. "Seeris, say something."

**{Can you hear me?}**

"Yes!" she exclaimed. "Seeris, you're alive!"

**{Yes, Uli. I've come to rescue you}**

"But how did you get here? Why aren't you still with the Yano detachment?"

"More importantly," I interrupted, "how can you help me complete my mission? And how do you even *know* about it in the first place?"

**{I became *aware* in the laboratory—when you were speaking with Eraz and Dyson. I know everything from that point on}**

"Then you know that being placed in this body wasn't my choice. And that I intend to leave it when this is all over."

**{Yes}**

"I assume you were scanning this fleet to find your sister,

but why were you spying on the Obas? And why aren't you *dead*? Queltz was convinced that he'd killed you in the attack." I futilely pulled against the straps again. "If you expect my help, get me off this gurney, doctor. And Seeris, I need answers. Tell me everything about what's *really* going on here."

**{Free him, Uli}**

She started to protest, but then thought better of it and undid my straps. Uli helped me sit up and gave me a cup of water as Seeris began to explain. I knew that her 'kindness' was prompted by a desire to preserve her brother's body, not out of any special care for me.

**{I am Yano, Udek. It is my clan—my sister's as well. This portion of the Brenin fleet is under the control of our chief rivals, the Saba. Uli is being held in hostage-servitude to ensure our loyalty. She is one of many, and we keep some of the Saba as well. All of the other clans do the same}**

I looked at Uli. "You are a slave?"

"*I am a doctor,*" she replied indignantly. Then she looked down at the floor to avoid my eyes. "But I am being held as part of our arrangement with the Saba."

**{I am a surveillance pilot for the Yano. My mission was to examine the Obas more closely. Our intelligence division had discovered something odd about their culture during the initial analysis, and I was dispatched to make a more thorough investigation of the planet—an attempt to reconcile the discrepancies found in the original data. But I saw it as an opportunity to sneak into this fleet and free my sister}**

"But why, Seeris?" Uli asked. "Why risk yourself like this for me? They told me you were dead. And *what* have you done to your face?"

**{I intercepted a communication between two Saba captains, Uli—they intend to kill all of the Yano hostages once we've finished crushing these backward races)**

"You shouldn't presume that you'll win," I countered.

**(It's a safe assumption, Udek. You are weak, all of you. Regardless, I altered my appearance so I could slip into this fleet and get Uli out. Due to the nature of our missions, surveillance pilots are very, high profile personnel; I couldn't take the chance that I'd be recognized. I hadn't quite finished disguising my ship yet when the Udek attacked me}**

"Tell me, Seeris, how were you able to pick Uli out from all of the other Brenin signatures?"

**{There are certain physical differences between the clans. I located and tracked all of the Yano life signs and she was the only one that frequented the infirmary...the only doctor. I was certain that I'd found her. And then the Udek found *me*. The scout ships aren't equipped with our shielding technology, and the Udek managed to disable my vessel. I remember being seriously injured during their attack, and my body must have placed itself in a healing coma to repair the damage. When they boarded the ship and found me, the Udek just assumed that I was dead. And then I awoke—watching through my own eyes as someone else controlled my body}**

"I wasn't happy about waking up under those circumstances either," I replied.

"Well, what are we going to do now?" Uli asked.

"*I* intend to kill Marshal Toz and find a way to sabotage this fleet," I said with finality. "Just as before. You can have this body back when I'm done with it."

“Or I can take you out of there right now,” Uli threatened. She went over to an equipment tray and picked up an injection kit. A sedative, I surmised.

“I very seriously doubt it, doctor. Now calm yourself before you get hurt.”

**{Listen to him, Uli. Don’t let his injuries lull you into a false sense of security. This savage is a killer, and I won’t see you harmed. In any event, I’m sure your scans will confirm that only the Bodhi can undo what they’ve done to me. Despite your considerable skills as a surgeon, even you can’t remove this filth from my body. There is an explosive device installed to prohibit tampering and I can’t find a way to defeat it. This technology is...odd.”**

“Perhaps we are not as backward as you’d like, eh Seeris? You Brenin are so arrogant.”

**{Don’t delude yourself, Udek. You are all barbarians by our standards}**

“Then stay out of the way while this *barbarian* deals with the marshal and gathers the intelligence he needs. Afterward, we can get off this ship and return to Bodhi Prime...where we can be rid of one another.”

**{I will help you complete your mission, Udek. As I said before, I only wish to escape with my sister. But when you’ve finished with your futile, little escapade, then we leave, *with* Uli. Agreed?}**

“Agreed,” I replied.

*The enemy of my enemy...*

But in this case, both sides were enemies, and I didn’t trust the Bodhi any more than I did the Brenin. But the Bodhi were a known quantity, driven by their archaic religious beliefs—their actions could be predicted based on past behavior. I had no idea what drove these Brenin to act. I examined Seeris’ goals—the ones he’d shared with me anyway—and realized that we were both motivated by self-interest. That was one character trait I *did* trust. And even though we would do our level best to kill each other in different circumstances, we had no choice but to work together now. I didn't like it, and neither did he, but if Seeris did anything to jeopardize my mission, he understood that he and Uli would die as well.

"I've convinced them that you have something potentially contagious," Uli said. "But that won't work forever. We need to do something...now."

I hopped off the gurney and stood up. "Yes we do, doctor. What's in that container?" I asked, gesturing at the liquid filled cylinder across the room

"From what they told me, that's the Obas pilot that attacked your ship. I've been ordered to perform some biological experiments on him."

Uli tossed me a fresh tunic to replace the blood stained one I was wearing. "What type of experiments?" I asked, pulling the new shirt on and fastening the lock strips. "And why bother? The Obas don't pose a threat to you—or anyone else for that matter."

**{The Obas have many secrets, Udek. And I found one of them. Now that this fleet has my ship, the Saba will learn it as well}**

"What *secrets*? They are weak and inconsequential."

**{Now who is arrogant? The Obas have a massive fleet of warships concealed beneath their oceans. My estimates gauge their strength at just below Udek numbers}**

"Impossible," I said cynically. "The Obas are isolationists. Why build such a fleet and not use it? It makes no sense."

**{Ask the Obas *why*. But it changes everything}**

The communications console beeped urgently and Uli triggered a switch to activate it.

*"Doctor Uli, the marshal has been informed of your situation and wants a status report."*

"Please tell him that I have everything under control now and the infirmary will be open again shortly. I have to finish sterilizing it first. Also, let him know that I may not be able to revive the Yano."

*"And the Obas?"*

"I'm starting the first experiment now."

*"We have changed course and are heading to the Obas home world, doctor. The marshal wants those results as soon as possible. We have preparations to make."*

"I understand. I'll forward my findings in the next few hours."

*"See that you do."*

A loud click signaled the end of the conversation.

"We're heading to Obas," she repeated.

"They've found out about the fleet and are re-tasking to deal with it," I explained. "They can destroy Bodhi Prime at their leisure, but they can't leave a fleet that size intact. If the Obas *did* decide to strike at the Brenin, your armada might find itself flanked—a serious threat that can't be ignored. That's assuming, of course, that the Obas really do have as many ships as the Udek, which I *still* find hard to believe."

**{Believe it, Udek. It's true}**

"Then we need to get there first," I replied.

**{No! We go to Bodhi Prime as planned. I don't care about you, the Obas, or this fleet. We escape and then return to the Bodhi—so we can rectify the insult those monks have done to my body}**

"But if we warn the Obas, they can engage the Brenin fully prepared. If they are as strong as you allege, they may even be able to inflict some serious damage to this fleet."

**{No matter how large their force is, they can't defeat our shield array}**

"Yes...I know." I made no effort to hide my contempt for the Brenin, or their advanced technology. "But I intend to do something about *that* problem as well. You can't control me, Seeris; you know that. You can immobilize this body and get us all killed, but you can't bend me to your will. We are going to Obas, *then* on to Bodhi Prime. I want out of here worse than you want me out; don't doubt my motivation. We will both get what we want...after Obas."

"And what about *this* particular Obas?" Uli asked, pointing at the container.

"Experiment away, doctor. They are expecting results from you soon, and sending over some data will keep them from growing suspicious. Besides, that bastard tried to kill me."

"I see."

**{No. We need him. You forget yourself, Udek. You are in a Brenin body. If you and Uli show up together at Obas, what type of reception do you think you'll receive?}**

"A fatal one," I agreed reluctantly. "He's right. We'll be lucky just to reach orbit in a Brenin ship. And even if they do let us land, as soon as they see *us* they'll shoot. They don't tolerate *any* visitors, much less Brenin ones. And after catching Seeris spying on them, they are probably more nervous now than ever."

Uli saw where the conversation was leading. "I'll wake him," she said. "Maybe we can come up with some type of mutually beneficial arrangement."

I walked over and stood with her beside the container, both of us peering inside.

"I've never actually met an Obas before," I said. "This should be...interesting."

# CHAPTER ELEVEN

Uli drained the murky liquid from the tank and a distinctly humanoid form grew visible as it settled down to the bottom. When the last of the fluid had trickled off his body—disappearing into a large hole in one of the corners—I got my first good look at the occupant.

I'd seen holos of the Obas before, but they'd always been standing upright and in atmosphere. They were bipeds, slightly smaller than humans, with rough, light-green skin. Their heads appeared over-sized for their bodies, and they had prominent gill slits behind the oval holes that served as ears. It was common knowledge that they could breathe water, but they'd chosen to live in their planet's oxygen rich atmosphere—building enclaves on the small islands that peppered the mostly water covered world.

Why had this one been immersed, I wondered. I decided to ask Uli.

"The poison I'm supposed to test is waterborne," she explained. "And the marshal wanted to confirm its efficacy. But to me this trial is rather pointless. This toxin is designed to mutate as it passes through an indigenous, aquatic plant species, transforming itself into an *airborne* pathogen.

Exposure through direct immersion is way outside its dispersal parameters. But I imagine they want to see if there are any collateral lethalities as well."

"But why even design an agent like that?" I asked. "It would be much simpler to just create an airborne poison in the first place and skip the mutation phase."

"You'd have to ask the bio-weapons section. They've been at it for weeks. But they don't *need* these tests, it's unquestionably deadly once it mutates into the final form. I'm sure it will work. They just obtained an unexpected and serendipitous test subject and wanted to take advantage of it."

She unlocked the seals around the container and lifted the lid. A small amount of water fell to the floor and splashed onto her shoes, but the Obas inside remained motionless. I was watching her examine him when Seeris began to speak.

**{What do you know of these Bodhi, Tien?}**

Wary of interrupting Uli, I responded in thought. *Surely you've studied them like you have the rest of us. Why ask me?*

**{We have. But I've been examining this device where your consciousness is stored—trying to fathom its purpose. It has a control mechanism, far more nefarious than anything we employ. According to the programming I can access, there is an override system built into the chamber called a Shepherd Personality. It allows the device to manipulate the individual's mind when it's activated. This machine can subvert and control the consciousness stored within it. Do you still wonder why we call you barbaric?}**

*You don't seem to be able to control me, except through excruciating pain, and that doesn't benefit either one of us. You continue to call us all barbaric, but the Bodhi aren't like the Udek or the Blenej. Or even other humans for that matter. We are all different.*

**{Yet, as we've proven, you all die the same. And I *can* control you...*my* body that is. This chamber has created a mechanical bridge between our minds. I can command my own body, but only if you acquiesce}**

*That won't happen.*

**{Nor did I expect it to, savage. It's a pity that this module wasn't fully programmed, or I could do as I wish with your mind. As it is, the device simply serves as a conduit for communication}**

The sound of coughing brought my attention back to Uli; she was helping the Obas sit up, and it was gasping for air and choking—expelling water with every cough from its gills and mouth.

"Where am I?" it demanded.

Uli handed me the Bodhi translator and I activated it. "On a Brenin ship," I replied. "Look around Obas; I think it would be obvious."

"I can't see...the transition takes a moment."

His eyes fluttered rapidly, then he spun his head around slowly, taking in his surroundings. I saw him focus in on me first, and then he turned to look at Uli. Before either of us could react, the Obas grabbed a scalpel off a nearby tray and pulled Uli up against his chest, placing the knife at her throat.

"My ship?" he said frantically.

"Destroyed," I replied. "And you will follow it into nothingness if you don't let her go."

The Obas looked scared, but despite my threat, he tightened his grip on Uli. "I don't think you are in a position to make threats, Brenin."

"And what position are you in?" I asked. I made a sweeping motion with my arm to indicate the infirmary, but it alluded to the entire Brenin ship as well. "Look around, Obas. You are trapped. You will never make it off this ship."

"I've failed," he forced out, spitting up some more water. "I must return to Obas and tell them." His stomach convulsed, and Uli tried to pull away as his grip relaxed. He snapped back upright and regained control of her.

"You are not going anywhere without our help," I told him.

"And why would you help *me*?"

"Because nothing here is as it seems."

**{Tell him that you know about the hidden fleet}**

"Who's speaking?" the Obas asked.

"We know your secrets," I told him. "The fleet at the bottom of the ocean..."

He eased the blade into Uli's neck, causing a pinpoint of blue blood to ooze out onto the scalpel.

"No!" he yelled. Then more softly, "No..."

"This ship, this armada, is on its way to your planet now," I said. "To destroy that fleet and enslave your world."

He looked around the room, examining it in the way a caged animal investigates its enclosure—looking for a way out that didn't exist. The Obas began to understand the gravity of his situation and realized that he couldn't fight his way out of it. He took a deep breath and calmed down considerably—yet remained very alert.

"Who *are* you?" he asked.

"My name is Tien. I am an Udek intelligence officer."

"But...you..."

"The Bodhi put me in here, temporarily. I've infiltrated this ship to find a way past their shields...and to kill the Brenin leader."

If I was going to bring him around and secure his cooperation, he needed to know the truth—just as I'd demanded from Seeris. There was no need to keep secrets from the Obas anyway; they stood to lose just as much as anyone else in this war. And now that this fleet was headed to their planet, those losses would come sooner rather than later.

"The Bodhi put you in... I suppose that's possible." He

furrowed his semi-rigid brow, forming a slight depression that made him look less maniacal and more pensive. "I have to warn my people. If we can launch our fleet, we can defend the planet."

**{Another over-optimistic fool}** Seeris' voice blared through the speaker.

"Who *is* that?" the Obas demanded, looking around for the source of the voice. Then his gaze returned to me. "How do I know I can trust you?"

"You don't. But just like everyone else in this room, what choice do you have?"

The Obas released Uli and handed her the scalpel. As she darted away from him, he pushed his arms out straight and exhaled forcefully—a steady mist of water flew out of his mouth. I watched his chest expand as he drew in a deep breath of air.

"My name is Boe." He said. "Well...what do we do now?"

Uli scowled at him and backed away further. "Well, whatever it is, we'd better do it quickly. My quarantine is looking more and more suspicious by the minute. And in an hour or so, the marshal may show up here for treatment...with an entourage."

"Treatment?" I asked.

"Sometimes he gets hurt while exercising," she replied, placing the scalpel back on the tray. "Every afternoon, he practices with his Veilcat. And at least twice a week, he stumbles in here with some type of injury—usually a bite, sometimes a claw laceration. Last week, he said my treatments hurt too much, and that he was going to let the creature bite *me,* so I could understand the pain he went through. Toz is just enough of a monster to actually do it too."

"What's a *Veilcat*?" I said.

**{A paired hunting animal. They use their innate mental abilities to connect and bond with a hunter—**

**allowing the two to stalk prey in tandem. It is a vicious combination. The cats can also use their minds to confuse and paralyze quarry, even sentient ones}**

"Where does that voice keep coming from?" Boe asked.

Seeris' words were being broadcast from Uli's scanner, where they were then picked up by the ambient sensors of the Bodhi translator and converted from Brenin to Standard—just as when Uli and I spoke. But the Obas hadn't a clue about the source of the third voice. I took a moment to explain what had happened on Bodhi Prime to clear up his confusion. As I spoke, I watched the disbelief on his face turn into understanding...and then revulsion.

"So *both* of you are in there?" he said, pointing at my body.

"Yes," I replied brusquely, then turned to Uli. "Doctor, exactly where does the marshal practice with this animal of his?"

"Toz has a private exercise room two decks down. I'll show you on a map of the ship."

She walked over to a wall terminal and keyed up a schematic of the large vessel. Just as she'd described, the room was located two decks away—linked by a communal transport network.

**{Uli, display the nearest hangar with a scout ship in it}**

"I'm not familiar with the ship's flight complement, Seeris, but I can do a search." Uli input some data and three similarly sized areas began to flash red on the map.

**{There. The closest hangar is five decks up. Memorize the location; I have an idea}**

"Then let us all in on it, Seeris," I said.

**{The Obas and Uli will go to the hangar and wait for us—while you and I deal with Marshal Toz. Then we can rejoin them afterward and escape on one of**

**the scout ships}**

"How will I get this Obas through the ship?" Uli asked, pointing at Boe and giving him a disgusted look.

"Boe," he offered defensively. "*My name* is Boe. And I do apologize for threatening you."

I looked over at the cylinder he'd come out of and got an idea of my own. "Put him back in that, doctor. Then fill it up with water and push him through the ship. And keep that scanner with you; we can use it to communicate if need be."

Boe was incredulous. "I'm just supposed to trust you two to put me back in there?"

"You will if you want to live," I replied. "Or we can leave you here and you can arrange your own way off the ship...and through the Brenin fleet's security cordon. Oh, and let's not forget the shield itself."

"But—"

Uli ignored him. "And what if someone asks me *why* I'm pushing an Obas prisoner down the corridor?"

**{There is a direct tube to that hangar from the station just around the corner, Uli. You shouldn't have any issues}**

"I still need to obtain information about defeating the shield before *any* of us leave this ship," I said forcefully, leaving no doubt that my mission still came first. The looks I got from Boe and Uli told me they got the message.

**{Marshal Toz has access to every piece of information on this vessel, Udek. We can get it from him}**

"Then let's go," I replied. "The faster we can get off this ship the better."

# CHAPTER TWELVE

I left Boe and Uli behind in the infirmary to begin their own preparations and stepped out into the hall. Following the doctor's instructions, the guards had sealed off this area completely; there was no one in sight in either direction. Fortunately, the nearest transport station was less than ten meters away, and fell well within the confines of the cordoned off area. Uli said that no one should be able to exit from that stop due to the quarantine, but I could use one the cars parked there to leave.

*Seeris, do you think we can trust this Obas?*

**{I don't trust *you*, Udek}**

*Then that's a sentiment we share. Tell me, what's that thing in my...your wrist? Something slid out of it when Uli showed my arm to Toz.*

**{It is a prehensile extension of our skeletal structure; a tool for when we need to grip something strongly. But it also has sharp edges and can be used in combat, more so in the past than now}**

*And how did it mark you as one of the Yano clan? As soon as Toz saw it, he knew.*

**{They are called, *bledi*. In the Yano, they extend**

**from the bottom of the wrist and curl upward, extending out past the fingertips. In the Saba, they come out of the top and curl down. The Isk have one on either side of their wrists, opening and closing in opposing directions—we are all different}**

*Interesting.*

I approached the transport station and two doors slid apart automatically—one receding into the ceiling while the other disappeared into the floor. I stepped into the waiting car and sat down in one of the rearmost seats.

The vehicle had six chairs in all—placed two abreast in three rows. Luckily, they were all unoccupied. Glancing down at the armrest, I noticed a control panel and tapped it lightly. A map resembling the one Uli had shown me in the infirmary popped up, and I quickly located the exercise room. When I pressed down on the blinking indicator the car quietly slid into motion. Brenin technology or not it was an intuitive interface, and I was thankful that I didn't have to ask Seeris for instructions on how to use it.

But I did have other questions for him.

*What do you know about Marshall Toz?*

**{He has a reputation for ruthlessness, even among the Brenin. But he is a good leader—enjoying victory after victory as we move through your systems. And he is *very* popular, Udek; his murder will bring reprisal}**

*Good. Then his death will matter.*

**{You have no idea what this will bring down on my clan if they learn that I was involved}**

*You weren't too concerned about that when you thought to rescue Uli.*

**{A rescue, even if I'd been caught, would have led to a personal punishment. If this assassination is traced to me, there will be violence between our**

**clans}**

*That's my plan, Brenin. And like it or not, that's exactly how it's going to happen. You heard Eraz, and you know what we intend to do.*

**{So sure of yourself, Udek. The marshal may well kill you instead...kill *both* of us}**

*We will see.*

But Seeris made a valid point, and it was one that I'd been suppressing this entire mission. I *was* a seasoned assassin, but I didn't have any of my usual equipment. I'd taken two long-handled scalpels from the infirmary, and even though they were surprisingly well balanced, they weren't designed for fighting. But there was a much larger problem; I wasn't even in my own *body*, and I had no idea how these creatures fought.

*What I wouldn't give for a gun right now,* I thought to myself, *any gun.* But Seeris had assured me that all firearms were heavily guarded, and the danger of trying to obtain one far outweighed any possible benefit.

The car stopped and a female Brenin boarded, taking a seat at the front of the shuttle. I was relieved when she didn't bother to look back or offer a greeting. Uli had repaired my head wound and covered it with a small bandage, and I was worried that it might draw attention to me and elicit conversation. Fortunately, that wasn't the case...so far, anyway. We started moving again and I prodded Seeris for any information that might help me win against Toz.

*What do I need to know to beat him?*

**{Stay far away...attack and retreat. If he grabs you with his bledi, it's over. And remember, they are *very* sharp—serrated on both sides and pointed like a knife}**

*Anything else?*

**{Yes. The Veilcat is going to be the real problem, and I have no idea how to counter it. If it**

**compromises your mind, it can slow you down—maybe even paralyze you. Toz would be able kill you in seconds...if the cat didn't take you for itself first}**

The car stopped again and the female Brenin stood up to leave; my armrest vibrated to let me know it was my stop as well. I got up and followed her out, then turned left and started down a long hallway. The design scheme here matched that of the infirmary—a white, glowing ceiling that provided light; shiny, metallic walls with various control surfaces and maintenance hatches, and a shadowy-black floor that defied any attempt to examine it closely.

I continued to question Seeris as I walked down the hall. *Won't he have guards?*

**{No. Not here. Training with a Veilcat is a singular experience, and other minds in the vicinity can disrupt the bond between the creature and its master. Intruders might even be perceived as prey and fall victim to the cat}**

*Two doors...three. This is it.*

I peered into the room through a small, square glass panel set into the middle of the door—just as a silver blur flew by. As I continued to scan the darkened interior, looking for Toz, the massive Veilcat's head slowly rose up from the bottom of the window to stare me in the eyes. Its nostrils flared and I froze.

**{Get inside, Udek. If the cat saw us, then Toz knows someone is here}**

I grabbed the handle and twisted it—there was a loud pop as the lock disengaged and the Veilcat vanished from the window. I pushed the door open slowly, and then cautiously entered the room. It was a large chamber, broken up into different sized sections by partial walls and pillars. I looked around for the marshal and Veilcat, but spotted neither.

I saw dozens of platforms—some square, others round—scattered throughout the room; ranging in size from short, squat pieces that were barely a meter tall, to large structures that almost reached the high ceiling above. I also noticed horizontal bars hanging from wire cables, and handgrips mounted vertically on every flat surface. The pillars, walls, even the ceiling, were littered with handholds of different types.

Unlike the rest of the ship there was only a modicum of light here, and the room was dominated by deep, black shadows. Between the copious dark spots, and the open areas hidden behind the larger pedestals, there had to be twenty or so places to hide from view.

Marshal Toz called out from one of them.

"Who are you?" he asked. "Who are you *really*? My cat senses your mind, Yano. You are the one from the infirmary, yes?"

"Yes."

"Then if you've come here, it can only be to kill me. This room is as far from *escape* as you can get."

"Did your cat tell you that as well?"

Toz stepped out into the light; he was standing on a high platform on the far side of the room.

"She didn't have to, it's obvious. But why, Yano? You know what will happen because of this treachery. After I kill you, I *will* make your entire clan pay for your actions."

"You needn't worry about that," I replied. "In fact, Toz, soon you will have no worries at all."

"I'm not so sure, Yano. You see, I'm up here and you're down there. And as you know, *the trees are life...*"

**{And the ground is death}** Seeris finished.

The powerful Veilcat slammed into me from behind and the impact knocked the air from my lungs. As I struggled to regain my breath, the beast stood on its hind legs, pushing me across the floor with its large torso. It grabbed at my chest from behind with both front paws—the razor sharp claws mere inches from my flesh. And it took all of my strength to push out against the gradually tightening grip. The effort left me no opportunity for escape or counterattack, but what choice did I have? It was an embrace I knew I wouldn't survive.

The animal grew frustrated, and instead tried clamping its jaws down on my neck. But its head was in a bad position and I managed to dodge the snapping jaws each time. The Veilcat shifted its weight for a better angle of attack and I spun sideways, dropping to the floor and rolling away. The cat's momentum continued to carry it forward, giving me just enough time to reach into my tunic and jump back up with a scalpel in each hand.

*I'd heard nothing!*

**{They are silent, Udek. Don't let it out of your sight}**

The animal circled around and stood facing me about three meters away. The cat was thickly built, and powerful muscles quivered and drew taunt as it shifted its weight from leg to leg. Even with my Brenin senses, I couldn't anticipate its next move. It was impossible to tell when it might leap, or in what direction. The cat bared its teeth as we stared at one another, and I got the impression that the creature was waiting for me to make the next move. Out of the corner of my eye, I saw Toz watching from the platform.

The Veilcat turned its head sideways and looked at me quizzically.

"What *are* you?" Toz asked. "You are *not* Yano! My cat can't fathom your mind. You are blank!"

The cat leapt.

I guessed correctly and spun off to the left, drawing both scalpels down its flank. I could feel the sharp knives puncture its skin and carve their way into the beast's flesh, but also intense pain as it reached out and raked its claws across my chest. I heard fabric rip away as the animal's nails dug deep into my body, and blood began to run freely from the long gashes. The Veilcat and I both cried out, then turned to face each other again; the beast pacing back and forth in front of me, confused. It was unable to affect my mind—to paralyze or suppress my actions—and it had never encountered this before.

Neither had Marshal Toz.

"That looks painful, assassin. Are you still so certain that you can kill me? Personally, I don't think you'll live long enough for us to even meet properly. Why don't you just go ahead and tell me who you *really* are."

"Oh, we *will* meet, Toz. But I'll tell you nonetheless."

There was no reason to hide who I was from him. If I killed Toz, my secret would die as well. And if *I* died, the chamber in my chest would tell the Brenin all they needed to know anyway. Even if they couldn't access the information inside, the construction alone would point to a non-Brenin source; the plan to seed dissent within their ranks would die along with me.

**{Watch the animal, Udek. Toz is trying to distract you}**

*Silence, Seeris! YOU are distracting me.*

I kept my eyes trained on the Veilcat as I spoke, watching it pace back and forth menacingly. "My name is Kiro Tien. I'm an intelligence officer in the Udek Special Corp."

"Udek? Impossible! There is no way those thick skulled, half-evolved animals could get past our defenses. No...no... You are something else."

"Believe what you will," I replied.

"No matter, assassin, I'll find out at your autopsy."

The cat lunged again, but this time I misread its attack. The large beast twisted in the air, dropping low enough to grab my legs with its claws. The nails punctured my skin, pushing deep into the muscle below. The cat used the firm grip to yank me violently toward it, and I fell hard to the floor. I knew the Veilcat had me, but it had left itself vulnerable as well. The animal's large head was directly above, and I reached up with both hands and plunged the scalpels into its neck—driving them so far in that the creature's tough skin closed over the wide flanges on the handles. The scalpels were lodged deep in the flesh, and even though the closing skin had seized the knives— resisting all of my attempts to pull them back out—it couldn't stem the flow of animal's blood. It ran down my arms in a steady torrent. The cat let out a guttural scream and ran off—taking my only weapons with it.

I tried to stand, but my legs gave out and I fell to my knees. My blood mixed with the Veilcat's in a blue and red pool on the ground.

**{She severed an artery, Udek. You must put a tourniquet on that leg or we will be dead in moments}**

I looked around and saw no sign of Toz or the Veilcat, then ripped off part of my tunic and wrapped it around the hemorrhaging leg. I pulled hard, tightening it as much as I was able, then knotted it several times to make sure it held. The blood slowed down to a trickle and I struggled to stand up again.

**{Toz is a pompous fool. If he and the cat fought as a true pair, we would be dead already}**

*Forgive me for not being disappointed.*

I didn't think the Veilcat would survive, not with those slash wounds and the two scalpels in its neck. More than likely, it had run off to die. But Toz was still uninjured, and undoubtedly watching me right now. His voice rang out loudly, echoing throughout the room and confirming my suspicions.

"You killed my cat, assassin! Do you know how long it takes to pair with these animals? Do you have any *idea* what you've done? Murderer! Oh... I won't kill you now. Oh, no. I'll keep you alive—but you will *beg* me for death. I will make you beg, assassin!"

Silence...

And then I heard him drop from the ceiling and moved aside just in time. Toz rolled away and hopped up as I staggered into a fighting stance. I watched as he calmly walked toward me, and as he got closer, I could see the barely controlled rage in his eyes. Two bony knives slowly extended from his wrists; they curved closed tightly, then snapped open straight and rigid.

*The bledi.*

"I am going to gut you, assassin...see what's inside. Then I'll sew you back up again for a nice, long interrogation. You *and* that Yano bitch." He shook his head. "That quarantine... I should have known. *She* let you escape." He stopped in front of me—just out of reach—then raised his arms and noisily raked the bledi across each other. "We are all going to have such fun together, Yano. Well...fun for me anyway."

*How do I extend the bledi, Seeris? Tell me now!*

**{You just *do*, Udek. It's not something I can explain}**

Toz lunged forward and stabbed at my head; I leaned off to the side to avoid it.

*A feint!*

I saw the other bledi coming toward me in an upward thrust and pushed his wrist to the side—falling back against a large pillar. The weapon missed its mark and became lodged in the column beside me. I pulled away from Toz as he struggled to free himself, hobbling as fast as my damaged legs would take me toward the back of the exercise room. I stayed in the shadows and tried to move quietly.

*I need the bledi, Seeris! If you want to get Uli to safety, I must have them.*

**{Give me my body, Udek. And *I* will fight him}**

*You're insane. You would never return control to me. I don't trust you, Brenin, and I must complete my mission.*

**{Dasi. Yes...I know}**

I heard a noise overhead and looked up to see Toz swinging across the ceiling, using his bledi as hooks. He moved from handle to handle with remarkable precision, then dropped onto a high platform nearby and started climbing down the side of it. At the halfway point, he leaned out and peered around the room; I ducked back further into the shadows.

Toz called out cheerfully, "I *will* find you, assassin. But even if I don't, sooner or later you will bleed to death, and then I'll find your body."

He looked around for a moment, as if trying to pierce the darkness through sheer effort alone, and then jumped off the pillar to a low hanging bar and swung off—back toward the front of the exercise room. In desperation, I turned my left wrist over and pinched it with my other hand; the skin separated and I saw a scant bit of bone, but then it slid back in again just as quickly.

*Damn it!*

**{Give me control. Do it, Udek! I can defeat him. I am Yano!}**

By the way Seeris was pleading with me, I could tell that there was a long history of hatred between the Saba and Yano. One that provided a wellspring of motivation for revenge—for affronts extending far beyond today's events. I *knew* that Seeris wanted to kill Toz, of that I was certain, but I was equally convinced that once he controlled his own body again, I would never complete my mission...never see Dasi again. And I wasn't about to let that happen.

*What is tha—?*

I sensed it more than heard it, a slight pressure change, an unnatural *feel* in the air. I was not alone. I flattened my back against the wall of a tall, square platform and tried to move quietly away from the presence. But creeping stealthily was impossible—my injured leg betrayed me with every step. The tourniquet had rendered it numb, and I was forced to drag the useless appendage along. But the slight, scraping sound I made was almost inconsequential, because I knew that if I could sense Toz, he knew *I* was here as well.

"Last chance to give yourself up, assassin. Why prolong your misery?"

The voice came from everywhere...and nowhere. With so many structures—so many different sizes and shapes—scattered throughout the room, the sound bounced around indiscriminately. I edged myself around a corner, emerging from the shadows where I'd been hidden, and found Toz standing there, waiting for me. But he was no longer calm; he'd put aside all pretense of the game we'd been playing. And when he saw my face, his demeanor changed even further. Something feral had been triggered, and now, Marshal Toz was enraged.

He growled, "Let's finish this, assassin."

He ran up a side wall and launched himself through the air, coming down on top of me as I tried to spin away. I felt two sharp punctures rip through my back, tearing the flesh aside as the bledi passed all the way through me...then again as they were withdrawn. His momentum, and my attempt to evade the attack, sent us tumbling to the ground. As we both leapt back up, I found myself standing behind him, and before Toz could turn to face me, I kicked out with my good leg—striking him in the small of his back and pushing him face-first into a partition wall. I leaned into Toz hard, pinning him flat against the smooth surface, then grabbed his hands while he struggled and yanked them down to his sides—trying to neutralize the bledi. It didn't take Toz long to realize that he couldn't break my grip from this position and he jumped up, placing his feet flat against the wall and pushing violently backward.

We both went down again and Toz landed on top of me; the hard impact forcing me to let go of him. I heard air passing through one of the holes in my back and knew that the bledi must have struck a lung. The organ was now collapsing, and robbing me of much needed oxygen. Toz hopped up and spun around as I lay there struggling to breathe. He placed a foot solidly in the center of my chest and held me down to the floor.

"Well done, assassin. Well done... Especially in your condition." The praise was as hollow as the sentiment behind it—the tone of his words announcing the return of the more clinical Marshall Toz. His anger had dissipated completely, replaced by the confidence an impending victory often engenders. "But I grow tired of this," he continued, "and I *do* have other responsibilities. You know... I think I've changed my mind; I will kill you. And then ship your body back to the Yano. Give them a message...a hint of what's to come."

Seeris' voice exploded in my mind. **{Give me control, Udek! NOW!}**

Everything I am told me not to do it, but watching Toz gloat—seeing him cherish his moment of victory—pushed me to my limit. But even more than that, I realized that I had no choice; I had to do *something*. Or die. I relaxed my control over Seeris' body and felt his presence grow stronger, soon eclipsing my own. The Brenin's mind surged through the primary physical connections in a desperate flight—like a long-caged animal fleeing its enclosure. Then he bypassed the unnatural chamber installed by the Bodhi and we switched places—like a ship taking on a new pilot.

I watched in fascination as Toz thrust his bledi down toward my head—even more amazed when I saw my own arm rise up and extend its weapon. But *my* reaction was nothing compared to the look on Toz's face, when Seeris deflected the killing blow, then used both his arms to stab the marshal in the chest and throat. Toz froze motionless, and then his eyes flashed wildly before the inner lids closed and stayed shut. Seeris snatched the bledi back out, and then pushed the Toz's corpse back onto the floor.

**{You killed him, Seeris! We needed that information!}**

*Relax, Udek. We can use one of his hands to get what you want from any console on this ship. They are all keyed to Toz's DNA. We may even be able to issue orders through the terminals, though to my knowledge, no one has ever tried it before. Nevertheless, I believe it will work.*

**{Put me back in control, Seeris. Put me in control...now}**

*I don't think so.*

**{Bastard! I *knew* better than to trust you}**

*You had no choice, Udek; we'd be dead if you hadn't. Toz has been slain, just as you wished, but I'm going to erase all evidence pointing to the Yano. My clan will not suffer for your schemes.*

He rocked to one side, using the momentum to help him stand, then leaned up against a wall, trying to catch his breath.

"Now, let's get out—"

Seeris stopped speaking...he stopped *everything*.

I could still hear the sucking sound coming from my damaged lung, but other than that, there was absolute silence. Seeris wasn't moving; he was dead still. And out ahead of us I saw why. It was the Veilcat...still alive, with both scalpels hanging down from its neck. The animal's mane was covered in matted blood, and a growing sanguine pool developed underneath where it stood. But it was still *very* much alive.

*I've often heard that life is fragile, but if that's really true, why are some things so damned hard to kill?*

Seeris broke the silence, confirming my fears. "It has me,

Udek."

**{Snap out of it! Concentrate. The cat is toying with your mind}**

"I can't... I can't move."

**{Then give me back control}**

"No...you will..."

The cat limped forward and roared defiantly.

**{Give me control, Seeris. Now! It can't affect my consciousness here in the chamber. I am immune. You must return the body to me!}**

The Veilcat leapt just as my mind raced back into Seeris' body. I jumped away from its mouth, landing flat on my back when my injured leg collapsed. The animal's breath was thick in my nostrils as it spun around and pounced on me, holding me on the ground with its two front paws, one on each shoulder. It stared in my eyes and emitted a low growl. It was taking its time, I realized, playing with me in a macabre game that would end with my death. But I kept my focus, and when it finally leaned in close to bite, I struck.

I reached out and grabbed the dangling scalpels, pushing the knives in hard, and then pulling them in opposite directions. The blades ripped the cat's throat apart, showering me in blood and gore. The animal went limp and landed on top of me with a sickening thud...finally dead.

I struggled to push the heavy beast off, and then pulled myself back upright using the nearest wall. Cautiously, I shuffled through the swelling puddle of blood and back over to where Toz's body lay. Clenching my teeth, I grabbed my left bledi and bent it back, hard. It was painful, but compared to some of my other injuries the discomfort wasn't that much of an issue.

**{What are you doing to my body, Udek}**

*What is necessary.*

The bledi snapped loose and I screamed. I had to painfully

wiggle it back and forth to sever some of the internal structures, but it finally came free. Then I fell to my knees and used the serrated edge to cut off one of Toz's hands. When I was finished, I buried the broken bledi in the neck wound where Seeris had stabbed him.

**{You can't do this, Udek! The Saba will know. It will bring chaos and death. You have no idea what you're doing}**

*I'm doing what I have to do, Seeris. And you know that you can't stop me. Now... If we intend to get to that scout ship unnoticed, we have to find a way to wash all of this blood off and get some clean clothing.*

I coughed hard and my chest started convulsing; a clear, blue-tinged fluid spilled out of my lungs and ran warmly down my chin. I barely managed a few gulps of air before the bloody mixture returned to choke me again. Huddled over and grabbing my stomach, I spit the fluid out and started searching the room for a way to clean myself up.

Each step I took brought intense pain, and blood oozed out of wounds all over my body. I felt my heart race as it fought to keep my tissues supplied with oxygen, but my lips were growing numb and I knew that soon, if I couldn't stem the blood loss, I'd join Toz and his Veilcat—wherever it was dead Brenin went. Despite what I'd told Seeris, I didn't really believe we were going to make it all the way to the scout ship.

In fact, I didn't think we were going to make it out of this room alive.

# CHAPTER THIRTEEN

Brother Kiva looked down at the monitor tracking the ship's progress through the vastness of space—the vessel represented by a small circle in the center of the display. The monk saw a much larger circle looming ahead of it, indicating the massive planet that lay directly in their path. He toggled a video feed on another monitor to take a closer look.

Kiva admired the beautiful world; it colorfully gleamed with varying shades of green and blue—each hue seamlessly diverging into the next, and all framed against the backdrop of a swirling, white nebula that lay just beyond the planet. Zooming in closer, he spotted the world's two moons. His actual destination wasn't visible yet, but Kiva knew that at this speed, it wouldn't be much longer before it appeared on the monitor as well.

"We are pushing the engines far too hard, Brother Dyson." Kiva's voice was pained but respectful.

"We have little choice, Brother. We need to meet our admittedly ambitious schedule if we're to have any hope of success."

Kiva nodded. "Of course. But perhaps we can reduce the velocity just a little? Surely it can't make that much of a difference."

Brother Dyson leaned back in the small, uncomfortable chair and closed his eyes. He was visibly tired and exhaled slowly before speaking. "The maintenance personnel promised me that the ship would last the mission, Brother Kiva. And mere *hours* could be the difference between success and failure...life or death." Dyson rubbed his eyes with both hands, and then opened them again to look at the young monk. "A few lost minutes could determine the very future of Bodhi Prime, Brother."

The old monk pushed himself up from the chair and started pacing around the small ship, shaking his hands to ward off the tingling sensation that had developed in them. He'd rested little over the past few troublesome days, and now fatigue threatened to overtake him. Dyson realized that he would fall asleep if he didn't start moving, and now wasn't the time. They were almost there.

Spirited conversation had kept him going until now, and Brother Kiva *was* good company, but they'd been working together closely for quite some time now, and there simply wasn't anything new to talk about. Brother Dyson had just finished counseling his young disciple on some of the more profound aspects of the Buddha's teachings—things he should reflect on further before going forward. Yes...he'd already given the eager monk *plenty* to ponder, and as they were the only two present on the little ship, Dyson's choices now were to either make small talk with Kiva, or drown in himself in his own troubled thoughts.

He envied Kiva in many ways, seeing much of himself in the young man—a prism into a past when Dyson himself had much to learn, and was just as enthusiastic, sometimes maddeningly so. He looked back with amusement at how he must have tortured his masters, never relenting in his search for answers. And he showed his adherents the same patience his teachers had afforded him, squelching the occasional irritations that arose from his other responsibilities to give them the counsel they needed. Yes...there was much familiar about how Kiva saw the world, so idealistic and excited. Even more familiar was how he looked to Dyson for answers, just as the old monk had queried his elders all those years ago.

But Dyson also understood the differences between then and now; his masters had never been forced to deal with an increasingly violent galaxy, or the technological advances that had so profoundly changed the order itself. *No*, he mused, *they never had to make the decisions foisted onto me over the last two centuries. They never had to adapt as I have.*

Dyson clung to the Noble Truths, believed in the Eightfold Path, but he also knew that life didn't often respect his beliefs. Sometimes you had to make hard choices...sometimes, you had to make *impossible* ones. He stretched his arms out and felt the weariness in his muscles, knew he needed to rest, but not yet. They were almost at the next stop—another chance at life—and another possibility of failure.

*No!* He thought to himself. Failure wasn't possible. He would say what must be said; promise what needed to be promised. He would make them see. And if his principles interfered, he would put them aside for the greater good and make the right maneuvers—just as he'd been forced to do on far too many other occasions.

Just as he'd been forced to do with Kiro Tien.

*What hell must that troubled soul be going through right now?* He wondered.

"Brother Dyson," Kiva called out, breaking the monk's reverie. "There are four ships on their way to intercept us."

"They are expected, Brother. They will escort us to the orbital platform for the meeting."

"Brother..." Kiva began nervously, "I know you are wise, and I'd never question your judgment, but are you certain that *this* is the right course of action?"

"No," Dyson admitted, surprising his subordinate. "*This* could be a tremendous mistake that costs us everything." He plopped back down in the seat and looked the younger man in the eyes—his gaze adding weight to his words. "But the alternative is even worse."

They both watched silently as the fighters took up escort positions around their vessel, then the five ships moved together toward the large space station. The collection of interlinked docking platforms and residence modules was perched in a low orbit around the bustling world below. As Dyson looked past the station and at the large planet, his thoughts turned to its peculiar inhabitants: the Blenej.

They were four-armed humanoids, very similar to humans, but interestingly, they had evolved over the eons into three distinct groups, each with a different colored skin. The Blenej were either blue, green, or red in appearance—each color having a unique psychological disposition that matched the physical disparity. The Blenej could be easily identified by color alone as philosophers, artisans, or soldiers, and the differences between them were much more than just skin deep—each group represented a fundamentally different aspect of the Blenej culture, and they filled their roles accordingly.

Brother Dyson so lamented this entire situation. How he'd love to debate philosophy with one of The Blue—compare the theological underpinnings of their society with his own. Or watch a performance by some of the highly gifted Green musicians and dancers—maybe even admire an exhibit in one of their art-filled galleries. There were so many wonderful reasons to visit this place—to take pleasure in their rich and diverse culture—but it was not to be; he was here for the one group that he had no interest in whatsoever. He was here for the soldiers; Dyson had come to meet with The Red. And his mission, the monk admitted to himself with a disturbing sadness, was a quest for violence. A goal that stood in complete opposition to everything he'd ever learned or taught. But there it was nonetheless.

The truth.

He looked out the window, beyond the planet and into the vastness of space, pondering this insanity. Through negotiation and subterfuge, he was becoming...had become, an agent of death. Not all that different from the Udek spy he'd unleashed on the Brenin. But where Kiro Tien was disturbingly comfortable with his ability to end life, it made Brother Dyson sick to his stomach.

*Yes*, the monk wondered as his ship automatically docked at the station, *where was that Udek assassin now? And what havoc has he wrought this day?* Was Tien already dead? Or was it *he* doing the killing? Either way, the blood being shed was on Dyson's hands.

And that blood was seeping into his soul.

# CHAPTER FOURTEEN

*Damn it, Seeris. Where is it?*

**{I'm not certain; there should be a preparatory room here somewhere. Toz wasn't in uniform, so he must have changed his clothing when he got here. He wouldn't walk through the ship in that attire}**

I painfully staggered around for a few more minutes before finally finding an unlocked door at the very back of the exercise room. It led to a staging area of sorts—a simple room with a sink and large wall locker—the latter containing different outfits of clothing, bandages, and miscellaneous medical supplies. The materials were all well used, and it was apparent that Toz had often treated his own injuries in lieu of going to the infirmary.

Locking the door behind me, I ripped off what was left of my clothing and evaluated myself in a large mirror mounted above the sink. Deep claw marks stretched across my chest, and tattered skin gelled together with coagulating blood to cake the wounds in a sticky mixture of gore. There were two smallish holes where Toz's bledi had pushed their way through the skin, and turning to the side, I was able to see their much larger counterparts in my back. The entrance wounds were jagged from the serrated edges of the bledi, and as I watched, a large flap of skin pushed out from one of the holes—flinging a small amount of blood in the air before being sucked back down again with the next breath I took.

I looked down to find that my legs were in no better shape.

There were no towels in the locker so I grabbed some of the clothing and wet it in the sink—cleaning the wounds and the wiping the dried blood off my body. Even though my injuries were life threatening and I desperately needed to get moving, I also knew that I must be meticulously clean. Any blood that I missed would draw unwanted attention, and *that* could also prove fatal.

Once finished, I placed gauze pads over the puncture wounds and skin-tape across the claw marks, pulling them tightly closed. Then I covered the gashes with the self-adhering gauze as well, throwing the empty packaging on top of the bloody pile of discarded clothing and used supplies on the floor. I checked everything over once more before finally turning my attention to my legs. I reached down and removed the makeshift tourniquet and the blood started flowing again.

**{There is an arterial clamp in the med-kit—a small tube with an intelligence chip. If you place it in the wound, it will find the rupture and repair it}**

I reached into the bag and pulled out the tiny device Seeris had described.

**{Just push it through the wound}**

I did as he instructed, squirming as I felt the device move through my flesh and into position. Within moments, the blood flow slowed to a trickle and then stopped altogether. I quickly cleaned up my legs with more wet clothing and bandaged the wounds, then pulled a green tunic and matching pants from the closet and started dressing myself.

**{No, Udek. Green is marshal's rank only. We would be discovered immediately. Put on the black**

**set}**

I tossed the green outfit aside and dressed myself in the black one instead. It was a chore to pull the clothing on; even the muscles that *did* work were sore, and the bandages restricted my limited mobility even further. But eventually, I got everything on and turned to look at myself in the mirror.

*Not bad.*

**{Not good either, Udek. Your posture and injured gait will draw notice. Stay as far away from everyone as you can}**

*I intended to do that anyway.*

**{This has all taken a great deal of time; the marshal's adjutant should be here soon to collect him. We must leave now}**

I wrapped Toz's hand in a clean shirt, and then stuffed it into a small, black carryall I found on the floor of the locker.

*Let's go.*

I unlocked the door and stumbled my way back through the exercise room, passing the bodies of Toz and his Veilcat along the way. I moved cautiously around them, trying to avoid stepping in the copious amount of blood splattered and dragged throughout the area—I knew that much of it was my own. I was pulling my bad leg along and leaning heavily toward my right side, but I eventually made it to the front door and out of the exercise room. I looked down the corridor in both directions before stepping out, heading off in the direction of the transport station. I concentrated on walking smoothly...normally, but there was a sharp pain in my stomach and I doubled over—quickly snapping back upright as another Brenin passed by.

He paused to look at me for a moment, but then kept walking without saying a word.

**{That was close}**

*And completely involuntary. My stomach muscles*

*spasmed without warning.*

I made it the rest of the way to the transport hub without incident, and when the next car arrived, I fell down hard into one of the seats. I winced from the impact, but neither of the other two passengers seemed to notice. Or maybe they simply didn't care. The pair were in the middle of a heated discussion about something, and seemed oblivious to my presence altogether. The car started moving again, and I pulled up the hangar's location on the armrest and selected it.

*As we get closer, Seeris, see if you can reach Uli on her scanner.*

**{I have already been trying, Udek}**

*I don't know anything about Brenin physiology, but these injuries appear damn significant. How bad is it?*

**{The punctured lung is the larger issue. The diminished oxygen flow coupled with the blood loss could make you lose consciousness}**

*That makes sense; I'm already dizzy, and every breath hurts.*

**{Uli can repair my body, but we must hurry}**

The car stopped and the other two passengers rose and got off, continuing their argument as they stepped out of the transport. The doors closed behind them and the vehicle smoothly slid into motion again. Just as it reached cruising speed, the armrest vibrated and a loud alarm began to wail. I looked at the display and saw that a general alert had been ordered.

They'd found Toz's body.

The car came to a stop and I forced myself up, holding on to the seats as I moved toward the doors. I was relieved to find that I'd arrived at my intended destination, and not been diverted to some other area of the ship as part of a Brenin security protocol. As I stepped out onto the main concourse leading to the hangar deck, I was greeted with a picture of my own face—Seeris' face actually—displayed on a wall monitor directly in front of me. Looking down the corridor, I saw that the same image was on *every* monitor.

*Not good.*

**{Uli is near. They are hiding in an airlock just down this corridor. Turn left, and then go straight ahead about fifteen meters; they are at the end of the hallway on the right}**

I remembered from the diagram that the scout ship was in the opposite direction, and toyed with the idea of leaving the pair behind, but I knew that I needed Uli to heal my injuries, and Boe to get us past the Obas military. I reluctantly started walking toward them just as four, armed Brenin came around the corner at the far end of the corridor. I slowed my pace to keep from appearing suspicious and focused in on the group. I could tell by their demeanor that they hadn't identified me yet; one of them was holding a scanner and leading the others.

**{They are following the Obas' life signs...maybe even Uli's. By now, they know everything that's happened}**

*Tell her to seal the airlock door from the inside.*

**{What good will that do? They can simply override the controls}**

*I'll take care of that. Ask her if there are any spacesuits in there as well.*

**{Why?}**

*Just do it! We don't have time.*

**{She said yes}**

*Then tell her to put one on.*

I stepped up to one of the wall consoles and pretended to work. When the Brenin turned down the hall leading to the airlock, I pulled Toz's hand out of the bag and placed it on the panel—everything lit up green and a dialogue box popped up.

*Ask her the number on the airlock.*

**{G-67. What are you doing?}**

I input the information and the airlock controls came up, presenting me with a series of commands. I sealed the door using the marshal's authority.

**{You've sealed her in there...but why?}**

*So they can't override her lockout. They won't be able to trump Toz's authority, and will have to cut their way in.*

**{What good does that do us?}**

*You will see.*

I stuffed the marshal's hand back into the bag, and then half-ran, half-shuffled back in the direction of the large flight hangar. At the entrance, I slowed my pace and calmly walked inside. I was greeted by the sight of many different types of Brenin ships, all in various states of readiness. Some were immediate response fighters, prepared to fly straight out and engage the enemy; others were torn apart and lay in different stages of maintenance—some merely framework. There were even a couple of the heavy bombers I'd seen in videos from Brenin planetary attacks; the ships they used to *pacify* their conquered subjects.

I followed a circuitous route to the closest, unattended scout craft, carefully avoiding the host of Brenin walking around performing their duties. When no one was looking, I crouched down low and unlatched the entry port, then I pushed it open and climbed up inside the ship.

**{We are not leaving her!}**

*Don't worry, Seeris. We are not leaving either of them.*

I resealed the hatch behind me and dropped into the pilot's chair, shaking my head to fend off the dizziness. Then I turned on the console and started the engines. As they warmed up, I pulled Toz's hand out of the bag and placed it on the control surface; a multitude of new commands presented themselves and I started issuing orders to different departments; I knew that Seeris was watching my every move.

**{Clever, Udek. Very clever}**

*I'm glad you approve.*

**{But will it work?}**

I ignored him and returned to the flight controls, raising the ship off the deck and nudging it slightly to the side to clear some maintenance equipment. Among the many orders I'd just issued was one granting unrestricted flight clearance to this vessel, and as I hovered across the hangar, lining up with one of the many launch doors, I watched in satisfaction as it opened automatically at my approach. I flew into the waiting bay beyond, and the large, metal door closed behind me. The exterior door began to slowly open, and when it reached the minimum height clearance for the scout ship, I launched into space—immediately turning left and diving back in close to the massive vessel. I came to a stop just outside the airlock where Uli and Boe were trapped.

*Tell Uli to get ready, Seeris. Instruct her to latch onto the Obas' containment tank so I only have one object to catch.*

**{You are a madman, Udek. But she tells me she's ready. Hurry...Uli says they've started cutting through the door}**

I rotated the craft sideways and positioned the bottom hatch parallel to the airlock's outer door.

"This would be a hell of a lot easier if this ship had a docking port," I grumbled aloud.

I stood up and hobbled back to the flight locker, where I struggled to put on one of the spacesuits stored within it. The process was difficult and slow, especially the legs.

**{Hurry up, Udek. They are getting in!}**

I sealed the helmet and hit the atmospheric purge switch—starting the pumps that quickly rid the ship of air. Then I opened the exterior hatch, locking it in place before going back over to the flight console. Using Toz's authorization, I overrode the safeties on the airlock where Uli was hiding and triggered a rapid depressurization. When I hit the final command, the airlock door flew open, shooting Uli and Boe out into space. A slew of debris followed them out, including at least one Brenin body. They'd already cut their way into the airlock by the time I opened it to vacuum.

I studied Uli's trajectory, then briefly fired the ship's thrusters to better align the hatch with her path. As I watched her approach the vessel, I was gratified to see that she'd locked herself onto Boe's containment tank as directed. The chamber gently bumped into the ship as I bent down through the hatch, reaching out to grab Uli's hand and pull them in. When she got close enough, I let go and she crawled onto my back, working her way over and past me to enter the ship. I held on to the container tightly as she squeezed by, and then tried to pull the tank in with me as I leaned back inside. It was a close fit, and I had to retract the rolling assembly flush into the carriage before I could finally drag it through the opening and set it down on the deck. I turned around to seal the hatch behind me, and then staggered to the flight console to restore the ship's atmosphere. As pressurized air loudly filled the cabin, I set a course away from the fleet and brought the engines to full power.

"The shield—" Uli started.

"I've already taken care of it," I said.

We sped away from the dense, central collection of ships, making our way to the outer perimeter of the Brenin fleet.

"Why aren't they chasing us?" Uli asked.

"Because Marshal Toz ordered all the hangar doors sealed, and then locked out the controls on every patrol ship. He also took the engines and weapons offline on the larger vessels."

"But why would he do that?" she asked is amazement.

I gestured to the severed hand, still resting on the console. "He didn't have much of a choice."

A hole opened up in the Brenin shield as we approached,

re-setting itself as soon as we passed through. Then my console beeped loudly, drawing my attention to an incoming message. I saw that it was a fleet-wide communiqué; the Brenin had finally realized what was happening and were rescinding Marshal Toz's clearances. But it was too late; I knew they couldn't undo everything in time to stop us now. I quickly checked my download queue and was relieved to find I'd gotten everything I was after.

At the same time I was issuing my departure clearances and locking down the launch bays, I'd also set up a program to ferret out all data pertaining to the shield technology, and directed it to make a local copy. It was *all* here. We had what we needed, and by the time the Brenin got everything straightened out and returned the fleet to normal operations, we would be too far away for them to catch us and get it back.

Toz's authority had been most helpful. It was a shame I'd been unable to find a self-destruct order; I could have taken out this entire Brenin armada with a single slide of one finger.

*But nothing is ever THAT easy.*

# CHAPTER FIFTEEN

I pulled off my helmet and placed it on the console, then reached over to engage the ship's autopilot. Once I confirmed that the computer had chosen the fastest route to Obas, I turned around to speak with Uli. She was sitting in the back on a pull-down jump seat, and before I got a chance to open my mouth, she started yelling at me—the shrill voice amplifying as she took off her helmet.

"Are you are *insane*, Udek? We could have been killed! Wait..." She tilted her head slightly to one side and regarded me closely. "Why are you breathing like that? What have you done to Seeris' body?"

"There was no other way to get you out," I answered. "And the injuries are courtesy of Marshall Toz and his Veilcat."

**{It's true, Uli}** Seeris' confirmed, his muffled words emanating from the scanner tucked underneath her spacesuit. **{It was necessary to jettison you like that to get you off the ship...and the injuries did occur during the struggle with Marshal Toz}**

Her features softened—but just barely—and she lowered her voice. "Get that suit off so I can see how badly you've been hurt."

I unsteadily got up from the chair, and Uli came over to help me peel off the spacesuit. Even with both of us working together, it was a major effort to remove the tight-fitting outfit. It was sticking to my body—now bleeding again from several of my wounds, and severed tendons and partially unresponsive muscles were reasserting themselves now that the danger had passed. But despite the difficulties, we finally managed to get it off, then Uli pulled the scanner out from underneath her suit and passed it over my body. She read the litany of injuries aloud as the machine discovered and evaluated them.

"Collapsed lung, broken femur *and* metatarsal on the right leg...severe lacerations on both extremities. Transected artery in the left leg—emergency patch in place. Two penetrating wounds on the torso, both passing all the way through... Your bledi! What happened to it? It's *gone*. Looks like it was broken off.

She looked up from the scanner and stared at my face. "How did you even make it this far?"

"The alternative was death."

"Good point. I'm going to get the ship's medical kit and address these wounds. I'll need to put you out for about ten hours—maybe longer—while I perform the necessary procedures to repair everything."

"Ten hours!" I protested.

"*At least*," she reemphasized. "It will keep you from waking up before I can adequately control the pain these procedures are going to cause. And believe me, you don't want to be awake for this."

"Very well."

**{And what about the Obas?}** Seeris said.

"We leave him in the chamber until I'm conscious again," I replied. "I don't trust him—he might try to subdue Uli and take control of the ship."

She bristled at the suggestion. "I can take care of myself,

Udek."

**{He's right, Uli. We needn't take that chance}**

"All right, Seeris," she agreed reluctantly. She gestured at the ground. "Lie down on the floor next to the Obas' chamber. We'll have to make do with what we have to mend Seeris body, and it's not like we have a bed in here."

I did as directed, holding on to Boe's tank and using it to lower myself down jerkily, while she went to the emergency locker to gather up the medical supplies. My mind raced as I laid down flat on my back; I was wary...uncertain of Uli's motives. Would she try to remove the soul chamber while I slept? I didn't think she'd do anything that might hurt her brother—especially with the lethal Bodhi precautions in place—but *maybe* she thought she could actually pull it off.

**{Relax, Udek. She will do as she says...nothing more}**

*So you can hear all of my thoughts now, Seeris? Even when they're not directed at you?*

**{No. I merely guessed at what you were thinking. But I am sensing more of your consciousness. Seeing more of who...of what...you are}**

*My mind is my own, Brenin. Remember your place in this arrangement.*

**{Heed your own advice, Udek}**

Uli returned with a circular, red box and pulled it open, digging out a thin, metal band, which she then placed around my wrist. She slid a finger down the edge of the device and I felt myself relax. The pain, which had been with me since I first awoke on the Brenin flagship, finally began to subside. I was still fully aware, could see and hear everything, but could no longer speak.

I watched as she took out a pair of scissors and cut away my clothing, occasionally turning aside to throw the scraps toward the back of the ship. She then wiped some milky-green fluid around the holes in my chest, and produced a scalpel and what I guessed were a pair of surgical spreaders from the kit. Uli laid the implements down on top of a sterile pad she'd placed on my stomach, and then leaned over and adjusted the device on my wrist again. My vision began to blur, and the last thing I saw before drifting off to sleep was the scalpel coming toward me.

And then Seeris was in my mind.

And I was in his.

I sensed his anger—the helplessness of being kept at bay and unable to control his own body. The disgust he felt because a *barbarian* was sharing his thoughts...along with his form. But above it all, there was rage. The overwhelming hatred he harbored toward the other clans, a loathing that colored every other thought or feeling he experienced. But then, the intense emotions started to recede, and his mind faded away, replaced by a growing sense of being somewhere...being *someone* else.

An awareness of a time and place far removed from where I now existed.

*I...*

*I was...in a tree?*

Perched on one of its highest branches and looking out over an expansive forest. The trees went on for as far as my eyes could see—all the way to the horizon—and melded into one another so thoroughly that it was impossible to distinguish where one stopped and another began. The thick foliage even blocked out the ground below, making it hard to determine how far up I was. But I knew it was *extremely* high.

Peering in closer, I saw scratch-built dwellings intermittently spaced throughout the thick canopy—some were large enough to house twenty or more people, while others were much smaller structures, designed for a single family or individual.

And they were all on fire.

I watched as two hands rose into view and extended their bledi, jumping out to grab a lower branch and swing away. I was gliding smoothly through previously unseen, open areas between the thick branches, and I soon realized that I was seeing all of this from *inside* someone else. My host was obviously Brenin, and moved swiftly through the canopy for a hundred meters or so, before spinning himself into a ball and landing squarely on one of the smoldering platforms—just outside a small tree-home. Then I felt another presence beside me, and the view turned to the side where I saw a massive Veilcat, primed and ready to strike. But not at me—this cat was mine—I felt that with complete certainty. I watched with apprehension as my Brenin host approached the door warily, bledi at the ready, and looked inside.

Three dead Brenin were visible through the burned and broken door—one adult and two children. I felt my host's pain at the sight, sensed the hurt twisting into rage as he focused in on the puncture marks left in the bodies. He analyzed the shape of the bledi wounds and knew that the murderers were Saba. And there were cat marks as well, especially on the children.

He stood there motionless, knowing that the house was on fire; realizing that soon, it would fall from the sky, raining charred wood and bodies down onto the forest floor below. He knew, as did every Brenin, that this type of wood resisted flames—that the live trees were almost impervious to fire—but sooner or later, the structure *would* succumb, and his mate and children would fall to the earth.

He vowed to himself that their killers would hit the ground first.

He called out to the trees, a shrill sound that brought his cat to attention, and drew reinforcements in from far afield. Soon, he knew, they would come. The Brenin looked around the village and saw destruction and broken bodies in every direction. He hoped that some of the Yano had managed to escape into the forest during the chaos—surely there would be at least a few survivors—but he also knew that when the dead were finally tallied, the price of failing to anticipate this attack would be unbearably high. For him...it already was.

The Saba cowards had attacked while most of the men were out hunting; the village was almost entirely occupied by women and children at the time. But there was blame enough for all here, the Yano knew how treacherous the Saba were, and they should have been more prepared—left more of the men behind for protection.

As he stared out over the canopy, he saw other Yano start to trickle in. They were gathering in the trees surrounding the village, and looking down to witness what has become of their homes and families. My host could feel the rage building in the air, saw the faces of his brethren, and knew that vengeance was near. One of the arriving Yano had spotted a Saba hunting party nearby, singing war-songs as they moved through the trees with their cats. And they had been covered in blood. He pointed out their direction and the Yano departed, leaving the sound of crackling wood and falling debris in their wake.

They swung through the forest with fierce determination—bledi grasping and releasing as required—each Brenin exhibiting a natural grace that many animals would envy. And every Yano hunter had his cat alongside him—the Brenin's rage transferring between master and beast through the mental attachment that bound them together. The feral wrath was contagious, swelling uncontrollably as the deep emotions shifted back and forth between the pairs. The animals roared in response, their anger growing beyond any hope of restraint.

This was not a silent hunting party sneaking up on a food beast. This was a merciless killing mob bent on revenge.

The Saba heard their approach and scattered off into the

trees, hoping to divide their pursuers and escape in the confusion. But it was far too late for that. There were now hundreds of blood-crazed Yano at their backs, and their screams continued to range through the forest—drawing in even more of their brethren from every direction. No matter which way the Saba turned, they found Yano hungry for retribution.

I watched as my host chose a target, and then saw the distinct gray flash as his cat pounced on the Saba. They both fell through the trees intertwined, landing hard on a large branch just a few meters below. My host swung down to join them as the two separated, and using the connection between them, the cat and Yano attacked in unison—the Veilcat grabbing at the Saba's legs while its master went for the neck.

The Saba lashed out frantically with its bledi, but it was impossible to fend off both attackers. The Veilcat reached out and shredded one of his knees and he stumbled forward—the Yano seized this opportunity to lean in and drive his bledi through his enemy's face. It emerged from the back of the Saba's head in an explosion of bone and skin. Blood spattered over my host as he pulled his weapon back out, then he stood back as his cat howled defiantly. The beast grabbed the body in its powerful maw and shook it side-to-side, flinging blood everywhere. The Yano started to call his cat away so they could find another target when the dead Saba's pair arrived, looking for its own revenge.

The Veilcat had become separated from its pair as the Saba scattered, but it must have sensed its master's peril and rushed back to defend him. The beast dropped down from above, pouncing on the Yano cat and sending the two tumbling off together in a deadly embrace. The animals rolled around violently, bouncing off thick, vertical branches and the tree's massive trunk as they grasped and slashed at one another—each struggling to land a killing blow. I felt my host's helplessness as he attempted to intervene, but the two cats had melded together in a ferocious ball of slashing claws and snapping teeth; it was impossible for him to get close enough to help.

Then a loud yelp pierced the air and thick globules of blood flew onto the tree's broad leaves, dripping down onto the branch at my host's feet. The Saba cat had found an opening—disemboweling the Yano's pair with one of its powerful claws. The Brenin saw his cat fall, and felt its injury through their mental connection. The Saba cat used its abilities to amplify the sensation, overwhelming my host's senses.

He froze as the animal flew at him, but the rage of losing his family acted like armor, shielding him from the Veilcat's full mental powers. He struggled heroically to recover his wits before it was too late. I knew that it wasn't me, that *I* wasn't there, but I felt the fear nonetheless. At the last possible moment, he fell flat on his back, stabbing the cat in its stomach as it overshot, and sending it flying off the branch and down through a small opening in the canopy...tumbling far away to its death on the forest floor.

The Yano jumped up and ran to its pair, finding the cat whimpering and trying to drag itself toward its master—still trying to protect him. My host dropped to his knees and cradled the cat's head, stroking the animal's mane and speaking softly to calm the beast. The cat's pain was beyond measure, and its entrails had spilled out in a sticky trail behind it, yet it was still trying to rise, to fight once more with its master.

Loyal...to the end.

The Yano placed his bledi at the Veilcat's neck and looked in its eyes. An understanding passed between their minds and the Yano felt his pairs' gratitude. Then it pulled the bledi sharply across and put the animal out of its misery. The

Brenin's own pain subsided as well as the creature's life ebbed away, the bond between them severed by death. He said an ancient prayer and closed the beast's eyes, then pushed it over the edge of the giant branch—sending it down to the forest floor where all of the dead things go. He then swung back out into the trees to join his brethren, knowing that after they finished killing these Saba, they would go to their lands; that they would burn *their* homes, and kill their families—just as they had so many times in the past.

And then they would return home to rebuild their village...again.

The vision faded, and I sensed Seeris' mind in passing as I rose up out of the haze—regaining my own psyche and then consciousness. I was still on the floor, and looked over to see Uli asleep in the pilot's chair. In a brief moment of clarity, I *knew* why Seeris needed to save her, and why he hated the Saba so vehemently—even why the Brenin fleet was now moving through our worlds. But then all of that understanding faded away and I was myself again.

Drifting back to sleep, I realized that my own mind had once again reasserted itself, and *whatever* I'd just experienced meant nothing to me. Seeris' thought's were his own, and not my concern; he could keep his nightmares to himself.

I didn't need them...

I had enough of my own to last a lifetime.

# CHAPTER SIXTEEN

When I awoke again, Uli was standing over me with her scanner, her mouth twisted up in a pensive scowl. One eye widened as she looked down at the instrument.

"You're awake," she announced, unnecessarily.

"Barely. Help me up."

She reached down and grabbed my arm as I struggled to stand; there was some residual discomfort in practically every part of my body, but thankfully no pain. I was wearing a fresh Brenin uniform, and reasoned that there must be a supply of them in one of the ship's storage lockers.

"How am I?" I asked, leaning back against the tank containing the Obas pilot.

"I've fixed the broken bones and patched and re-inflated your lung, but your oxygen exchange will be hampered until it fully heals. The gashes and punctures were an easier fix; I expect you'll make a full recovery from all of your injuries."

"But?"

"What do you mean?"

"I *mean* that I saw your face when I regained consciousness. I'm trained to evaluate people, Uli, but even someone who wasn't could read that expression. I know something is wrong."

That same expression returned as she ran the scanner over my head, then brought it down again to look at the display. "I really don't know what's going on in your brain, but the synaptic readings are *extremely* hyperactive." Then the confused look vanished and her face grew angry. "The way the Bodhi tied that container into Seeris' neural network is damaging him; I'm sure of it."

"Yes, well I got the impression it was something they'd never tried before."

"Anima—"she started, and then caught herself.

"Don't worry about insulting me, doctor. I have my own reservations about the Bodhi."

"You are all the same to me, Udek...backward and uncivilized. At any rate, the sooner we get you out of Seeris' body, the better."

**{Tell her about the dream, Udek}**

*What...?*

**{Tell her about the attack. About the Saba. And the forest}**

*You saw that?*

**{It is *my* memory}**

*Your memory?*

**{Tell her, Udek}**

"I saw a forest while I slept, one that stretched out forever...and the aftermath of an attack. I saw Brenin hunters with Veilcats, and witnessed homes burning in the trees."

*"What?"* Uli said, incredulous.

She walked to the front of the ship and fell down into one of the chairs, then put her scanner on the flight console and turned back to stare at me—as if trying to look inside my mind using only her eyes.

"But how is that possible?" she asked.

"I still don't understand *what* I saw," I replied. "Much less, how it's possible. But I'm sure it has something to do with the way the Bodhi linked our minds together."

"It is Seeris' dream; he has told me about it many times. And *you* saw it?"

"I felt like I lived it," I confessed.

"You witnessed an ancient memory," she said, clearly shocked. "No non-Brenin has ever..."

**{Ask her about hers, Udek}**

*What difference does one of her dreams make? Does any dream make, for that matter?*

**{It's important. Do it}**

My immediate reaction was to ignore him, but it is always good policy to gather *whatever* intelligence one could about the enemy. And who knows, maybe it was important.

"What about your memory, doctor? What is it *you* see?"

"I would *never* tell some barbarian about my sacred memory!" she spat out. "I will not! You have *no* right. And you wouldn't...you couldn't...even begin to comprehend."

**{Tell her that I wish it. So I can make you understand}**

I repeated Seeris' comment, but Uli insisted on speaking with him through the scanner to confirm it. They argued loudly for several moments, and just as I was becoming convinced that she would never agree, she finally, reluctantly, acquiesced. I sat down beside her in the other flight seat as she began speaking.

"Consider yourself fortunate, Udek. I believe you are the first being not born on Bren to learn about our visions, certainly the first to actually see one. They are genetic memories from the ancient history of our world—from a *very* long time ago." She took a deep breath before starting—preparing herself, it seemed.

"In my dream," she began, "I am Yano, giving birth to my child—a daughter. I am hurt and bleeding...and she is early.

It's not her time yet, but there is no stopping it now. I was injured in an attack by the Saba, stabbed in the stomach with a bledi, and now she is coming. My sisters are there, each holding one of my hands as I push, and I see their concern...feel their anger."

Uli stops to take a breath, and through the trembling, I can see the hate on her face. She's telling the story as if it had happened to *her*—the strong emotions surging across her face and guiding her animated gestures.

"I'm pushing hard, and feel a wetness release inside me. Then I look down to see a puddle of blood underneath, staining the white linen as it spreads out from my body. I feel my daughter move...she's starting to make her way out and I push even harder. Her head breeches, spattering blood all over the midwife, and then my child's shoulders break free. I lean forward for a final push and her feet emerge, followed closely by the placenta."

"The pain lessens and I'm able to sit up...to see my daughter for the very first time. My mother has taken the child now, balancing her on her forearm as she tries to breathe life into her little body. She's gently rubbing her granddaughter's back, and I can see my child's tiny chest rise and fall with each breath pushed into her lungs. Over and over again my mother tries...but it's not working, and my sisters begin to wail."

"My mother is undaunted—her face a mask of love and determination. Somehow, I'm able to hear her softly spoken words, filtering in through all of the screaming. "No, child, you *must* live. You have to make the Saba pay for what they've done to you."

Uli's voice breaks and she looks into my eyes, searching for understanding. "But my mother's words fall on deaf ears, Udek. On ears that have never heard...on ears that never *will* hear. My child is dead. And the Saba have killed her."

I watch Uli's face as she starts to cry, sobbing so hard that it becomes difficult for her to speak. I know that she isn't here, on a ship bound for Obas. She is *there*, in the distant past with the Yano, watching her child die.

"My mother finally sees the truth and joins in with my sisters, screaming at the limits of her voice. And then she cries, squeezing my daughter's body tightly against her chest. My baby's tiny arms swing around lifelessly, and I can see that one of her eyelids is partly open. I look in my daughter's eye, but there is nothing there...nothing except death.

Outside the hut, I hear my Yano sisters grieving with us and our screams fill the forest, but then I sense something else as well, a low rumble that begins to swell in intensity. It's the voices of our men, quickly rising above those of the women. But they aren't wailing in pain, no...they are screaming for revenge. And I know that soon, very soon, they will exact it. By the end of this day, the Saba will be crying over their own dead, and through my tears, I pray that one of them is a child, just like mine."

Uli stops speaking and I know that her story is finished. Her vision, her ancient memory as she called it, was over. Her tears subside quickly and she regains her normal bearing. I sense that she's hiding a trace of embarrassment from sharing this experience, but her contempt for me swiftly quashes it.

"How long ago?" I asked, realizing that these really were ancient memories—from an era long before the Brenin developed even the most basic of technologies. "Just how old *are* these recollections?"

"Our scientists have discovered thousands of skeletons, and the remains of villages dating back nearly fifty thousand years—at the evolutionary cusp of our present form. But even though the events occurred long ago, to us, the memories feel as if they occurred only yesterday."

"It was like that for me as well," I agreed.

**{So now you see, Udek. Now...you understand**

**what you've done. *Every* Brenin has a memory like this, and we re-live them each time we sleep. When the Saba find my bledi in Toz's body, it will rekindle the ancient hatred. And there *will* be vengeance}**

"Better the Brenin slay each other, than continue their advance through our systems, destroying our civilizations."

**{Your civilizations? Pa! You are nothing, all of you. On Bren, we have technology you could only dream of...possibly never even understand. And our literature and art have reached a zenith that we ourselves can't surpass. All of this made even more remarkable when you consider the constant, internecine clan warfare that has plagued us over the generations. But now...finally, we have risen above that hatred, and even greater things await us}**

"You consider exchanging hostages rising above it? And what about the Saba captains' plot to kill them? You are deluded, Seeris."

**{Am I? What about you, Udek? I have seen in your mind as well. Do you really think you can lecture anyone about their faults?}**

"What are you talking about?"

**{I have seen some of your memories—witnessed your vaunted military in action...how they have oppressed others and seized their planets. The only thing that holds the Udek in check is the combined forces of the other species. You only push as far as you dare without inciting a galaxy-wide revolt against you. You are *no* different than we are, and certainly no better. And what about you personally, Tien? How many lives have you taken? I have seen some of your victims...the things you've done...what the other Udek have done to *you*. The clans are right to bring you all to heel; the Udek are diseased in both thought and**

**actions}**

"Enough!" Uli shouted. "For now, we are stuck with one another. It's understood that we each have our own, very different agendas, so let's leave it at that and do what's necessary to finish this, then go our separate ways."

She was right, of course, but so was I. Hell...even Seeris was correct about some things. The actions of every race, *everyone* for that matter, could easily be called into question. I didn't feel compelled to defend the Udek culture or their actions; I wasn't even sure it could be done. But the Brenin were more of a menace than the Udek had ever managed to become—though not for lack of trying. Regardless, all of this introspective nonsense was pointless. And none of it really mattered to me anymore. This entire universe could go to hell for all I cared. I just wanted Dasi and my freedom.

Nothing more.

Yes...once the Brenin are gone, I will be perfectly content to leave everything and everyone else behind and never look back. But first things first.

I got Uli's attention and gestured over at the tank. "Let's wake him up. We need to find out what he knows and prepare for our arrival on Obas.

# CHAPTER SEVENTEEN

Uli repeated the procedure she'd performed on the Brenin flagship, and once again the Obas pilot coughed his way to consciousness—waking up in yet another location not of his choosing.

"Where...am..."

Boe fought to speak, but then gave up, leaning forward to spit water out all over the floor instead. Some of it splattered on Uli's pants and she gave him a disgusted look. He drew a deep breath of air and then tried again. "Where am I...now?"

"You are on a Brenin scout ship bound for Obas," I replied.

"So the escape went well, then?"

"I wouldn't say that. In fact, if that chamber hadn't been spaceworthy, you wouldn't even be here right now."

Boe looked down at the container and shook his head. "I see." The Obas then dropped down to the floor and stood up straight, stretching his limbs as he took a long look around the ship. "How much longer until we arrive?"

"A little more than a day. And the Brenin will be following in right behind us."

"Have you contacted the Obas yet?" he asked excitedly.

"And tell them what? 'Please ignore this Brenin ship as we

land on your planet. We'd appreciate it if you wouldn't blow us out of the sky.' That *is* why we are brought you along, Obas. Remember?"

"Yes...of course."

Boe took a few tentative steps before finding his balance, and then strode up to the flight console with an air of authority. He looked around for a minute, moving his hands from panel to panel, and then stood back. "I can't figure out the communications system," he admitted. "Actually, I can't even find it."

Uli stepped forward and turned it on, tuning the radio to the Obas' general frequency. "There," she spat.

"Thank you...and I really am sorry about the scalpel."

She ignored him, turning back to rearrange the items in the medical kit.

*It seems the Yano bear grudges,* I thought.

**{You know our history now, Udek. What do you think?}**

Before I could reply, Boe started speaking into the com. "This is Master Pilot Boe, issuing a priority contact request."

There was an immediate reply. *"Master Pilot? Your voice prints matches...but we thought you were dead. When you chased off after that Brenin ship and didn't return, we were certain of it."*

"I'm alive, and heading toward Obas now—in a ship very much like the one we discovered spying on us from behind the third moon. But this one is under *my* control, and I require clearance to land in Edo."

*"Edo? In a Brenin ship? You know we can't possibly grant that. You will have to land on the surface."*

"But you must!" he yelled. "The Brenin are coming to Obas. We have to prepare."

I leaned in close to Boe's ear, lowering my voice so it couldn't be picked up by the microphone. "Tell them you have gathered intelligence that can help them fight the Brenin," I suggested.

As I backed away from him, the Obas stared at me, trying to evaluate the truth of my statement. I nodded confirmation.

"I have information that will help us fight them," Boe said into the microphone, his eyes never leaving my face, "You have to let the Ki Assembly know."

There was a moment's silence, and then the voice returned. *"I'll need a few minutes to relay this, Master Pilot."*

"Of course," Boe replied.

"Edo?" I said. "I don't think I've ever heard of that Obas settlement."

**{That's because it's *very* well hidden}** Seeris' voice called out from the scanner.

Boe's face paled. "How do you know that?" he demanded.

**{We've known about your hidden population for some time, Obas. You might be able to keep your secrets from these other pathetic races, but you can't hide them from us}**

"But if you know that—" Boe was interrupted by a tone indicating the communication system had again gone active.

*"Master Pilot Boe, the assembly has granted you permission to land at Edo. I'm sure you understand full well the position you've placed us in, and won't be surprised by the armed escort as you get closer to the planet. We've located your ship based on this transmission and anticipate your arrival in approximately 26 hours."*

"Seeris," I said aloud, "can we find out how far behind us the Brenin fleet is now?

**{Yes. But if you turn on our active scanners, the fleet will be able to pinpoint our location as well}**

*I have a feeling they already suspect where we're headed.*

**{That is a safe assumption, Udek}**

I walked up to Boe's side, prompting him to step away and

give me access to the console, then I pushed in the control pin to activate the sensors. A new interface popped up, and I slid my fingers across one of the yellow lines it projected into the air, directing the sensors aft—back along the exact path we'd followed to Obas. Within seconds, a large pattern of ships appeared on the screen indicating the position of the Brenin fleet. On the small display the hostile armada looked extremely close, but the distance indicators actually put it at a little over a day and a half behind us. I told Boe as much.

"The Brenin will arrive at Obas in two and a half days," he said into the microphone. "Tell the assembly to mobilize the fleet; the ships need to be fueled, armed, and launched into space as quickly as possible."

There was a brief pause, and then the voice replied, *"Do you have any idea what you are asking us to do, Master Pilot?"*

"Yes. I do. And I'll need to speak to the assembly as soon as I land as well."

*"They have already told me as much. I really hope you know what you're doing, sir"*

Boe turned around to look at Uli and me and then replied, "So do I."

The lights dimmed on the com panel as the channel went dead, and Boe turned silent. I knew that there was a somber deliberation going on in his mind—logic and necessity struggling to determine how much to reveal about his world. But there was an overriding curiosity as well; he wanted to know how much we *already* knew.

The Obas lowered himself slowly into one of the pilot seats and placed his hands on his knees. "How did you know about our hidden cities?"

"What hidden cities?" I asked.

**{We discovered them when we first started scouting your civilizations for conquest—before we**

**even moved our fleet into this area of space. Your agricultural output on the surface was *far* too much for the known population, and you don't engage in trade with the other races. In fact, you don't export anything at all, so we wanted to find out where all of this extra food was going. As part of this investigation, we sent undersea probes to the bottom of your oceans, finding the caverns, and your *real* cities; the *true* size of your population}**

"The caverns..." Boe looked shocked, and then afraid. "We've stayed hidden from the rest of the galaxy for so long. We never imagined being discovered."

Hiding their numbers had been easy for them, I realized. No one ever paid any attention to the Obas; there was nothing important about them or their planet. From a practical standpoint, they had nothing of value to trade for...or to take. And as far as the other worlds knew, the Obas had only a small population, housed in modest settlements scattered across the few pieces of dry land the planet possessed. Their tiny fleet of outdated and underperforming ships simply strengthened this perception of harmlessness. Who would ever bother to take a closer look when there were so many more interesting and profitable systems to explore?

"How many of you *are* there?" I asked.

**{Tell this clueless Udek, Boe. Let him know how foolish his race is, and how little they know about their own tiny part of the galaxy}**

The Obas sighed, knowing he had no secrets left to protect. "Our last census counted nearly eight billion."

"Eight *billion*," I asked, incredulous.

"Yes, and that was taken almost forty years ago. You only know about our land settlements, but we have many large cities built on the seabed as well. And, of course, the natural undersea caverns we inhabit."

**{And still, they were considered harmless, until I discovered their submerged fleet on a follow-up mission}**

"We feared you'd found something," Boe confirmed. "That's why I trailed you to Bodhi Prime. I was chasing after you when the Udek attacked and took your ship, but I didn't dare intervene. The Udek are...unreasonable. Beyond that, I needed to keep our secrets, and wanted to avoid any potential questioning. So I followed the Udek to Bodhi Prime, and then again when they left the planet. Watching and waiting. When the scout ship launched again, I was elated. I'd been given another chance to destroy whatever information you'd gathered about Obas. But I wasn't expecting the Udek to defend you, and I certainly wasn't prepared for the Brenin."

"I still don't understand," I replied. "According to the Brenin, your military power almost rivals that of the Udek. But why? You never *leave* Obas. And you ignore all attempts at trade or political alignment. What possible use could you have for all of that firepower?"

Boe's features hardened. "Just because we *choose* not to interact with the galaxy, doesn't mean we are ignorant of its dangers. We are prepared to defend our isolation."

"I see."

**{The Obas were first deemed a minor threat, and when we split the fleet into its constituent clans—soon after our initial victories in the outer systems—they were given little priority. But now that they know about your ships, the Saba contingent is coming for you. The irony is that your *protective* fleet is going to doom your world, Obas}**

"Eight billion?" I repeated, ignoring Seeris. I shook my head, still not believing it. But my brain never got the chance to digest the information.

Because the Udek chose that exact moment to attack us.

# CHAPTER EIGHTEEN

The small ship lurched upward, then rocked violently side to side—sending the three of us forcefully colliding into one another. A second impact hurled Boe back into his confinement tank, knocking it over and sending the last bit of water still inside all over the floor. He slipped on the wet surface and went down hard. I lost my footing as well, and quickly grabbed the flight console to keep from joining him on the deck. I saw the Obas pull himself back up using the blunt edge of a bulkhead, then looked beside me to find Uli holding onto one of the flight chairs as tightly as she could manage—fighting to keep from being tossed around the ship.

I gazed down at the sensor display and saw that it was an Udek patrol vessel attacking us—one with more than enough firepower to eliminate this little ship. I hit the com switch and hoped for the best. "Call off your attack now. We are not the enemy!"

But the Udek ignored us, just as I expected they would—just as I would have done in their position. Two more powerful blasts hit us in rapid succession, and this time we all hit the floor. Uli landed on top of me, and I helped her back up as the ship regained its attitude. I grabbed at the console and tried again. "This is an Udek special operation under the direct authority of General Queltz. Cease your attack immediately."

The pounding abruptly stopped, and a harsh voice barked out over the com system. *"Who is this?"*

"Kiro Tien, Udek Special Corp. I'm working under orders from General Queltz himself."

*"It is my understanding that General Queltz is dead. Why should I believe a disembodied voice coming from an enemy ship? Show me your face, Tien. Prove you are who you say you are."*

"Our communications system was damaged in your attack," I lied. "The video feed isn't working. Contact Colonel Eraz, acting captain of the Ral 97M. She can confirm my identity, and my clearance."

At this point, I *really* hoped she'd survived the engagement with the Brenin.

*"I will,"* the voice replied. *"And I'll also come aboard to verify it for myself."*

**{You can't permit that to happen, Udek. As soon as he sees my body, and Uli's, they will start shooting}**

*Believe me, Seeris, I know.*

"This mission is extremely classified. The nature of this vessel alone should suggest that to you. And *no one* comes aboard without clearance from Eraz," I said.

*"You don't command me, Tien. Prepare to be boarded."*

I sat down at the flight controls and toggled the engines, ramping them up to full throttle...and then a little beyond. Slowly edging the ship sideways, I pointed it away from the Udek craft in what I hoped were small, imperceptible movements, and then I darted off when I had a clear path—using an aggressive escape pattern that I knew would push the patrol ship's maneuvering and targeting systems to their limits. I was very aware of the ship's capabilities...and its few weaknesses.

"You can't outrun them," Boe stated flatly.

"No," I agreed. "And we can't outfight them either."

"Then what *is* your plan?" Uli asked.

"To stay alive long enough for them to get a response from Eraz. So she can vouch for me and call them off."

**{How do you even know they contacted her?}**

"I don't. But there is nothing else we can do now."

I banked the ship up sharply in relation to the Udek craft, and then turned hard and flew back down the side of it. The larger patrol ship couldn't match our maneuvers, but did manage to target us as we passed by. Our ship shuddered under the blasts of multiple energy cannons.

*Of course they'd have a competent weapons officer,* I lamented.

I flipped over backward and dropped our velocity—causing the turning Udek ship to overshoot us—then dropped into a wide loop to spin back around. But they'd managed to hit us again as they flew past and one of the engines was damaged; I realized just how badly when I came out of the loop and tried to bring it back up to full speed.

"Damn...damn...damn..." I muttered.

The Udek had matched our course and were now overtaking us, and there wasn't a damn thing we could do about it. I powered down the remaining engine to wait, and then turned to speak with the others. "Prepare to be boar—"

*"Kiro Tien,"* a voice rang out, filling the scout ship. The Udek patrol vessel had come to a complete stop, stationing itself just off our port side.

*"Colonel Eraz has just confirmed your status and directed us to aid you in any way possible. I don't mind telling you, Tien, that I don't like being bossed around by a mere colonel. But she was General Queltz's aide, and that gives her...additional authority. Until they rescind it anyway. And with him dead, that shouldn't be much longer. But for now,*

*what do you require?"*

"To proceed unimpeded," I replied. "That is what I *require.*"

I checked the engine's diagnostic display and saw that the self-repairing systems had already brought the efficiency back up to seventy-five percent. Shortly, it would be fully operational again.

"But there is one other thing," I added. "Give Eraz a message from me. Tell her that the marshal is gone, and that the Brenin are headed to Obas. Tell her to bring every warship she can summon to the system."

*"Obas?"*

"Yes, Obas. A good portion of the Brenin fleet will be there...in just a little over two days. And let her know I'm still working on the shield problem. She will understand."

*"Very well. I'm just going to re-transmit this exact audio...after I examine it for any hidden Brenin code, of course."*

"Of course. I've been unable to establish a secure channel from this ship for much the same reasons. Udek security protocols forbid accepting any transmission that originate from enemy ships."

*"If I hadn't enabled a local override to allow your original broadcast, you would be atoms right now...my curiosity got the better of me. But believe me, Tien, with the level of Brenin technology we've seen so far, I'll be thoroughly scrubbing my short range radio after we disconnect."*

"A wise precaution. Tien, out."

I re-input the course for Obas and we resumed our trip, slowly gaining velocity as the damage engine healed itself. The Udek patrol ship sped off in the opposite direction, on a mission of its own.

*That was close. Too close.*

I stood up and stretched my arms, causing the one

remaining bledi to slide out from underneath my wrist and protrude slightly. It retracted again automatically. Seeing the bledi reminded me of where I'd left the other one, and what would result from that action; a Yano spy, killing the Saba leader and then working with the enemy to escape. The plan couldn't have gone any better.

Thanks to the dreams, I had a much better understanding of the Brenin. I knew that the assassination would set off intense fighting between the clans, and send a wave of bloodlust rippling through the fleet—a hatred powered by their ancient memories. It *would* weaken them, of that I had no doubt, but would it be enough? Only time would tell. But right now, the Saba contingent was bearing down on Obas, and they would be incensed when they got there.

I truly hoped that there was something useful in the information I'd stolen. Something that could help us fight them. Something that would at least give us a *chance*.

If not, Obas will become the final resting place of us all.

# CHAPTER NINETEEN

The tranquil, turquoise ball grew larger as we swept around the last of Obas' eight moons, diving steeply toward the thick atmosphere ahead. According to the sensor readings we took as we flew by, some of the planet's moons were habitable—even if only marginally so—but the lone signs of settlement were extensive scanning arrays pointing out in all directions; it was as if the Obas were watching the entire galaxy to make sure it didn't intrude on their solitude.

*What were they so afraid of?* I wondered.

The flight console beeped for attention, warning us that four ships were rising up from the surface on an intercept trajectory; they reached orbit at the same time we did, and took up positions around all four sides of the Brenin ship.

The newly arrived Obas craft were impressive—larger than Boe's ship had been, but covered with similar markings. Most notably, these vessels bore *many* more guns. As they drew in closer, tightening up their escort positions, I got a better look at their full complement of weapons.

For their size, the ships were immensely over-gunned, almost ridiculously so. I saw energy cannons, ion arrays, and obvious missile tubes with unknown tools of destruction hidden behind them. The ships bristled with so many armaments that I wondered if there was any room left inside for a crew. Seeris made a similar assessment.

**{Peaceful isolationists? They've fooled you all, Udek}**

*Maybe, Seeris. But it will be interesting to see what effect those weapons have on the Brenin when they arrive.*

**{None at all in my estimation, even if they do manage to breach the shield. And despite the information you've obtained, I highly doubt they'll find a way through it. And even if they did, our hulls are designed to be incredibly resilient. I scanned this Obas 'Secret Fleet' myself, Udek; I know its capabilities. They will be lucky to present even a minor impediment to our armada, certainly no real danger. Regardless, I suggest we drop our passenger off with the stolen information and leave for Bodhi Prime—so we can straighten out our own peculiar situation. You've met your obligation to that misguided monk, Brother Dyson. Bodhi Prime is safe...for now}**

*You seem to forget, Seeris, if we can't stop the Brenin, regaining my own body, and Dasi, will do me little good. Where could we go with your people destroying everything in sight? My future depends on stopping the Brenin. And now that I know more about your race, about how you view the universe and your place in it, I'm even more convinced of that than ever.*

**{Then we will all die in this futile pursuit of yours}**

*Maybe. Do all of you Brenin believe yourselves so infallible?*

**{Our successes speak for us. I see no reason to *think* otherwise}**

"We are preparing to descend," Boe announced.

He and Uli took the two chairs, while I grabbed a ceiling mounted handgrip, leaning forward to get a better view out of the forward window. Soon, we were dropping through the moisture-laden clouds of the lower atmosphere; our passage buffeted the ship slightly, causing it to gently sway side to side. As we broke through and into the open sky below, we were greeted by an expansive sea-view—azure waters stretching off to the far edges of the horizon in every direction. It was beautiful, and haunting at the same time; hundreds and hundreds of kilometers of water with no visible signs of life...or so it seemed. I heard Boe say something to the escort ships and then we veered off to the left—within minutes, a small land mass appeared in the distance. Details started to emerge as we got closer, buildings, vehicles, and finally, people. I recognized the island from Udek intelligence reports; it was Nuvrep, one of the few known Obas settlements.

"Understood," I heard Boe say, then he spun his chair sideways to explain what was happening. "We will land here for a few minutes so our military can board and search the ship. They will be scanning for hidden weapons or explosives...anything that may present a danger. And they *will* search our bodies as well. I implore you to cooperate, we won't be allowed to proceed if you don't."

"Is this *really* necessary?" Uli asked.

"What would you do in our position?"

"The same," she admitted after a short pause. "Probably worse."

"Very well," I added. "Let's get it over with."

**{Frightened children, terrified of their betters}** Seeris commented.

I ignored him, and watched Boe bring the ship down in a small clearing—the escort craft continuing to hover high above us in the partially overcast sky. I was forced to admire the Obas' skill in piloting the ship. It had only taken him a few minutes to gain proficiency with the vessel, and his first attempts were much better than mine had been back in Eraz's hangar—a Master Pilot indeed. We touched down so softly that I barely took notice of it, my attention instead drawn to the group of heavily armed Obas filing out of a nearby building to approach the ship.

The majority of them took up guard positions, while a few others wrestled scanning equipment out of containers and then disappeared underneath the ship. I watched on the exterior monitors as they examined the entire hull—not a single port or extension remained untouched—then all of the Obas gathered together in a group to share their findings. Even through the window it was clear that the deliberations were heated. But eventually, they all agreed on a course of action and one of them held up a communication device to call Boe. The booming voice bounced throughout the ship.

*"We are coming aboard. Back away from the hatch and make no threatening moves."*

The three of us remained at the front of the ship, away from the hatch as directed, listening as the voices grew louder outside. I checked the console to confirm that the security latch was off, and then watched as the hatch lights blinked red twice, before changing to yellow. The door clanked open and a gun rose up slowly though the opening. I saw that it was fitted with a remote camera sight, and the weapon pivoted around in a complete circle—looking for any signs of danger—before its owner popped up through the hatch to level the gun at the three of us. His mouth sagged open as he stared at Uli and me, almost as if he couldn't believe his eyes, but then the Obas recovered himself enough to speak.

"Hands above your heads," he directed. "All of you."

We complied as Boe tried to explain the reaction. "Other than in pictures, or a few learning videos from their time at school, many of my people have never seen an off-worlder before. In fact, the majority of us haven't; some even think you are all mythical. Certainly, no Obas has *ever* seen a Brenin."

The soldier stepped up through the hatch and was quickly joined by two others; the first kept his gun trained on us the entire time, while his comrades scanned and searched every part of the ship. I watched in amusement as one of them picked up Toz's hand and examined it closely. He showed it to the soldier guarding us, and I saw his grip tighten on the rifle. The Obas then held the hand out far away from himself, dangling it by one of the fingers as he yanked a plastic bag out of his waist pouch with his other hand.

"Decontamination procedures," the other two Obas reminded him.

"I know. *Believe me*, I know."

He hit a tiny blue patch on the bag with one of his fingers and it spread itself open, then he dropped the hand inside and the container re-sealed automatically.

"Ivos," he called down through the hatch. "Catch."

He dropped the hand through the opening, and then unclipped a canister from his belt—spraying his hand and arm repeatedly with disinfectant. Even though his hand dripped with the clear fluid, he appeared unconvinced that it was clean.

**{I find it amusing that this barbarian feels the same way about us as we do about him}**

"Where did that voice come from?" our guard asked nervously, his eyes darting around the ship.

"Look over there...on the counter," I replied, gesturing toward it with one hand while continuing to hold my arms up in the air. "It's a medical scanner."

"And why would a voice be coming from a medical scanner?" he asked skeptically.

"It's a long story."

"Well...you are not going anywhere until I hear it."

"We don't have time for this nonsense," Boe interjected. "I need to see the assembly. Now. Scan the device and finish your examinations. We must go on to Edo."

The soldier was respectful, but adamant. "We have to be certain there is no threat, Master Pilot. I apologize, but we must be thorough. We don't understand some of this technology."

Boe snapped. "You will *never* understand this technology. Finish your work and get us on our way!"

The soldier's attitude shifted rapidly. "Yes, Master Pilot."

The guard gestured for the other two to hurry up, and they quickly finished checking the ship's interior. Then they came over to us and meticulously scanned our bodies. They kept their distance, I noticed, reluctant to actually touch us. I expected alarms to go off when they detected the soul chamber inside of me, but because of the strange Brenin physiology, all of their readings probably seemed equally suspicious. The soldier scanning me *did* pause when he got to my arm with the missing bledi; he re-scanned my other wrist and frowned at the difference. But eventually, they were satisfied and our guard dropped his gun...mostly. The other two Obas stepped back out through the hatch and closed it behind them. As the tension in the air lessened, we lowered our arms.

"My name is Corporal Miz," the Obas announced. "I will be accompanying you to Edo." He spoke into his communicator, never taking his eyes off of us. "This is Miz. As far as we can determine, everything is safe. The alien ship may resume its flight now. I will be remaining aboard as a precaution."

*"We await your liftoff."*

Miz turned to Boe. "Whenever you are ready, Master Pilot."

Boe nodded at him, then sat down in the primary flight chair and engaged the ship's flight systems. We gently rose back into the air, barely reaching a hundred meters before starting to cruise forward slowly. I watched the display as our escort craft resumed their previous stations, so close now that I could see flashes of movement as their crews moved around the flight deck. We'd traveled barely two kilometers over the placid waters before Boe slowed the ship to a hover, then pitched the nose down to begin gliding toward to the ocean's surface; I grabbed one of the hand-grips and saw Miz do the same. It was impossible to tell when we hit the water, sliding below the surface in a smooth, light movement—trading air for water in a seamless transition that could have easily gone unnoticed, unless you were looking out one of the windows...which I was.

As we sank into the sea, I saw one of our escorts peel away, and then another—leaving one ship ahead of us and one behind. A brightly colored school of tube-shaped fish swarmed over the area, their skin flickering in the filtered light as they darted through the water. The mass of creatures flowed over, under, and between our ships, before moving off in a synchronized wave to find something more interesting to look at.

Diving even deeper, the natural light faded away, and our escorts turned on their running lights and rotating search beams. Boe did the same with our ship, although its comparative illumination was minimal; it was designed for space flight, not deep-sea diving. Regardless, it was holding up well under the ever-increasing pressure.

For several minutes, there was nothing visible outside the radius of our external lighting, *nothing* but an ebony void—the type of deep darkness that causes the mind to conjure up monsters. But then I saw a glow in the distance, a pinpoint of light that grew larger as we descended—becoming exponentially brighter every hundred meters we traversed. Soon, its source filled our field of view; it was a massive undersea city, one whose illumination rivaled that of the sun's natural light, far above. Its brilliance extended for kilometers in every direction, as did the city's structures.

I was astonished by the sheer size and complexity of what I was witnessing—the sprawling metropolis clearly housed millions of Obas. And then I remembered Boe's confession to us during the journey here; that this was only one of *many* such cities, scattered across the ocean floor—and that they also inhabited the undersea caverns located all over the planet. All of this...in addition to the token presence on the surface.

*Eight billion Obas?*

That might be a conservative estimate.

# CHAPTER TWENTY

Boe leveled the ship off and moved slowly over the city, giving me plenty of time to look around at the impressive structures and unique architecture. There were large, clear domes—reaching hundreds of meters above the ocean floor—each mounted on thick pillars that jutted out from the bedrock below. I could see buildings inside the domes, with small, open vehicles ferrying passengers back and forth between them—the Obas going on with their normal lives as if oblivious to the impending danger.

Beneath the massive domes were even larger structures, stretched out across the ocean floor. Spaced between them were smaller, individual buildings—some connected by clear travel tubes, others completely set apart with external airlocks to the ocean outside. And the surrounding water was *full* of vehicles, ranging in size from large, clear-canopied ferries, to smaller single-person transports. There were even construction vehicles, and I watched as one of them landed on a dome's exterior; the crew grabbed their equipment and stepped out onto its glass-like surface. But none of the conveyances ever came close to us. In fact, *all* of them steered far clear of our ship. Sometimes, obviously so.

And everywhere...*everywhere*...there were Obas.

In the distance, I saw a dark wall rising up from behind the city, pushing through the deep water to ascend out of sight. And as we got closer, I realized that it was an underwater mountain. The immense wall of rock was dotted with small buildings and elaborate rows of lights, all set in obvious, purposeful placement. But the majority of the surface was undeveloped, and thickly covered by bright, red sea-grass that swayed in the gentle ocean currents. A pink-tinged glow surrounded each source of light, as the illumination caught the diluted color of the ubiquitous plants and broadcast it away from the mountain.

We were on a collision course with the rock face, and I noted with increasing alarm that we'd barely slowed down. But before I had a chance to say anything, two large doors parted through the red grass and a bright light came spilling out from within the mountain. Two ships emerged and situated themselves on either side of the doors, and then our leading escort veered off to the right, turning around to head back over the city. The rear guard abandoned us as well.

"We will be landing in approximately five minutes," Boe announced.

Our speed decreased, and we passed unimpeded through the doors—entering a rock chamber carved out of the mountain and coming to a complete stop. A metal wall stood solidly in our path, and the ship's lights reflected brightly off the large, gray monolith, illuminating the entire chamber. I heard a loud clank as the exterior doors closed behind us, and then air bubbles started to rise all around the ship—some as large as a meter across. The water level began to drop rapidly, and I watched as it drained past the front window to recede below the ship. Boe kept the craft steady and level throughout the transition, and within a few moments, the entire chamber was dry.

The 'wall' in front of us began sinking into the floor, and as it did, a huge space became visible on the other side of it. I leaned forward as far as the strap I was holding allowed and peered inside. As my eyes adjusted to the light, I saw twenty-five...maybe thirty ships, just like the ones that had escorted us from orbit. Parked between them and beyond were hundreds of other smaller craft.

"This is one of our small-craft maintenance and servicing facilities," Boe explained. "The capital ships, destroyers, and other large vessels, are all kept in the bigger caverns."

"*Bigger* caverns?" I remarked.

**{Much larger}** Seeris answered.

"He's right," Boe said angrily. The Obas was visibly upset that their secrets were out, but he also practical enough to realize that further deception was pointless.

I looked out of the window again, taking in more detail this time and reflexively making a tactical assessment; there were more ships in this one hangar, with much greater firepower, than we thought all of Obas possessed. But despite this impressive display of ships and armaments—and the enormity of the space itself—I was still able to easily pinpoint our destination as we moved deeper into the hangar. There was a large clearing ahead of us, set far apart from the other ships, and around it were standing at least fifty armed soldiers—presenting a perimeter of firepower more than enough to deal with any potential threat our ship contained. As we came to a stop and descended into the carefully prepared area, I noted four Obas in civilian attire also awaiting our arrival, each flanked by personal bodyguards.

"Do you afford all visitors to Edo such a hospitable welcome?" I asked.

Miz, who'd said nothing the entire trip, chose this moment to break his silence. "There have never *been* any visitors to Edo before. This is a simple precaution, nothing more."

"I see."

Boe adeptly put the ship down in the middle of the gathering and shut the engines down.

"Let's go," Miz said, reassuming the alert, military demeanor he'd possessed on the surface.

I walked over to the hatch and opened it; a pop sounded when the latches released—no doubt caused by a slight difference in pressure between the ship's interior and the hangar's atmosphere.

"You three go out first," Miz directed.

I helped Uli down through the opening first, and then Boe followed her out. Once they'd moved out of the way, I stepped through myself, walking out from underneath the flight wing to join them at the front of the scout ship. Miz made his way out as well and took up a position behind us with his rifle at the ready.

The four civilian Obas approached us confidently, leaving their guards behind. But by the wary looks on the soldier's faces, I knew that if anything untoward happened they would be ready to react within seconds. The Obas came to a halt a few feet in front of us and stared.

"Amazing," one of them exclaimed. "Even for off-worlders, these two are so...different." The others nodded in agreement, and then they all gawked for a few more uncomfortable moments before one of them finally stepped forward.

"I am Lews, Speaker for the Ki Assembly. I'm sure that designation means absolutely nothing at all to you, but I am the elected leader of Obas."

He glanced over at Uli for a second, and then back at me, unsure of which one of us to address. "And you are...?"

"That requires a complicated answer," I replied.

"Then do give me an abbreviated version, please. As you can see," Lews spread his arms out wide and spun slightly to indicate the armed perimeter, "there is some concern about your presence here."

"Of course. I am Kiro Tien, Udek Special Corp, placed inside this body by Brother Dyson...one of the Bodhi."

"Dyson? Yes...yes...I know him. We've had limited dealings with the Bodhi in the past. That would certainly explain that chamber in your chest our crew on the surface detected, and *some* of your actions, but I wasn't aware that the Bodhi could transfer someone's consciousness into an alien body like this."

"I don't think *they* were aware they could it either," I replied. "But this whole situation is rather unique."

"Indeed it is."

"But there is something...more," I confessed. "The Brenin that this body belongs to is in here as well."

*"What?"* Lews exclaimed.

"It's true," I admitted, pointing at my chest. "Dyson thought the creature was dead when he jury-rigged my consciousness in here. Unfortunately, that wasn't the case."

"Then...*who* controls the body?"

**{He does. For now}**

The Obas delegation looked around nervously for the source of the voice.

"The device this female is carrying can relay the words of the Brenin trapped inside," Boe explained.

"Fascinating," Lews said.

"Yes, Speaker Lews, but irrelevant. The Brenin are coming here, to Obas," I said forcefully. "And they are not far behind us. They know all about your true population...and your fleet."

"We have confirmed their course and are taking the appropriate measures to protect ourselves. As to what they know, we have only your word."

"It's the truth," I replied, making no attempt to hide my frustration. "I have acquired information that may help you defend yourselves."

"Your prior communications alluded to as much—and we

will look it all over—but how do we know it's not disinformation seeded by the Brenin, to draw out our fleet and annihilate it? For that matter, how can you convince me that you aren't simply a Brenin spy, sent to help us destroy ourselves?"

"Ask Master Pilot Boe about our actions and motivations. Speak with Brother Dyson, and the Udek military; they will each confirm everything I've told you."

Lews shrugged. "Unfortunately, Boe is under a cloud of suspicion himself right now—for chasing after that Brenin ship in the first place. He may well have been compromised during his absence, we just don't know. And the Udek? No, I think not. We've had a less than stellar history with them over the years. But I *will* contact Brother Dyson; maybe he can shed some light on this whole situation."

"Good. You can give him a message from me as well. Tell him I said that the marshal is dead, and that the Brenin have been diverted from Bodhi Prime. And tell him to remember our bargain...because I do."

"I'll see that he gets your message. But until we've confirmed your story, I think you'll agree it would be best if we kept you all secluded."

"You mean imprisoned," I scoffed.

"Nothing so malevolent; a simple precaution, nothing more."

"Where have I heard *that* before?" I replied, looking back at Miz.

Lews waved his hand and several of the soldiers left the perimeter to join us. "Take them to holding," he directed. "And be careful—see that they aren't harmed."

"Of course, sir," one of them replied.

"And take Master Pilot Boe as well...just in case."

"A simple precaution, nothing more?" I asked sarcastically.

"I'm glad you understand," Lews said. Then he and the other civilians rejoined their personal guards and walked away.

I turned to Boe. "Aren't you upset about being lumped together with us—being held under suspicion just by association?"

"Of course not," he replied. "All Obas understand how devious off-worlders can be. In fact, I'm shocked that we've even made it this far. But Speaker Lews has always taken a much softer approach to aliens than any of his predecessors. If the last Speaker were still in charge, our body parts would probably still be drifting down from orbit."

"I see," I replied.

And then our guards took us off to jail.

# CHAPTER TWENTY-ONE

As far as prisons went, especially compared to a hellhole like Nilot, the conditions of our confinement weren't bad. They'd placed us all together in one room—a small space furnished with a single bed and a square table with two chairs. I dropped down in one seat while Boe took the other. Uli lowered herself onto the mattress, glaring at the lone door leading in and out of the room; she sighed heavily.

"These stupid fools," she complained.

"They'd better deliberate quickly," I said to Boe. "That fleet needs to be manned, fueled, and launched into orbit as soon as possible."

"For what it's worth," Boe replied, "I agree with you. But we are a cautious people, Tien. We learned some violent lessons when we first ventured out into space...and we have not forgotten them." The Obas looked up from the floor where his gaze had wandered to lock eyes with me. "Some of those *lessons* were at the hands of the Udek."

"So you decided to withdraw from the galaxy entirely? Choosing to hide from everyone and everything that wasn't Obas forever? That seems like an extreme solution."

"To you, perhaps, but not to us. We have everything we

need on Obas; we don't need to participate in your capitalistic economy, and certainly not your self-serving galactic politics—driven by whoever holds the most power, not what's best for the masses. To put it plainly...we don't go *looking* for trouble like the rest of you."

"The Udek didn't start this fight," I said testily. "The Brenin came to us."

"They aren't anywhere near your worlds—the systems they've devastated are light years away. But the Udek rushed into battle regardless." The Obas shrugged, and his gills flared out slightly before sealing shut again. "It is in your nature, Tien. You can't deny it."

"They destroyed one of our mining colonies," I countered. "The Brenin killed over a hundred Udek in that attack."

"A hundred? They've killed *billions* on other worlds. And now that their fleet has broken up into smaller groups, they will be able to move even faster throughout the galaxy, spreading death everywhere they venture."

"Until they eventually make their way to us," I interrupted, bringing my point home. "You Obas prepare for the worst, and then wait in fear for the animal to show up at your door. We Udek are more proactive, we hunt...*before* becoming the hunted." I calmed myself and my tone turned even more serious. "But there is something else as well, something that most of the other races have already learned. Something the Obas should know, and the Brenin *will* learn. We embrace the concepts of vendetta and retribution—*revel* in the act of vengeance. If you wrong us, we will respond in kind. In most cases, overwhelmingly in kind."

**{Like true barbarians}** Seeris interjected. **{Unable to control your fear and anger. Lashing out with your pitiful militaristic displays—like children brandishing toy swords. The universe will be better off when you've all been brought to heel}**

"Ah, so we should control our anger," I replied. Like you do against the Saba?"

**{*That* is different]**

"No...it isn't."

I decided to change the subject—to avoid an argument that neither side would ever concede. "Tell me, Boe, what kind of designation is Master Pilot?"

"It's an honorary title," he responded, with obvious pride. "One reserved for Obas pilots that have left the planet and travelled to other worlds. There are not very many of us. So few dare."

"Well that certainly confirms what I already suspected. Over the years, I've seen a few reports mentioning Obas off-planet, but probably less than twenty overall. Where all have you ventured?"

"Two planets," he boasted. "Grenub and Bodhi Prime—both times to pick up...things."

"Thanks to the Brenin, Grenub is now all but gone. What were you doing in the Bodhi system?"

"I'm not allowed to discuss it. But why does anyone other than religious adherents go to Bodhi Prime?"

"Consciousness transfer," I answered for him.

"As I said, I'm not allowed to discuss it." But his tone confirmed what his words did not. *The Bodhi have a very long reach,* I thought. *Even the Obas...*

**{Base, little animals, trying to exercise some small amount of control over your sad lives— transferring yourselves into new bodies when you get old...it's pathetic. Life is to be lived, and death equally embraced. You are all so afraid of what you don't understand}**

"The Brenin have all the answers, eh Seeris? Then why don't you enlighten us?"

**{We live as we see fit. And then die as nature and**

**circumstance demand. It's that simple}**

"Then why have you come here with your armada? Did nature demand that?"

"Tell him nothing, Seeris," Uli snapped. She leaned forward as if preparing to launch herself out of the bed.

**{He has seen our dreams, sister. He will understand}**

"Maybe," she replied coldly. "But he has no *right* to know."

**{Neither he nor the other barbarians can stop us, Uli. This information will gain them nothing}**

"Then why..." Uli started, but then she gave up, lying back down on the bed and closing her eyes.

**{This fleet...this expedition, is the first grand cooperative project the clans have ever been able to accomplish. And the only reason we've managed to succeed *this* time, is because we're driven by a self-serving goal that we all share. We assembled this large force to search for other worlds like Bren, forested planets where we can thrive independently—apart from one another and in peace. We seek a new world for each of the four major clans on Bren. Our belief being that if we segregate, we can nullify the compunctions of the dreams and stop killing one another, rid ourselves of the...instability that holds us back as a people. Despite the adversity built into our nature, Udek, we have accomplished magnificent things. You've witnessed first-hand our technology, our power; you see what we've built. Imagine what we could do apart from the enmity that divides us}**

"But there are hundreds of habitable worlds—just in the local group," I protested. "Surely it can't be that difficult to find what you need."

**{We have examined *thousands* of planets since we left Bren, and have only found one in the last sixty**

**years that suits our special needs. Our ancestors were arboreal—it is who...is *what* we are. And there are specific requirements that must be met for settlement. Although there are hundreds of planets technically within the habitable zone of our species, many of these exist on the very fringes of it. Those too close to their parent star are mostly desert worlds, and the planets on the furthest edge are covered in ice. These marginal worlds typically produce single biome planets that are unsuitable for our purposes. And there are many, many planets that are simply covered in water, with no appreciable land masses whatsoever, like Obas. So the search continues until we are successful}**

"But why kill and subjugate the indigenous populations along the way. Why not just bypass those planets that aren't suitable?"

**{We leave overseers behind on the worlds we conquer to gather supplies needed by the fleet. When their work is done, they rejoin the armada before it moves on. It is a simple matter of necessity. As to why we destroy, you've already explained it yourself. Where the Obas are reactive, we are *proactive*, like the Udek. Anyone that can potentially threaten us is eliminated}**

"Most would consider the Brenin to be the threat," I scoffed.

**{That, is a matter of perspective, Udek}**

I realized that there were never going to be any major points of agreement between anyone seated at this table, especially the two inhabiting *this* body. Seeris saw the universe as something to be controlled—it existed to suit the needs of the Brenin. Every other race was either a potential impediment to their goals, or a minor nuisance to be eliminated.

They were the polar opposites of the Obas, who feared the universe as a rule, and saw anything outside the confines of their own world as extraneous and unnecessary. They would be more than content to pretend they were the only race in the galaxy, and indeed had lived that way for centuries. But the Brenin weren't going to allow them that luxury much longer.

And as for my own people, the Udek, what could be said about us? Our race is strong-willed and stubborn; at times, even to our own detriment, and we continually expand our influence as far as we dare, without uniting all of the other races against us. We don't hide from the universe—nor do we think we are the reason for its existence—but we are determined to exploit it for all that its worth.

"There is something else my brother hasn't shared with you, Udek, something you alone are uniquely qualified to understand." Uli sat up on the bed and took a deep breath before continuing. "We will *all* leave Bren to resettle on the new worlds...only returning home for The Pilgrimage. It's why we can't leave any threats in our wake; we need unfettered access back to Bren after the migration is complete."

"What pilgrimage?" I asked.

"All Brenin compare their personal visions to a universal database, one that helps them locate relatives and common villagers from the Time Before. Using landmarks like rivers and mountain ranges, our ancient dreams have all been traced and mapped. We've conducted extensive archaeological research to find the exact locations of our visions, Udek. I have grieved at the site where I lost my child. Seeris knows where his village was burned—quite literally—to the ground. And he's stood on the exact same tree limb where he was forced to take his cat's life. The trees never die, Udek, our history remains. And we make The Pilgrimage every hundred years to honor our ancestors—by visiting our ancient homes and reflecting on the past. *Nothing* must interfere with that."

"So you kill *everyone*, just to make sure you have a clear path back to Bren?" I asked, incredulous.

**{Not everyone...only enough to ensure our own safety}**

"How very comforting for the survivors," I said sarcastically. "I thought we were no threat to your ships. So why even bother."

**{Many pilgrims will be in smaller vessels, Udek, most without escorts. Even with your limited weaponry, you might prove a risk to them}**

A loud knock on the door interrupted our discussion before I had a chance to challenge Seeris' reasoning; it swung open to admit three Obas—two soldiers and a physician if I read their outfits correctly.

"Kiro Tien," the doctor said. "My name is Eil. I'd like a moment to examine you if you don't mind." She darted a look over at the two soldiers with her to let me know she was going to do it whether I *minded* or not. "I only need a quick scan of your chest. It will be completely painless, I promise."

"You are wasting your time," I answered. "You know as well as I do that the Bodhi install safeguards to protect their technology. But go ahead and get it over with...just don't get your hopes up."

She nodded, smiling, and then came over to the table—turning on a hand scanner as she approached. Boe got up and joined the two guards waiting by the door.

"I'm sure you are right," Eil said. "But imagine if we *can* decipher some of it. It would change everything. I already have a copy of the scans they took of you on the surface—and the Brenin physiology is *fascinating*—but I have to admit that I'm much more interested in this consciousness chamber the Bodhi have devised. I'd love to know how it works."

"So would everyone else," I replied.

I shrugged as she waved the device slowly across my chest, watching as her happy, excited face twisted into a frown. Then she pulled another instrument from her medical bag and pressed it hard against my sternum. It had small silver wheels on its base, and she used them to meticulously roll the machine over the entirety of my torso, front and back. There was a glint of hope in her eyes as she removed it and pressed a series of lighted buttons on the top of the device, but then she read the results and scowled.

"Those Bodhi certainly are a cautious order. That's for sure."

"Anything useful?" I asked, already knowing the answer.

"No," she admitted. "Nothing. Not only is the container heavily shielded against scanning technology, but it's also emitting a static broadcast across all frequencies detailing the explosive power of its failsafe—a boast that my scans *can* confirm. If I tried to tamper with that device, the explosion would be large enough to cause a catastrophic hull rupture in this section of the dome."

She threw her tools back in the bag and brusquely signaled to the guards. "Let's go back to the lab; there is nothing else I can do here. At least there I can learn more about Brenin physiology...without fearing an explosion."

One of the soldiers pushed the door open and the three of them filed out. But before it swung shut again, the doctor stuck her head back in for a final look.

"What an amazing pair of specimens," she said. "I really hope they don't kill the two of you."

Then she pulled the door closed tightly behind her.

# CHAPTER TWENTY-TWO

*Kill?*

No. I didn't think so. Up to this point, the Obas had been almost hospitable...scared and cautious, yes, but hospitable nonetheless. But the doctor was privy to information and *motivations* that we knew nothing about, so the remark had to be taken seriously.

All of the intelligence I'd ever seen on the Obas pointed to their pacificity and ironclad policy of non-engagement. It would be remarkably out of character for them to just kill us outright, particularly in our present circumstances. But my recent experiences were beginning to change how I saw them entirely. Before the Brenin arrived and took him captive, Boe had done his level best to blast me into atoms. And the Obas *had* managed to build and conceal an impressive fleet of powerful warships.

*Maybe we really didn't know them at all.*

The four of us spent the next few hours resting silently, alone with our own thoughts—which in my case was a real blessing, as I didn't hear from Seeris at all. Boe kept his eyes closed for the duration, and even though he was seated, I suspected that he'd drifted off to sleep for at least part of the time. Uli and I remained wide-awake.

I was beginning to think they'd somehow forgotten about us when the door opened without warning—jolting us all alert. Four, armed soldiers walked into the room, followed by Speaker Lews and another Obas I hadn't seen before.

"I hope you are all well," Lews said. "Please, forgive our caution, but we've had our share of bad experiences with off-worlders in the past, and...well...I'm sure you understand. There is also the issue, technically speaking of course, that you are both part of the enemy force en route to attack our planet."

"I understand your apprehension," I replied, "as well as the need for caution. But time is an issue here, Speaker Lews, for all of us. Have you spoken with Brother Dyson?"

"I have. And I must say that he was extremely surprised to learn you were on Obas. I thought that man implacable until I saw his reaction to *that* bit of news."

"And what did he say?"

"He asked me to assure you that he would keep his end of the bargain, whatever that means. He refused to explain it to me, or anything else for that matter. The Bodhi and their secrets..." Lews frowned and then shook his head. "I also told him that the Brenin fleet was coming here now, instead of Bodhi Prime. He seemed very relieved, although I can honestly say that I don't enjoy the reason for his good fortune. Regardless, he confirmed everything you've told us, and recommended that we examine the information you've brought along with you."

"I find it hard to believe that you wouldn't at least take a look at it, no matter what Dyson said."

"Well..." Lews admitted, "We have tried. It's just that we can't decipher this offwor...the Brenin language."

"I can assist you with that," I offered.

"Ahh...I'd so hoped you would. This," he gestured to the man beside him, "is Ni Peq, our chief scientist for extra-planetary affairs, and a very competent physicist. He will be heading up the team we've assembled to analyze the data."

I nodded at Peq and he inclined his head slightly.

"I'm not a scientist," I admitted. "But I *can* tell you what it all says, so maybe you can find a way through their shielding. According to Seeris, their ship's hulls are extremely tough, and our previous engagements with the Brenin bear that out. But despite this, we've still been able to destroy a few of their vessels in the past—those on the periphery of the fleet's formation anyway. The shield has always stopped us from doing any real damage to their numbers, but if you can get past it, you can hurt them."

"We will find a way," Peq said confidently. "We have no choice."

"Can I assume, then, that we are no longer prisoners?" I asked.

"Prisoners?" Lews said. "You were never prisoners, simply guests with restricted access."

*Restricted to one small room,* I thought to myself.

"Master Pilot Boe," Lews called out, bringing the Obas to attention. "I'd like you to stay with our guests for the duration of their visit and aid them as required."

"Of course, sir."

Lews turned to me and reached up with one hand, hesitantly placing it on my shoulder. The gesture was uncomfortable for us both, but the effort and his facial expression conveyed a message he couldn't say out loud: *I'm sorry I misjudged you.*

"Tien, if you would *please* join Peq and his team at the research area we've set aside, we can get the work underway immediately."

I nodded assent. "I'll take Uli with me as well; I'm sure she can provide us with some valuable insights into the finer points of the Brenin language."

"Whatever you think is best," Lews replied.

I could tell that he was a charismatic leader, accustomed to using consensus and congeniality to guide his people, but the current crisis was weighing heavily on him and straining Lew's good nature to its limits. He managed a smile nonetheless. "As I'm sure you can well imagine, I have other matters to attend to, but I'll check in on your progress later." The Speaker stepped aside and motioned for Boe, Uli and myself to leave with Peq. The scientist turned to depart and we followed him out the door.

As we started down the corridor, Peq spoke up. "Speaker Lews is unsurprisingly tolerant of you, off-worlder, it's in his nature. He is part of a minority of our population that has a new *vision* for Obas. The Speaker's party favors greater engagement with the galaxy at large, and I think that misguided goal taints his judgment. He has the dangerous notion that the Obas should take their rightful place in galactic society, and is always touting the benefits of mingling with off-worlders." Peq gave me a disdainful look. "I don't mind telling you that I completely disagree. If anything, I think our present circumstances argue for continued isolationism."

"You can't hide from the galaxy," I replied. "*That* is the lesson the Brenin are bringing to Obas. If you'd left the planet and formed alliances with other races—colonized proximate worlds—you wouldn't be in the danger you are right now." I looked at his face and realized Peq didn't understand just *how* serious a predicament the Obas were in; I decided to *enlighten* him.

"How many Obas are currently off-world?" I snapped.

The question caught the scientist off-guard and he grew defensive. "You know nothing about us, Udek. All of your assumptions are incorr—"

"How many?" I repeated forcefully.

Peq glared at me. "I'm not privy to that information, but

certainly less than a hundred."

"And if the Brenin annihilate this world? What will happen to the Obas then...as a race?"

"Even their fleet couldn't kill *all* of us living on the planet," he argued.

"For your sake, Peq, I hope you are right. But what if they could?"

"Then we would cease to exist as a people," he admitted.

I slowed my pace to get his attention. "I've been on one of their ships, Peq. I have seen the technology they possess. Ask the Grenub or the Yilj what the Brenin can or cannot do—*if* you can find one of them still alive. Don't let your hubris over what you've created here cloud your judgment. The Brenin *will* annihilate this planet if we can't find a way to stop them. And the best chance of doing that is by deciphering the information I've brought on their shielding."

He came to an abrupt halt and locked his gaze on me; the expression on his face told me Peq was weighing my words carefully—trying to decide whether or not to trust what I was telling him...whether he could trust *me*. And even if he couldn't bring himself that far, could he ignore the *possibility* that I was telling the truth?

I watched as the struggle played itself out in his eyes, a lifetime of prejudice and fear fighting against the possibility of failure. Knowing that if he chose poorly, his entire race would pay the price for his decision.

In the end, he made the right choice.

"If that data is as important as you say it is, then we'd better get to work."

We started walking again, albeit much faster this time.

* * *

I took a measured glance around as we stepped into the room set up to study the stolen Brenin intelligence. Constant, situational awareness was a hallmark of Special Corp training—becoming an ingrained habit over time. And it was one habit I hoped to never break.

Upon entering any space, regardless of size, I methodically evaluated the people and environment—considering the value, danger, and implications of everything extant. My eyes automatically scanned the room for weapons or hidden dangers, and then generated an overall threat assessment. I also noted each entrance and exit, and identified potential enemies or allies. Quite simply, I looked for anything that could harm or help me.

This room was decidedly benign.

Two large walls were covered floor to ceiling with display monitors, each highlighting a different file from the records I'd taken from the Brenin. Several Obas were moving from screen to screen, conferring with one another and making notes on ubiquitous dataslates. I assumed that most were scientists, but a few seemed to be more purpose-driven, issuing orders to the others and admonishing them when they became distracted by minutiae. Obas intelligence specialists, I guessed. I noted with some interest that there were no soldiers present, and other than the people milling around in every direction, the room was completely empty, except for a low table with a few chairs spaced around it. Everyone turned to look at us as we entered the room, a few nodding at Boe in recognition.

"This is Kiro Tien," Peq announced. "An Udek operative disguised in a Brenin body. You have all seen the preliminary reports about his situation already." Many in the group nodded in confirmation as Peq gestured past me. "And this is Doctor Uli...an *actual* Brenin."

The assembled scientists made no pretense of social propriety whatsoever—either it was a trait the Obas didn't possess, or they were so overcome by their proximity to actual aliens that they forgot themselves. Whatever the circumstances, they stared at us unapologetically; pointing out the various anatomical features they'd never seen before. The talk grew even louder as they began to openly speculate about the uses and capabilities of the unique Brenin physiology. Peq took appreciable delight in disrupting the collective conjecture.

"Enough!" he snapped. "Doctor Ko, what progress have we made so far."

The room silenced and a very thin Obas stepped forward. There was hesitation in his gait, and even though he didn't appear that different from the others, something told me he was aged.

"We've been able to decipher the Brenin numerical system, and using that, decoded the timestamps on each document. The information on the left wall is more recent, within the last few weeks we believe. The other wall displays much older files."

"Numbers?" Peq said, condescendingly. "*That's* your progress? Numbers?"

"Actually," I interjected, "I think he might be on to something, at least as far as categorizing the information goes." The scientists parted to let me through, and I moved up closer to the walls to get a better look. "I wasn't sure how long I'd be able to access the system, so I set up the search to find the shield specifications first—that would be the older files on the right. The other *bonus* files were based on a broad, secondary search I implemented—looking for the current military plans of the Brenin fleet."

"You can read them for us?" Ko asked excitedly.

"Yes. Well...as I told Peq, I can tell you what it all says, but I wouldn't *understand* any of it—certainly not the scientific underpinnings of the shield technology. It might be faster if I helped you develop a translation matrix, so your entire team could read the documentation for themselves."

"I agree," Peq said. "Everyone get to work on the

translation program first. With all of you collaborating together it shouldn't take that long."

As the scientists set about their work, conferring excitedly about how best to build the program, Ko walked over to join us. The Obas started to hand me a dataslate and then hesitated. "Can you read Standard as well?" he asked.

"Of course," I replied. "I *am* Udek after all."

"Sorry...I'm sorry. It's just that the Bodhi...well, it's so hard for me to believe. I mean...I used to think you Udek were strange, but *this* body."

"We don't have time for this, doctor," I said.

"No we don't," Peq agreed.

"Gah! Let's get this over with," Uli barked, stepping forward assertively to face me. "You may be able to read Bren, Udek, but I doubt you know enough about the proper syntax or subtleties of the language to do this correctly. And I guarantee that much, if not all of the science will confound you...all of you." No one escaped the look of disgust she flashed across the room. "But *I'll* help these cretins get it done, so we can leave this planet and end this interminable nightmare. Seeris, you should assist as well to speed things along."

*Yes, Seeris, you've been quiet for a while now. Ready to be useful for a change?*

But there was no response and the silence stretched on.

"Seeris?" Uli repeated, and then pulled out her scanner to check the settings. "Everything's working," she said. "We should be able to hear him. I don't understand."

"He hasn't spoken for some time," I told her.

"Step aside," she yelled at Ko. The old Obas backed up so quickly that he almost fell down as she flew by. Uli stopped at arm's length away from me and passed the scanner across the front of my body. She checked the results, and then adjusted the instrument—walking around me in a slow circle and scanning my head.

"We need to go to Bodhi Prime," she snapped. "Now! Seeris is dying. Those damned monks have no idea what they've done to his brain. The way they attached those couplings...it's degrade—"

"We are not going *anywhere*," I interrupted. "Until this information is translated and something useful is found."

"That is correct," Peq added. As if on cue, the door opened and two, armored guards stepped into the room, brandishing large weapons to emphasize their presence.

*Sub-dermal vocalizer?* I wondered. *Or are they simply monitoring everything from outside?*

"Barbarians," Uli spat. "If my brother dies, I'll make sure you all follow closely behind; *if* you somehow manage to survive the next few days."

"Then help us get this done," I responded sharply. "Believe me; I want out of this body just as badly as *you* want me out of it."

I'd already discovered that Brenin faces could be very expressive, and right now, her's was projecting unfathomable amounts of rage and hatred—an unbridled loathing that typically led to violence. But what could Uli really do? She was alone and trapped; she had no choice but to help us. The alternative was to watch her brother die slowly, synapse by synapse.

"Give me that pad," she barked, snatching the dataslate away from Ko. "I will work with these Obas to create the translation matrix, Udek. Why don't you start reading the military plans so these fools can attempt to defend themselves?" She pulled on my arm hard and leaned in toward me, placing our faces mere inches apart. "But once they have the information we leave for Bodhi Prime, agreed? No further delays."

"Agreed," I lied.

It was an arrangement I had absolutely *no* intention of keeping. We would leave after the battle for Obas...or not at all if we failed. Uli released me and walked away, with a very unnerved Doctor Ko trailing behind her.

"How do I control the screens?" I asked Peq.

"They are all touch capable, but you'll need a dataslate to access the higher ones."

I took up a position in front of the left wall and began searching through the files, my eyes darting from folder to folder looking for anything useful. Boe and Peq stood beside me staring at the wall of information as well, although I knew neither one of them could make out a single word of the Brenin text.

"Well?" Peq said impatiently.

"Give me a moment," I snapped.

There was so much information to pore through. Hundreds of status updates, material requisitions, personnel transfer orders, maintenance requests... But also...yes... There it was. I walked over to one of the screens mounted low in the far corner and tapped on it, magnifying the information displayed there. Yes, *that's* what I was looking for. I didn't understand everything I saw, but I got the gist of it. And that was enough to cause nightmares.

"Summon Speaker Lews," I said to Peq, not bothering to turn around. I continued reading the screen, attempting to glean as much information from it as I possibly could.

"What is it?" he asked.

"I think I've found out how the Brenin intend to kill you," I replied.

"*All* of you."

# CHAPTER TWENTY-THREE

"Poisoned missiles?" Speaker Lews repeated. "But that doesn't make any sense. If they taint the water, we can simply place filters on our intake pipes and stop it before it reaches the supply lines. And if they poison the atmosphere, we'll just move everyone undersea. The influx from the surface would be inconvenient, I'll grant you that, but there are remedies for both those possibilities. Do the Brenin seriously believe that they can wipe us out with these toxin-infused warheads?"

"I don't know," I admitted. "But I *do* know that the Brenin aren't stupid, they must have thought this all out...including the defensive actions you've just described. According to this document, the plan has been in development for quite some time."

And then something jogged my memory; a recollection from my time on-board the Brenin ship—when Uli had been ordered to test the poison on Boe. Something she'd said...

"Uli," I yelled across the room, earning a reproving look from her. "Didn't you tell me that your people developed the poison to affect a specific type of flora, one native to Obas? I believe you said the agent was designed to pass through the indigenous plant, triggering a mutation into an airborne pathogen."

"I did," she replied distractedly. "It was designed to make the flora release a deadly poison into the air, before culminating in the death of the plant itself. But they didn't tell me *what* plant, or even how it fit in with the planet's ecology."

"The brill," Speaker Lews breathed. He said it quietly, but every Obas in the room heard him, and they all reacted with same shocked realization.

"What are the brill?" I asked out loud.

Uli ignored us and went back to her work, using curt gestures to bring the majority of the distracted scientists back to the table. They'd all been situated around it working on the translation protocols when I'd interrupted them.

Boe spoke up first. "You saw the red plants covering the mountainside as we entered the hangar?"

"I did."

"That is the brill. It covers most of the undersea mountains—all of those with natural caverns inside. The plants filter oxygen from the water and push it through the semi-porous rock face—forcing air into the caverns beyond and creating a breathable atmosphere inside the mountains."

"So they intend to poison the brill," I stated. "That's bad, but still not an extinction-level event. Can't you just abandon the caverns and send your populace into the cities?"

"No," Speaker Lews said gloomily. "You don't understand. The brill provides *all* of our oxygen, for *every* city and habitat; it produces an overabundance of air in the caverns, and that's what we channel out to the cities. We have no artificial oxygen generators; if they poison the brill, the toxin will travel throughout our air supply. And if we shut down the ventilation system to stop it, we will all suffocate."

"And you can't go to the surface," I finished for him, beginning to comprehend the situation more clearly. "Not all of you, anyway. And even if you could, you would be left open to Brenin attacks."

"So now you understand the danger," Lews stated.

"Yes," I replied, hiding my reluctant admiration. The Brenin had indeed done their homework; they'd be able to destroy this entire race of beings with a single missile barrage. But why? Because of the hidden fleet? The Brenin had seriously...viciously, culled other races during their advance, but they had never gone so far as to wipe out the *entire* population. This was so...deliberate.

"I will order the fleet into orbit," Speaker Lews announced. I knew that his confident tone was more for the benefit of the other Obas present than it was a reflection of his true feelings. "Every ship we have will assemble to defend the planet, and then I'll dispatch half of them to intercept the Brenin. Maybe they can buy us some more time to work on the shielding problem. With any luck, they may even be able to thin out the Brenin force before it arrives."

"Your entire fleet couldn't harm us," Uli stated flatly from across the room. "Much less half of it."

"Then why do you feel so threatened that you have to poison us from afar like cowards!" Speaker Lews snapped.

Uli said nothing further, instead going back to work with the now even more anxious scientists.

"Speaker Lews," I started, trying my best to be diplomatic, "maybe sending half your ships out to engage the enemy isn't the best use of your forces. It might be better if they stayed together as a larger fleet, arrayed in a defensive formation to protect the planet."

Lews gestured over at the scientists collaborating with Uli and lowered his voice. "Look at them, Tien. They are motivated and highly competent, but confused by the strange language and technology. They need time to sort this all out. A battle *away* from the planet will slow the Brenin advance and give them that time."

“But right now,” I protested, “the Brenin are a known quantity, maintaining a steady course and speed. We know exactly where they are, and how long we have to prepare. If you provoke them, they may react unexpectedly and change the game.”

“This is no game, Udek,” he said testily. “This is our *lives.* Besides, I think you underestimate our chances.”

“And I think you *overestimate* them,” I countered.

“Enough!” he said with finality. “I appreciate your input, Tien. But the decision is mine. And I have made it.”

Lews swiftly regained his composure, raising the volume of his voice, but softening the tone. “Master Pilot, please take Tien to the vents and show him *everything.* Explain our unique biosphere as much as you are able. Maybe his off-wor...his different perspective can provide a unique solution to this crisis—one that we ourselves can’t fathom.”

“Of course sir,” Boe replied.

“But the translation—” I began.

“Go, Udek,” Uli said dismissively. “I don’t need you. You overvalue your importance here.”

*Maybe,* I thought, *or was she just trying to get rid of me?*

But to what end? Even if she did have some nefarious plan, Uli was being so closely monitored by the Obas that she couldn’t possibly implement it. No, they were perfectly capable of managing her in my absence, and I *should* take this opportunity to learn more about the Obas, if for no other reason than my own intense curiosity. I nodded to Boe, and we followed Speaker Lews out of the room as he departed with his entourage.

Lews moved with deliberate haste down the hall ahead of us, barking commands at those in his orbit, and issuing orders to others more remote through a com unit on his forearm. His retinue was struggling to keep up with him, and even his personal guards were pressed into jogging to stay at his side. I was satisfied that the Obas were completely motivated now; the fleet would launch and prepare for the Brenin.

At least we'd made *that* much progress.

As the Speaker rounded a corner and faded out of sight, Boe veered off to the left and down a short hallway; I followed closely behind him. The small corridor terminated at a rock wall with a polished, metal door set firmly into its center. Boe grabbed the diagonally mounted handle that ran the full length of it and yanked hard, pulling it open. We both stepped through, emerging out into the large hangar where we'd first entered the sprawling mountain complex.

We were standing on a metal walkway that spanned the width of the cavern—high above the busy hangar floor below. I looked down to see Obas technicians rushing around dozens of ships, frantically preparing each for combat. There were various types of armaments scattered around the staging zones, all waiting to be mounted on the vessels. In fact, there were *so many* missiles and directed energy batteries strewn about that even an uniformed civilian could see the truth; the Obas ships were little more than giant weapons platforms, offensive craft with a single purpose—to inflict as much damage as possible, as quickly as possible.

"I should be going with them," Boe said.

"Don't worry," I replied. "Before this is all over, I'm sure you will get your chance. The Brenin will see to that."

We crossed over to the other side of the hangar, encountering a metal door identical to the one we'd just exited. It was also set into the natural cavern wall, but instead of a hallway leading back into the complex, it opened up to reveal a small elevator, barely large enough for four people. We boarded it and Boe pulled the door closed behind us. He slid a finger all the way down the control panel, setting the lowermost floor as our destination, and then the lift started smoothly on its way. As we made our descent, Boe read information scrolling across a wall-mounted monitor sitting adjacent to the elevator controls, occasionally frowning at what he saw there. They were readiness reports, I reasoned. The door opened automatically when we reached the bottom.

"This is it," Boe announced. He stepped aside so I could exit first then walked out himself.

We'd arrived in a rounded, stone chamber, approximately ten meters in circumference, with a high, cone-shaped ceiling. It was empty and otherwise featureless, except for two large holes in the opposite wall, directly across from where we stood.

"Those are just two of the thousands of air vents that crisscross these caverns," Boe said. "This particular pair forces air all the way up to the surface—connecting with other vents along the way that reinforce the stream where needed, or bleed off excess pressure as required. The end result is a constant, steady flow of air."

"All the way to the surface? The brill create *that* much pressure in the chambers?"

"And more. Some vent chambers, like this one, are quite mild. Others generate enough airflow to rip a body apart. Most of those are installed with collectors to harness the wind as energy. As our technology has improved over time, we've been able to reroute and repurpose the distribution of air to better suit our changing needs."

He pointed up at the stone ceiling high above. "The natural rock itself provides illumination, so no artificial lighting is necessary, and geothermal vents prevent the caverns from getting too cold. We had everything we needed to evolve here—air, heat, and light, all naturally occurring in the cavern systems that stretch out across the planet."

"What do you mean you *evolved* here?" I asked.

"Come with me," Boe directed. "I have something to show you. We are going into the vents."

He walked over to one of the jagged, jet-black holes set into the wall and motioned for me to join him.

"Are you serious?"

"I am. Don't tell me you are afraid, Udek."

"Not at all," I replied, already in motion.

As I approached, I could hear the wind rushing out of the chamber and flowing into the hole; it tugged at my clothing as I got closer.

"No need to worry, Tien. We installed repeller fields long ago. They will hold your body in the center of the shaft during the ascent so you don't slam into the rock walls."

"Where are we going?" I asked.

"Up," he replied, and then Boe backed into the vent. I watched in fascination as he rose slowly up into the air and out of sight, then I followed him in.

I looked down just in time to see my feet rise off the stone floor, instinctively reaching out to push away from the walls as I wobbled unsteadily. But it wasn't necessary. Just as Boe promised, my body remained centered in the shaft—far away from the coarse and jagged walls. I tilted my head back to look up and saw the Obas about five meters above me.

His voice echoed through the shaft. "Are you okay, Udek?"

"I am," I replied.

"Good. We will come to another chamber in a few moments, where you will see several sets of handgrips set around an egress hole leading out of the shaft. Grab one of them and use it to pull yourself through the portal and out of the vent."

"Understood."

The walls of the vent glowed faintly—just as the ceiling had in the chamber we'd just left—providing more than enough light to view my immediate surroundings. As my eyes adjusted further, I was able to take in an even greater amount of detail. I caught my reflection in a polished section of rock adjacent to where the Obas had mounted one of the repellers—experiencing a moment of confusion when I saw the Brenin face looking back at me. But then I remembered who and what I was...and where. I was an Udek spy, trapped in a Brenin body, ascending through a mountain deep beneath the oceans of Obas.

*Surreal* didn't seem adequate to describe the situation.

"We are here," Boe announced.

I studied his movements as he grabbed one of the metal handles, tucked in his legs, and then pulled himself through the brightly lit portal. When my turn came, I repeated the actions, grabbing another of the handgrips and following him through, albeit much less elegantly.

We lightly dropped to the floor of another stone chamber, naturally carved out of the mountain, but this small room was dominated by a dark pool of water that disappeared underneath the far wall. Diving suits hung on a bar suspended from the ceiling, and two small benches were placed side by side along one of the rounded walls.

"This," Boe said, gesturing at the water, "is one of our breeding pools. Every Obas that has ever lived came from a pool just like it. There are countless thousands of them, branching off from hundreds of vents around the planet."

"I'm not sure I understand," I admitted.

Boe walked over to the pool, motioning for me to follow. "Look in the water," he directed.

I peered down into the murky shallows and saw intermittent flashes of white; I leaned in closer to try to determine what they were.

"Eggs," I stated.

"Yes. The water here is pure and full of nutrients; it's constantly being replenished from the ocean and filtered by the rocks. There is a tunnel leading from this pool directly out to the open sea." Boe tapped me on the shoulder to draw my attention and I turned away from the water. "These pools," he said, "are how we came to inhabit the caves in the first place."

"Are you telling me that the Obas evolved from the ocean?"

"I am. The eggs have always been deposited here, and when they hatched, our young used to swim out through the channels to live out their entire existence in the sea. But long ago, our ancestors began swimming back into these caverns—exploring them. Eventually, they began to crawl out of the pools and adapted to breathing the air pushed in by the brill. Over time, we evolved accordingly, able to live in both environments. And as the eons passed, we eventually chose to inhabit the safer mountain spaces exclusively, eschewing the deep water for a dry existence. We still swim of course, and our internal structures allow us to adapt to any depth or pressure—this was critical to our early survival when the cave environments varied so greatly. But as you can see, all of the caverns are now pressurized to sea level, and the excess air is converted to energy, or vented out high above us into the atmosphere."

"But what about the Obas on the surface?" I asked. "Certainly they didn't swim up from this depth."

"No. The original surface dwellers rode the vents up. We don't know if it was accidental or intentional, but some of them made it all the way to the top. It was a perilous journey without repellers, and the bottoms of the vents are still littered with the bones of those that were unsuccessful. But some of them *did* survive, and they settled above—on the mountaintops that broke through the surface of the ocean. Over time, a few even made their way back, weighing themselves down with rocks and using low-flow vents to gradually sink back down to the caverns."

Boe gestured over at the shaft we'd used to get here. "Eventually, it became commonplace to use these vents to travel to the surface and back. And as technology improved, we found different ways to make the journey much safer. But with the advent of ships, this manner of transport fell into disuse altogether—except for fishing at different depths for hard to find food species, or for sport. And, of course, to use the breeding pools."

I looked back down at the eggs, marveling at the journey the ancient Obas had made from the ocean floor to the surface, ultimately making their way into space. From everything I knew it was a singular experience, one not shared by any other race. The humans may have similarly evolved from the oceans of their home world, but certainly not into—and beyond—such a unique biosphere.

Boe stood at my side and stared into the pool as well. "Imagine, Tien, crawling out of the sea and into these massive caverns—thinking that you'd found a whole new world, and then again, when the first Obas saw the surface *and a sky full of stars*. When they brought this news back to the caverns there was chaos. We have records of the madness that ensued. But we eventually adapted...as we always have. But *then*, we learned that we weren't the only inhabited planet in the galaxy—that the stars were full of life—and some of it was extremely violent. Well...it was more than even we could manage."

He took a deep breath and shuddered. "Now, do you understand why we keep to ourselves? Why we stay on our own world? It is enough, Tien. We have seen *enough*."

Maybe I did understand; I certainly saw how their history drove them to this reckless view. But understanding it didn't make it right. Isolation wasn't a valid response to the problems the Obas were facing, and I told Boe as much. "So you arm yourselves to the teeth and hope no one comes knocking on the door. It's a foolish approach to life, and quite frankly, it doesn't work."

"Maybe not for you, Udek. But it does for us. It is *our* way. It will always be our way."

*For one more day, perhaps.*

But I knew better than to continue the argument; it was no use trying to convince the Obas to be anything other than what they were. They had generations of evolution and experience telling them to stay home—to stay safe through subterfuge and isolation. And to their credit, it *had* worked up till now.

Frustrated, I decided to change the subject and gestured over at the hanging dive suits. "Why would you ever need those?"

"Ah," he smiled. "Occasionally, the eggs need tending or medical examinations. We use the suits to dive without having to make the switch to water breathing. The transition takes time and is often...unpleasant. Our scientists speculate that eventually, we may even lose the ability to breath water altogether. But I think that would take several more generations for that to happen."

He grabbed one of the suits off the rack and tossed it to me.

"Let's go for a swim," he said. "There is something else you need to see."

I caught the outfit midair and looked it over skeptically. "I don't see how I can possibly get my legs in here."

Boe walked over and hit a release button that caused the legs to pop open wider—deploying built-in side panels that greatly increased their size.

"For egg bearers," he explained. "Pregnant Obas do get rather large.

Despite the adjustments I still struggled pull the suit on, but I eventually managed, sealing my head inside the clear, round helmet last. It was tight where it should have been loose, and loose where it should have been tight, but Boe assured me that it would be fine before donning his own suit with practiced precision.

We stepped up to the edge of the pool and started shuffling down the gently sloped decline, barely noticing the water as it swept over our bodies to submerge us completely. I moved slowly—mindful of where I placed my feet—then Boe walked ahead to guide me. I followed his path step for step. There were eggs everywhere—some smaller and harder to spot than others, so it was best to be extremely cautious.

Boe's hollow voice rang through my helmet, sounding tinny. "I didn't think you'd be able to swim in your present form...as a Brenin, I mean. But it's only a short distance to the outside, walking there won't take long."

His voice fell away, and I was left with the sound of my own breathing filling my ears. I took a moment to look around; noting with interest that the path we followed was barely tall enough to walk upright. Fortunately, the walls gave off plenty of light, and we were able to avoid the occasional sharp rock jutting down from the ceiling. That same illumination sparkled off tiny, transparent organisms that were drifting along with the mild current; one of them alighted on my helmet briefly before propelling itself away again.

The buoyancy felt pleasant as we moved forward through the water, reminding me of my own Udek body and the last time I'd actually *been* swimming. It was almost two years ago, on Hyer.

I'd been sent there by the Corp to recover from injuries I'd sustained on an exceptionally dangerous mission—one that I'd rather forget, but would probably never would. Dasi joined me while I recuperated, and it was the first time in years that we'd been able to spend so much time together. I recalled how much she enjoyed swimming there—going to the beach almost every single day, and spending hours at a time in the ocean. It was a good time, a *great* time...a time we needed to have. My assignments had always kept me away, and Dasi never knew when, or even if, I was coming back. But there, on Hyer, she was happy.

I remembered the planet's rich methane atmosphere, and how we'd been freed from the respirators we were forced to wear on almost every world but our own. I recalled fondly how relaxed and content we'd been...for a few months anyway. But then I was healed, and sent off again on another mission. And Dasi returned home to Rilen, to wait patiently—without complaint—for my uncertain return.

*She deserved better.*

"We are almost there," Boe said, interrupting my thoughts. "Watch your step at the edge."

*The edge? The edge of what?*

And then I saw it, the cave opening that lead out to the open ocean. And beyond it, a field of lights extending as far as the eye could see. We were high above Edo, and as we stepped out of the cave, I stared down in wonder at the massive city below—doubting that anyone could ever grow immune to *that* view. We were even higher than the giant, pedestaled domes, and I could look down inside them with ease. I realized then how deceptively far we'd travelled up the vents during our short journey.

"Follow me," Boe said, stepping out onto a narrow ledge that snaked out across the face of the mountain.

I trailed along behind him, placing my back against the rock wall, and my feet end to end on the uneven sliver of rock extending out from the face of the mountain. We followed the trail carefully as it led away from the mouth of the cave, Boe setting a slow yet steady pace. After ten meters or so of stinted progress, the footpath became gradually wider, and we were able to step out away from the mountain and move normally.

The trail reminded me a little of the perilous route I'd taken on Nilot, of when I'd tried to save Dasi and failed, but when I spun around to look back at the mountainside that remembrance died. This was definitely *not* Nilot...not even close.

The red sea-grass, the brill, completely enveloped the mountainside, silently...peacefully, swaying with the current. This close to the plants, I was able to see hundreds of tiny fish swimming between the thick, flat blades that extended out from the brill's center stalks. Further up the mountain, at the point where the city's light faded away into the blackest nothingness, I saw the dark shapes of much larger fish, hovering over the brill and searching for the prey hidden in its midst. There was life *everywhere*; the entire mountain was covered with it. Curious, I reached out to touch one of the brill and it slowly withdrew from my hand, retracting back into its thick center core. When I pulled my arm back, it re-emerged, expanding again to full size.

"*This* is our life," Boe said through the helmet speakers. "The brill fed us when we lived in the oceans; to this day, we still capture the fish it attracts for food. It brought us out of the sea and gave us air, eventually sending us to the surface to tame this world...and to learn all about the threats beyond it. The powerful vents it feeds provide all of the electricity for our cities. It is our food, our air, and our power. The brill *is* Obas. And if the Brenin poison it, we will surely die. They know this."

"Yes, they do," I said, flicking my fingers across the top of the brill and watching the response. "But I also know that we'll find a way to stop them. I've never given up on anything before, and I certainly don't intend to do so now."

This was about more than just one planet; we had to stop the Brenin here...at Obas. If not, Bodhi Prime would be next to fall, then Jilo, Blenej, Volas—eventually, even the Udek Confederation would succumb. There would be nothing left, and Dasi and I would have nowhere to go.

I looked over to see Boe's lips moving inside his helmet, but quickly realized that he wasn't talking to me. My helmet speaker crackled and he was back.

"We have to return to Edo, now. The Brenin are sending out a vanguard to meet our advance fleet."

"Let's go," I replied, sensing his urgency.

But before we started our journey back to the breeding pool, I took one last look at the brill, then at the brightly-lit city below—curious about what this would all look like a day from now.

Wondering, if any of it would still be here at all.

# CHAPTER TWENTY-FOUR

I was stepping out of the breeding pool when I collapsed.

Lying curled up on the floor—rolled up tightly in a trembling mass—memories flashed through the unbearable pain. I remembered ducking my head often as we returned through the rock passage we'd taken out to the ocean—walking as quickly as we could while still avoiding the eggs. I recalled seeing the bright light emanating from the pool opening just ahead of us, and quickening our pace just a little more in response. Finally, I remembered the difficult walk up the sloped, stone floor to exit the water, my Brenin legs occasionally bound up by the ill-fitting Obas suit.

It was during that exertion that the discomfort first started; a mild ache that rapidly exploded into a searing agony—shooting through my head like a thousand needleblades. I may have screamed; I'm not sure. I *do* know that I pulled off my helmet and fell to the floor, clutching at my temples. My eyes squeezed shut involuntarily, but I forced them back open to find Boe kneeling down over me.

"What is it?" he said with concern. "What's wrong?"

"Seeris," I panted, finding it hard to breath...even harder to think. "Seerrrii...aaaaaaaaa!"

I rolled over on my back and my head hit the stone floor. *Relief!* I lifted it up and slammed it back down again, this time intentionally. I did this over and over again until Boe grabbed my head to stop me.

"The pain! I must...stop...the..."

Then I heard myself screaming. Yes, I was sure this time; it *was* me—a blood curdling cry so disturbing that it would push people back in horror rather than pulling them in closer to help. I was yelling *so* hard that my throat choked up from the effort. Again, I found myself fighting for air—my chest rocked by useless spasms in a futile attempt to breathe. But it was an effort that brought no relief. And then, as abruptly as it began, the knives slicing through my mind began to retract, receding back to where they'd originated—returning to the tortured pit of Seeris' failing consciousness. As the pain diminished, I was able to think again.

*He was struggling to be heard,* I realized. Seeris is not dead yet.

I opened my eyes again and fought to sit up. Boe helped me lean forward.

"Are you alright," he asked.

"I believe so. But this Brenin is dying..." I explained. "I can feel it now."

"And what happens to you if he dies?"

"I really don't know; I doubt anyone does."

With a great deal of difficulty, I managed to get my legs back underneath me and pushed myself up, standing solidly. I ran my fingers across the back of my head and was surprised to find no blood or torn skin. I quickly checked over the rest of my body and found no discernible damage from the incident.

"Are you healthy enough to travel?" Boe asked.

"I'm fine. Let's go."

He looked at me dubiously before walking over to the vent and peering down the shaft to make sure it was clear. "We are going up one more level," he explained. "We can board a seacar there and make our way to the operations center to join Speaker Lews and the others."

We pulled off our diving suits and I handed mine to Boe; he tossed them both back over the hanging bar where they sent a steady trickle of water onto the floor below. The Obas looked at me once again—making sure I was ready to go—before stepping into the vent to begin drifting upward. This time, I followed him into the shaft without hesitation.

When we reached the next level, I grabbed one of the waiting handholds, just as I'd done before. But this time I found myself dropping into a much larger room. Several Obas ignored us as they went about their business, re-fueling or otherwise servicing the dozen or so seacars lined up neatly in the garage. I noted that one of the vehicles was set apart from the others; its dome was open, and a technician was leaning inside, looking over the flight panel.

The entire back of the chamber was open to the sea, and I saw a ten-meter high wall of water being held back by a familiar type of technology—albeit one I'd only seen used in space before. It was a semipermeable force field.

"Master Pilot," one of the Obas said, turning to greet Boe. "We were told to expect you. The one out front is ready to go."

"Thank you," Boe replied, making no further comment as he strode toward the craft.

I followed him over to the two-person vehicle, dropping into the passenger seat and stuffing my legs under the console as best I could. Boe leapt into the car as well, pulling the clear dome closed as we rose into the air. We hovered for a moment as he switched on an opaque display set into the car's dome; a multicolored representation of the city popped up, each dome identified by name and purpose. I watched as he zoomed in on one section of the metropolis and tapped twice on a medium-sized dome, causing a blinking dot to appear. A green line extended out from the dot, linking our present location and obvious destination, then Boe flipped a switch on the control panel and leaned back in the seat. We flew slowly through the force field and out into the ocean beyond—the seacar now ferrying us to the blinking dot on autopilot.

Boe continually adjusted the engines as we hurtled toward Edo, coaxing every bit of power from them—pushing so hard that an alarming, high-pitched whine became audible inside the cockpit. And that velocity remained constant, even as we reached the city and began winding through its intricately placed structures. But despite our speed, I was still able to look inside the domes, noticing far less movement than when I'd first arrived at Edo. The Obas were securing everything, preparing for the Brenin attack, and other than the heavy flow of military spacecraft heading to the surface—to eventually make their way into space—the local water traffic was *much* lighter than before.

The total trip took less than fifteen minutes, ending when Boe turned off the autopilot to take the controls himself—manually piloting the seacar toward one of the domes. I watched out ahead of us as a round portal irised open, and then we flew straight inside the traditional airlock. The door sealed up tightly behind us, and Boe tapped on the console impatiently as the water drained out. When the cycle was complete and the interior door finally opened, we sailed through it and into another garage—roughly the same size as the one where we'd procured the seacar. The canopy popped open before we even touched down, locking into place as Boe expertly nestled the craft into a parking space between two other cars.

The garage personnel stared at me as we hopped out of the seacar and started heading toward the exit, but they didn't challenge our presence. They'd obviously been informed of our impending arrival, but for an Obas, hearing that an alien is coming and actually *seeing* it in person were two very different experiences. I was grateful for their subdued reactions.

"I never imagined that I would be bringing an off-worlder to one of our military domes," Boe said, echoing the unspoken sentiments of his fellow Obas in the room.

"If it's any consolation," I replied. "I never imagined you even *had* military domes."

"That was by design, of course."

"Of course."

We left the hangar, passing through hallway after hallway at a brisk pace, moving ever deeper into the dome. I discovered quickly that the building was full of soldiers, and each one we encountered gave me the same look of disbelief—they all stepped aside to give us a wide berth as well. Finally, we came to a large door at the end of a particularly long corridor. Two, armed guards, one male and one female, were stationed at a desk in front of it.

Boe approached the pair first. "I am Master Pilot Boe," he announced. "I am expected."

"Yes, we know," the female guard replied. Both soldiers looked at me warily as she turned to her display and tapped in a few commands. "I've informed them that you are here."

The guards sat silently while we waited, and then the door flew open and Peq came out. "Finally," he exclaimed. "Come in...quickly now..."

He darted back inside and we strode past the desk to follow him in. The guard's eyes never left us—more specifically, they never left *me*.

I found myself standing in a large room full of military personnel, most seated at four rows of interlinked work consoles—arranged in the shape of a chevron. The "point" faced an immense video screen mounted on a wall at the front of the room. The seated technicians were intently going over the information that flashed across their respective displays, but some of them did look up briefly as we entered the room before returning to their work.

Approximately twenty other Obas stood together in a group at the front of the room, all staring up at the large display—their attention drawn there by another Obas in military garb. From the structural design visible behind his seated position, I could tell that he was on a ship; his deep voice was echoing throughout the room.

*"No, Speaker Lews. They haven't responded to any of our attempts at communication. Scanners indicate that exactly one hundred ships have broken away from their main formation and are headed our way. Our combined speeds will place us in contact in approximately nine hours."*

"Thank you, Master Pilot Mems. The balance of our fleet is now gathering in orbit to prepare. We continue to work diligently on the shield issue as well."

*"Understood, sir. Our sensors indicate that their shield isn't currently active, but I'm certain it will be by the time we converge."*

"Unfortunately," Lews replied, "I think you are right. If we develop any new information, we will let you know immediately."

*"Yes sir."*

The screen blanked for a second and then Mem's image was replaced by a map of the local sector. Both fleets were shown heading toward one another on a nearly perfect trajectory, along with the current position and corresponding velocity of every ship in both formations. The Obas advance fleet outnumbered the Brenin vanguard two-to-one, but I knew that those numbers were utterly meaningless.

The Obas were rightfully proud of their heavily weaponized ships, and hopeful that they could prevail against this threat. It was, after all, the culmination of their worst nightmares—the outside galaxy finally coming to Obas. They had meticulously planned for just this event—used their abundant resources to build and maintain an impressive fleet of warships. And now, they were relying on that tremendous firepower to save their planet.

I just didn't think it would be enough.

Many races had already faced the Brenin, and they had all lost. Most had fielded smaller or less ably equipped fleets than the Obas, but the Udek had sent comparably armed forces into battle against them on several occasions, and we'd still ended up licking our wounds...each and every time. No. Unless we came up with something more, I didn't like the Obas chances at all.

I looked down from the screen to see Speaker Lews approaching us.

"Master Pilot...Tien. I'm sure you both just watched the update."

"We did," I confirmed.

"Our first trial is in nine hours. And I don't mind telling you that I'm concerned."

"As well you should be," I said.

"Yes, well... Have you gained any insight into why the Brenin have so strongly devoted themselves to poisoning our world?"

"Actually, Speaker Lews, I think I have. Boe showed me one of your breeding pools, one of thousands if I understand correctly. Am I also right in assuming that you intentionally limit Obas reproduction?"

Lews looked surprised. "Well, we did in ancient times, based on available habitat. But that hasn't been an issue for a few thousand years. There are plenty of environmentally regulated caverns, and we can adapt even more of them if we wish...and we have our cities, of course. Reproductive constraint is no longer an issue."

"Actually," I disagreed, "that *is* an issue for the Brenin. An egg bearing species could re-populate quickly after the Brenin fleet moves on. You would be able to replenish your numbers, and rebuild your civilization, much faster than the rest of us. And the Brenin know it."

"But if they destroy our habitat..." Lews said.

"Exactly. You will be gone, for good. The Brenin may have tried to subjugate or exploit you, if Obas had anything they needed, but there is nothing here for them. That, coupled with your deviousness in hiding both your population and the fleet, convinced them that they are better off annihilating you completely. In doing so, they no longer have to worry about you becoming a problem later."

"*Later?* They plan on coming back?"

I gave him the short version; they could find out the rest when they undoubtedly debriefed Boe later. "They want to assure safe passage for themselves back to their home planet—so they can return whenever they wish without any possible interference from us."

"I see," Lews said tiredly. "I always saw this as an all or nothing scenario, but I'm even more convinced of it now."

He waved an assistant over. "Vilk, provide these two with guest quarters so they can rest. I'm going to try to relax as well...while we have the opportunity. There is nothing to be done now, and we will all need our wits about us when the battle begins. I'll send for you in eight hours to witness the engagement with the Brenin."

Vilk stepped forward and motioned for us to follow him out.

I caught Speaker Lews before he walked away. "May I have a dataslate with library access? There is some research I'd like to do."

He looked at me curiously for a moment, and then over at Vilk. "Get him one...with limited access of course. Lock out anything even remotely classified as a precaution." The assistant nodded, and then Lews left to confer with some of his waiting advisors.

We promptly left the room and were escorted to separate quarters, very close to the command center. We dropped off Boe first, and just as I was stepping into my room on the opposite side of the hall, another Obas jogged up to Vilk and handed him a dataslate.

"It has been thoroughly scrubbed and locked down," he said. "It can only access the main library for unclassified, scientific inquiries...and general information that any off-worlder would already have access to. This dataslate has also been tamper-proofed; any attempt to modify the device will fry it out permanently."

*They do work fast around here,* I thought. These Obas were far more technologically sophisticated than any of the other races realized.

Vilk stared at me through the doorway before handing over the device. "Did you hear everything he said?"

"I did," I replied. "Don't worry; I won't pry where I shouldn't."

Under normal circumstances, I would have found a way to circumvent their safeguards, but what I was looking for wasn't classified so it wouldn't present an issue. As the door slid closed, I turned on the device, walking over to take a seat at the small desk situated in the corner of the room. I connected to the Obas main library and navigated to the section I needed, and then started my work.

Three hours and a lot of diligent searching later, I finally found what I was looking for and shut the dataslate off—putting my head down on the desk and falling asleep instantly.

Three hours after that.

All hell broke loose.

# CHAPTER TWENTY-FIVE

"What happened?" I asked, running straight past the startled guards and into the crowded command center. "The intercept wasn't supposed to happen for hours yet."

Vilk had awoken me abruptly before darting back out the door—saying only that I needed to get up, now, and report to the command center immediately. I'd sensed the urgency in his voice and jumped up from the desk, running out of the room. As I'd raced down the hall, I noticed that Boe's door was open and he was already gone.

"The Brenin have increased their speed immensely," Peq answered, turning to face me while the others continued to stare at the massive wall screen. "Both the vanguard and the main fleet. We've investigated every other encounter with them to date, and there are no prior reports of them ever reaching this velocity. Either they have deliberately withheld this capability, or they are truly taxing their engines for some reason. The intercept will now occur within the next few minutes."

It was just as I'd feared; we'd forced the Brenin into action ahead of their own timetable. And while it was usually good policy to catch your enemy by surprise—to disrupt their schedule and throw them off balance—you had to make sure that disruption suited your own purposes. I looked up at the screen and saw the two fleets almost on top of one another—there looked to be enough Obas ships to swallow the Brenin formation whole. But I also saw the black, semicircular line surrounding the smaller enemy vanguard.

"Is that the shield?" I asked.

"Yes," Peq replied. "It went active almost ten minutes ago."

"Where is the Speaker?" I said, his absence perceptible, even amid the clamor and heightened activity going on in the room.

"He will be along shortly," Peq assured me. "He is in a meeting with our intelligence chief."

"About?"

"I honestly don't know," he answered, making no attempt to hide his disappointment at not being included.

Master Pilot Mems' face popped up on the view screen, overriding the tactical display—just as a side door opened to admit Boe and Speaker Lews.

*"We are ready to begin our attack,"* Mems announced.

"Proceed," Lews said. "We have every confidence in you, Master Pilot."

*"Thank you, sir"*

The Speaker and Boe joined me at Peq's side and we all watched the screen with equal anticipation, eager to see what the next few minutes would bring.

"Any interesting news from your briefing?" I asked Lews.

He glared at Peq before responding. "Nothing you need concern yourself with, Tien."

But now I *was* concerned, because the uncomfortable glance told me two, disturbing things. The first was that I wasn't supposed to know about the meeting, which meant it probably had something to do with me. And the second, and even more troubling deduction, was that whatever it was, it was a problem separate from the Brenin. They wouldn't hide information from me that might hinder my aid and advice, so what else had gone wrong? *And what did it have to do with me?*

As the battle began, we all turned back to the display.

Just as in every other recorded engagement, the Brenin held fast behind their shield, sending out barrage after barrage of weapons fire through the protective barrier. Unfortunately, the similarity to earlier battles didn't stop there. None of the Obas' impressive firepower could penetrate in the opposite direction, and as a result of the uneven exchange, the Obas ships began disappearing at an alarming rate.

"Speaker Lews," I said. "We've had some limited success by concentrating our attacks on ships at the outside edges of the shield. It seems to be a little weaker on the periphery."

"Thank you, Tien."

He directed one of his officers to relay the information to the Obas fleet and they nimbly re-grouped in response—forming mid-sized squadrons that began attacking the Brenin ships on the outer edges. I marveled at the amount of damage the Obas could inflict, and their efforts were bearing fruit. Four of the Brenin warships broke apart, and several large hull fragments could be seen drifting outside the shield boundary. Emboldened by their success, the Obas pressed their attack even further, destroying two more Brenin vessels. I looked over and saw hope on Speaker Lew's face.

And then it all fell apart.

The Brenin began directing their own considerable firepower on one of the individual attack groups—every Brenin gun trained on the small collection of ships. They were vaporized instantly. Then they targeted another group, reducing it to tiny fragments as well. The Brenin were taking advantage of the concentrated Obas formations to focus their assault, mowing through the advance fleet section by section. Onboard munitions erupted on some of the damaged Obas vessels, causing secondary explosions that destroyed almost as many friendly ships as the enemy fire had. The destruction was *so* quick and absolute, that I realized the Obas had installed all of that impressive weaponry at the expense of proper shielding. Their warships were nothing more than glass canons.

The Udek had been able to manage the perimeter tactic because our ships were designed to withstand tremendous amounts of damage. But when the ever-paranoid Obas laid out their fleet designs, they focused on inflicting terrific destruction—which their ships were more than capable of doing—but without a history of internal conflicts to draw from, or the experience of waging war against other races, they'd severely underestimated the importance of defensive capabilities. There were always compromises to be made when designing warships, but the Obas had relied far too much on offensive capabilities. And while their hull designs were impressive to look at, the vessels crinkled like paper under heavy fire.

As the battle continued to unfold, I realized that the Obas also lacked the tactical knowledge of races that spent a great deal of time in conflict with others—the Udek, for example.

And they were paying dearly for that dearth of experience now.

*"Disperse! Disperse!"* Master Pilot Mems' voice blared from the speakers, the need to salvage his fleet suddenly more important than maintaining radio silence.

The Obas broke away, hurtling toward safety on different trajectories, but the Brenin were still managing to pick them off, one by one. Almost half of the Obas ships were already gone, and more were disappearing by the second.

Speaker Lews' head hung low, his face devoid of all

emotion. "Sound a retreat, Master Pilot Mems. Regroup and return to Obas; we make our stand here. Try to stay ahead of them if you can, but follow them in if you must."

Mems face popped up on the display. He looked harried, yet resolute. *"But, Speaker, we can try again. I can—"*

"No," Lews instructed in a resigned voice. "Follow my orders."

Mems started to argue, then caught himself. *"Yes, sir,"* he replied.

I watched as the Obas sped away from the battle, regrouping far away and behind the enemy vanguard. The fight was clearly over. For their part, the Brenin ignored Mem's ships, continuing on their course for Obas and ramping up speed as they moved past the remnants of the battle.

"Why aren't they pursuing our ships?" Lews asked.

"I'm not sure," I said. "It is an uncharacteristic act for certain. One of the very few I've seen from the Brenin."

"Maybe they think the main fleet will finish them off," Peq offered.

"No," I replied. "Take a look at the chart. The rest of the fleet is coming in on a different trajectory altogether. And they've made no course corrections to indicate they are diverting to pursue Mems. No...the Brenin are in a hurry to get to Obas. But why? It's not like you are going anywhere."

"No, we're not," Boe said. "But the Brenin aren't the only ones en route to the planet." He looked at Speaker Lews, who inclined his head.

"Go ahead and tell him," Lews directed.

"The Udek are on their way here as well. Our long range sensors detected a large Udek attack force; they will arrive at roughly the same time as the Brenin."

"Excellent news," I said. "So that's why the Brenin are ignoring Mems' ships; they know the Udek will help defend the planet and want to get here first."

"Tien," Lews began, "I think you actually *believe* that, and I would like to as well, but it's more likely that the Udek will do nothing as we struggle against the Brenin—let us perish while we do our best to save our world—and then only attack once we've done what damage we can and are defeated. They don't care about the Obas—except as far as we can help them slow down their enemy."

"My people may not be altruistic, Speaker Lews, but they aren't stupid either. If it's in their best interest to become your ally, they will. We just have to *convince* them that it is. How is the translation program coming along?"

"I'll check," Peq said, stepping over to one of the consoles to call the research room.

"Do you really think the Udek will help us," Lews asked.

"My people may not care about the Obas," I answered honestly, "but if they see you as someone they can exploit to get what they want—namely, stopping the Brenin—they *will* join the battle. And the end result will be the same; they will fight for Obas."

His face turned grave. "Well then, let's hope they see us ripe for exploitation. After the battle we just witnessed, I'll take all the help we can get...whatever their motivation." He lowered his voice so that only Boe and I would be able to hear him. "I should have listened to you, Tien. I should have kept the entire fleet here, together—prepared to defend the planet."

"You did what you tho—"

"Speaker Lews!" one of the officers called out excitedly. "The approaching Udek fleet is hailing us."

"Well, put them through," Lews directed, his face cautious, yet hopeful.

A familiar, caustic voice blared through the room, and I couldn't fight my blossoming smile. *"This is Colonel Eraz of the Udek. Is that bastard, Kiro Tien there?"*

"You can relax, Speaker Lews. I'm pretty sure I can

convince *these* Udek to help us."

"May I?" I asked, motioning toward the wall where Eraz's face featured prominently on the video screen.

"By all means," the Speaker answered.

I strode up to the large monitor. "Hello, Colonel Eraz. Strange meeting you here."

*"That it is, spy. I'm sure you can imagine my surprise when I found out you were headed for Obas."*

"No doubt. You received my entire message, then?"

*"I did. But I had one hell of a time convincing headquarters to send these ships. Forgive me for speaking in nebulous terms, but I don't trust these Obas; our plan regarding the marshal was successful?"*

"You needn't worry, Eraz, the Obas don't trust you either. And yes, everything went just as we planned—there *will* be a reckoning within the Brenin ranks. I was able to retrieve the information we needed as well, and the Obas are working on the shield problem as we speak."

*"Then Queltz was right about you, spy. You got the job done."*

"It was the *only* thing he was right about," I replied brusquely.

*"Yes, well...I will be joining you planet-side shortly, right after I get a closer look at this surprisingly large fleet of Obas warships we've discovered in orbit."* She looked down at something, frowned, and then faced the screen again. *"Assuming the Brenin can't go any faster than this ridiculous speed they've already managed, our estimates put us arriving an hour or so before them. That still leaves plenty of time for me to land and take over the operation."*

I looked over at Speaker Lews and saw the anger on his face. "She is rather presumptuous, isn't she?"

*"If you prefer, we can detour to another system,"* Eraz said matter-of-factly.

Speaker Lews shook his head sharply and readied a reply. The other Obas looked over at him intently, anticipating a defiant response that would put this off-worlder in her place. They were already uncomfortable with the Udek simply *coming* to Obas, but to have them actually enter the atmosphere and dive to one of their secret cities...well, that was simply too much. I decided to intervene before this got out of hand.

"Actually, Eraz, it would be best if you remained in orbit and *helped* coordinate the defense from there. The Obas have limited combat experience, and it has recently become apparent that their fleet is over-gunned and under-shielded. If you and your engagement coordinators can map out a plan with those considerations in mind, it would be most helpful."

*"I'll remind you, Tien,"* she said icily, *"that you don't command me, or this fleet."* Eraz leaned back in her chair and pressed her hands together contemplatively. *"But...what you say does makes sense—send me data on the Obas fleet's tactical capabilities and we will figure something out."*

"Absolutely not!" Speaker Lews yelled, clearly exasperated. "Those details are closely guarded military secrets! I'll not hand them over to some off-worlder for examination."

Eraz leaned in closer to the screen. *"Then I'll just wait until after the Brenin leave and examine the wreckage for what I need."*

"How dare y—" Speaker Lews started.

"Allow me to point out to both of you that while we bicker over how or whether we will fight together, the Brenin are drawing ever closer." I gently grabbed Speaker Lews arm, drawing not only his attention, but that of his bodyguards as well. "Eraz is right," I told him. "She needs that information to plan an adequate defense for your planet. Without knowing your ship's strengths and relative weaknesses, she can't do that." I released his sleeve and turned to the screen. "And Eraz,

I think you will be surprised by the firepower these Obas wield. They may not be able to sustain as much damage as our ships, but they can certainly dish it out with an amazing ferocity. The Udek would do well to fight at their side."

Eraz sat back and clasped her hands together once again, staring at my face. *"I am beginning to wonder what being in that body has done to you, Tien. You are changing from an assassin into a diplomat. I want to stop the Brenin—it's why we've come—but I need the information necessary to do my job."*

I looked back over my shoulder to see Speaker Lews conferring with Peq and several other Obas officials. But despite the flailing arms and determined faces, they were practically whispering, and even with my Brenin senses I couldn't make out what they were talking about. Whatever it was, it so incensed Peq that he threw his hands up, and then stormed back to the console where he'd been checking on the translation project. Soon afterward, another Obas, this one in a military uniform, spun around and left the room in a huff. Speaker Lews dismissed those remaining and rejoined me at the wall display to face Eraz. He looked tired; the argument had obviously taken its toll on him.

"We will cooperate," he announced. "I've detailed my military attaché to transmit the information you require. Peq informs me that the translation program is now complete, and that our scientists are already sifting through the data—looking for a way to defeat the Brenin shielding."

*"Excellent."* Eraz said. *Then send me that information as well."*

"I have a better idea," I interrupted, trying to stem any further arguments. "Go ahead and send the shield specifications, Speaker Lews, but also set up a line of communication between the Obas and Udek engineers. That way they can work on the problem together. It might speed things along."

I knew it was a good idea when neither Eraz nor Speaker Lews seemed happy with it. But both of them *did* see the wisdom behind the recommendation.

"Very well," Lews said. "We will send everything along promptly and set up a data link."

*"Good,"* Eraz replied. *"I'll notify my personnel and be in touch soon."* Then she disappeared from the screen.

"What have I done," Speaker Lews asked himself softly. I doubted that anyone other than me heard him.

"The right thing," I said reassuringly. "The *only* thing you could do to save Obas."

# CHAPTER TWENTY-SIX

Eraz's fleet arrived without incident, but there were some very nervous faces in the control room when the nearly 250 Udek warships approached the Obas vessels, waiting in orbit. The Udek came to a full stop barely a hundred kilometers away from them, and then sent out a steady barrage of active scans. Lews had provided Eraz with the ship specifications as promised, but she seemed bent on doing her own assessment as well. The proximity of the Udek warships, and the sheer intensity of the examination, made it obvious that she had no intention of hiding those actions either.

"I don't think your people trust us, Tien," Speaker Lews stated sarcastically.

"You can't blame them for being cautious. You wouldn't act any differently in their position."

"Actually, we'd never even *be* in their position. We wouldn't have gotten involved at all."

"Of course," I replied. The Speaker's honesty was a refreshing change from the environment I normally operated in—one where lies were frequently told, even when the truth would serve.

The door slid open behind us and Uli strode into the room

with an armed escort. As an Udek spy, and potential but untested ally, I was being tolerated—but not completely trusted. As an unrepentant and remorseless Brenin invader, Uli was a true enemy in their midst, and was being afforded all the caution her status demanded.

"Now that your usefulness is over," I said to her, "I suppose you'll just sit back and just watch the fireworks?"

"Believe it or not, Udek, at this point, if I could do more to help I would. After you lose this battle, the Saba will kill me. As Yano, and sister of the marshal's assassin, I *will* die today. There is no other possible outcome. My only hope of survival is a victory by you pathetic barbarians. As such, I am resolved to my fate."

"I'm glad to see your lack of confidence in us hasn't wavered," I said.

"I've seen *nothing* to convince me that you have even the smallest chance of victory. Have you?"

I didn't answer her, turning back to the display instead, not willing to admit that her assessment of the situation matched my own. I watched as the Brenin vanguard slowed their ships slightly to reform with the main fleet; they were consolidating their formation before attacking. Thankfully, this maneuver gave the Obas advance force enough time to return to the planet and rejoin their own flotilla—now entrenched behind a shifting wall of Udek warships. Eraz was clearly arranging her own vessels for the coming attack based on what she'd learned about the Obas capabilities.

On the tactical display, the two sides looked like an even match, number-wise anyway. The combined Udek/Obas force actually outnumbered the Brenin, but history told us that numerical advantages meant little against their shield technology. No...Uli *was* right; there was no reason at all to be optimistic. But as a rule, I never gave up. *Ever*.

And I wasn't about to start today.

"One hour," Boe called out. "The Brenin will reach Obas in one hour."

"Very good, Master Pilot," Lews replied. Then he turned to Peq. "What news on the shield problem?"

"We've made some excellent progress, Speaker. I'm forced to admit that the Udek engineers are very proficient. Not as capable as our own, of course, but quite helpful. We have a much better understanding of how the shield works now...but we still haven't discovered a way through it."

"*Find* a way," Lews responded sternly.

"We will, Speaker. We will."

"Colonel Eraz is hailing us sir," Boe interrupted.

"Go ahead."

*"Speaker Lews, I have placed my ships between the Brenin and your fleet. My planners tell me this is the best way to handle their...deficiencies."*

"Deficiencies?" Lews bristled, clearly angry. "Are you implying that our fleet is weak, Colonel?"

*"Actually, Speaker, if you will calm down for a moment, I'll explain that it's just the opposite. Your ships have immense firepower, but let's be truthful— they aren't very resilient. By placing my ships at the forefront, we can protect yours, allowing them to shoot at the Brenin through firing solutions spaced throughout our formation. Our combined offensive capabilities should do a hell of a lot of damage, shield or no."*

Speaker Lews breathed out heavily. "My apologies, Colonel Eraz, these are trying times."

*"For us all, Speaker. But we have an opportunity here, and need to establish a clear command structure before the Brenin arrive. We can't have orders coming from your ships, the planet, and me. One person needs to be in charge, and quite frankly, that person should be me. I have the requisite experience that your captains lack. No insult intended."*

"None taken, Colonel. I will place Master Pilot Mems in

command of our fleet, and then instruct him to coordinate our actions with you directly. I will also notify him to put our ships at your complete disposal during the battle. Master Pilot Boe will transmit those orders now." Lews nodded at Boe, but the other Obas stared back at him, clearly stunned.

"Do it," he ordered.

"Yes, sir," Boe replied, hesitantly opening up a channel to relay the instructions.

*"Thank you, Speaker Lews. I'm going to meet with my staff first, and then contact Mems myself to discuss battlefield communications protocols."*

"Understood, Colonel." Lews stepped forward and stood directly in front of the monitor, drawing Eraz's full attention; they looked at one another intently. "Use our ships well, Colonel Eraz. The fate of my planet rests in your hands."

*"I will, Speaker. I promise."*

Eraz disconnected, and Lews looked back at me with a surprised expression on his face. "For an Udek, she seems most reasonable."

I repressed a laugh. "She's happy now, Speaker Lews. Commanding a large fleet in an important battle is a field officer's dream assignment."

I didn't bother telling him that just a few scant days ago, Eraz was merely the underling of the general normally commanding this fleet—or that I'd killed her former boss and was directly responsible for Eraz's recent promotion. It might cause Lews to lose faith in her, and he had enough to worry about already. Besides, I knew Eraz was competent; she didn't get to where she was through failure.

The Speaker and I watched the screen as the distance between the two fleets narrowed. The scale made it seem as if they were right on top of each other already, but then the view wobbled, readjusting itself to zoom in closer. The gap between the two armadas returned, along with a distance gauge on the right-hand side of the display.

And those numbers were dropping rapidly.

*Not long now,* I thought. *Soon, this will all be over.*

One way or the other.

# CHAPTER TWENTY-SEVEN

The Brenin attacked without a word: no warnings, boasts or demands, just energy weapons and ship-to-ship missiles—hundreds of them flying toward the combined fleet guarding the planet. But the Obas and Udek weren't sitting idly by; they sent out waves of destruction of their own.

I watched as the heavy clusters of merging munitions slammed together—causing massive explosions that vaporized or deflected both barrages. Very few weapons from either side survived long enough to meet their intended targets, and both factions saw this and took remedial actions.

The Brenin focused their substantial firepower on small sections of the allied wall of ships, blasting through the thick-shelled Udek vessels to get at the more fragile Obas behind them. Dozens of ships died as a result. The allies responded by targeting ships on the extreme edges of the Brenin shield, methodically blowing them up, one by one. But every time one of them burst into fragments, the shield simply reestablished itself at the next Brenin ship behind it.

And the shield never fell.

It was taking a tremendous amount of effort to destroy each individual Brenin ship, and just as in every battle prior to this one, the attrition numbers were favoring the invaders. For every enemy vessel the allies managed to destroy, they lost ten of their own. And that ratio was untenable—pointing to a very short fight if nothing changed. But unfortunately, it did...

For the worse.

"They've fired missiles at the planet," Boe yelled out, and all eyes in the control room shot up to the display. "Scans indicate toxin in the warheads."

I watched as the missiles exited the Brenin shield, sailing through a hole punched in the Udek line. There were twenty of them in all, and as they pushed past the last of the defending ships, they started to change course—spacing out to follow different parabolic trajectories across the planet's sky. Twenty Obas ships broke formation and sped after them, each choosing a missile and accelerating after it.

"They will never be able to shoot them down at those speeds," I said under my breath.

Speaker Lews heard me. "That's not their intention, Tien."

Eraz's face burst onto the screen, disrupting our view of the chase. *"Speaker Lews! What the hell is going on? I need those ships back here. Now!"* Her image shuddered as her ship was hit; a second impact sent her flying forward but she caught herself and regained her seat.

"They are following orders, Colonel," Speaker Lews said somberly.

*"Whose?"* she demanded. Static began to fill the channel and white flashes distorted her image.

"Mine," he replied.

Eraz's face was replaced by the tactical display, just as it focused in on an Obas ship sailing through the atmosphere. The vessel was noticeably gaining on one of the Brenin missiles, and according to the display was within a hundred meters of it. The video was being beamed in from an orbital surveillance platform and was crystal clear. I could make out the ship's markings easily, and realized that I'd seen them before—leading the fleet against the Brenin vanguard.

It was Mem's ship.

I was just about to ask Lews what they hoped to accomplish when the vessel exploded in a massive fireball, taking the missile, the ship's crew, and Master Pilot Mems with it. The image then zoomed back out to show the entire planet, before splitting into nineteen different screens, each displaying one of the other pursuit ships as they all followed suit—each one exploding as they neared the missiles they were chasing. The hushed command center watched intently as in less than two minutes, all of the missiles were wiped out—along with the crews of the ships sent to destroy them.

"It was the only way to be sure," Lews explained. "We discussed this with the fleet as soon as we found out about the missiles—deciding to place proximity devices on nearly every one of our ships for just this contingency. The on-board computers made sure they would be close enough before detonation...we had to be certain that the toxin would burn up in the explosion as well."

Despite the Speaker's obvious conviction that he'd made the right decision, his shoulders sagged forward and his voice wavered as he spoke. "There was just no other way to be sure."

The view changed once more, this time to encompass the entire battlefield. I watched helplessly as Eraz tried to close the many holes blown through the defensive line by the Brenin. But now, she was also struggling to compensate for other weaknesses in the line—created when the Obas ships left the formation on their suicidal charge. It was simply too much to overcome.

She didn't have a prayer.

The Brenin continued to pound the weakened areas, moving their fleet in even closer—turning the conflict into a face-to-face shooting match where ordinance could no longer be intercepted by countermeasures or opposing fire. As a consequence, the allied ships were being shredded to pieces, while most of *their* shots bounced harmlessly off the Brenin shield.

I made a quick calculation based on what I was seeing; the ratio of destruction had jumped up to twenty-to-one, in favor of the Brenin. This battle's outcome would be decided in minutes at that rate. Eraz needed to come up with something fast.

"Speaker! Speaker Lews!" Peq yelled, drawing everyone's attention away from the catastrophe unfolding on the screen. "We've found it! A weakness in the design."

Lews pushed aside the melancholy that was consuming him—the result of watching so many brave Obas die. "Well don't just stand there," he barked. "What is it?"

Peq took a deep breath and collected himself, but it did nothing to curb his enthusiasm about the discovery. "The shield links every ship in the Brenin fleet together," he began. "They each have an on-board generator that accepts an incoming connection from one vessel, and then sends it on to the next; it is a closed, serial system. When we destroy one of their ships, the shield signal just falls back to the next generator unimpeded. It's why it never fails."

"But how does that help us?" Lews asked impatiently.

"Because we've uncovered a flaw in the way the shield signal is compiled and maintained. Any ship can start its construction, but that first ship becomes primary and *must* remain part of the matrix. If it's destroyed, the shield will fail completely, and the Brenin would have to spool up the entire thing again from the beginning, with a new primary. That process can take up to five minutes from what we've witnessed. And they can't simply bunch other ships around it for protection; they have to maintain a minimal spacing for the shield to form—the primary will *always* be exposed to attack.

If we can determine which ship it is and destroy it, we can get inside their defenses before they have a chance to raise the shield again."

"But how can we tell *which* ship?" I asked.

"We are working on that now. Neither our scanners nor the Udek's can detect the subtle signal changes between ships—those slight variations that would help us to pinpoint the primary vessel."

Speaker Lews pointed up at the wall display—where Obas and Udek alike were dying with increasing regularity. "We don't have *time* to develop a new technology, Peq."

"We don't have to," I said. "We can use the scout ship I stole to get here. Its scanners should be able to analyze the Brenin shield and find the primary. We can then pass on the target's location to the fleet."

"Then allow me to go," Boe said. He jumped up from his console to stand at Lew's side. "I'm the only Obas that has ever flown that ship, Speaker. It must be me."

"Yes...yes," Lews said. "Then go. Go now."

"Yes sir."

"I'm going as well," I announced. "I will explain everything to Colonel Eraz on the way."

"Very well," Lews said, and then he waived to dismiss us.

But we were already moving.

We ran out of the room and headed straight for the hangar—using a dome car to reach the mountain cavern in just a few minutes. The scout ship was open and waiting when we arrived, and we ran past some very confused maintenance personnel to hop aboard—powering up the systems and sealing the hatch behind us. Neither one of us said a word as Boe spun the ship around and glided toward the exit.

I watched with annoyance as the airlock doors wound through their slow and deliberate cycle, tapping on the console in front of me as we waited. When the exterior doors finally opened, we burst out into the ocean, continuing to build up speed as we left Edo behind. Boe brought the nose of the craft up and pointed it toward the surface.

We were ascending so rapidly now that the scout ship started to shake—vibrating so badly that I feared it might violently fly apart. The metal hull groaned under the enormous strain, filling the ship with disconcerting noises as it underwent rigors its designers never envisioned. I looked over to challenge Boe—to tell him to throttle back before we found ourselves swimming—but his face told me that he had it all under control. He was concentrating on the system readouts with total focus and determination, competently pushing the ship to its absolute limits while still keeping it all together in one piece. And his face also told me something else, but it was information I already knew.

I wasn't the only one desperate to get into space while there was still a fleet to save.

# CHAPTER TWENTY-EIGHT

The scout ship blasted out of the ocean and into the bright sunlight of Obas; there was no seamless transmission between mediums this time, it was a hard jolt, followed by an even harder acceleration. Boe was flying the ship as if his life depended on it, because it did—all of our lives did.

As we rose higher into the atmosphere, I was able to see the battle taking place ahead of us. It was difficult to make out individual ships from this distance, until they exploded—then they flashed brilliantly, screaming out for notice at the end of their lives. And those telltale explosions were everywhere; the gradually darkening sky was filled with them. Before we achieved orbit and threw ourselves into the midst of all that fighting, I pulled my gaze away from the forward window to call Eraz.

"We've found a way to disable the shield," I told her. "For a few minutes, anyway. It all hinges on destroying a single Brenin ship; the Obas engineers should be sharing the particulars with your people now."

I was so excited to tell Eraz the news that I neglected to look at her...*really* look at her. When I did, I was shocked to see her face covered in blood—running down from a deep laceration across her forehead. Her tunic was also ripped at the right shoulder, and a black burn mark stretched across the top of her chest. But despite these obvious injuries, she reacted as if all was going according to plan.

*"Good news,"* she said. *"Unfortunately, we are in a full retreat. I've ordered all of our ships into erratic defensive maneuvers and directed them to scatter out in small units. The Brenin are currently pursuing the largest surviving group...which would be mine."* I heard a loud explosion in the background and her image flickered.

"We are heading toward you now, Eraz. Try to swing the fleet back into some kind of attack formation as soon as you're able. We hope to have a target for you momentarily."

*"I'm on it,"* she said, signing off.

We broke through the upper atmosphere and into space, where I immediately turned on the scanners and started sweeping through the Brenin formation. They were just ahead of us now, chasing Eraz's group just as she'd said—picking off the slower and damaged allied ships as they fell behind. Using information uploaded by Peq, I adjusted the scanners to single out the shield signature—measuring the strength of the transmission as it moved between the Brenin ships.

*Got you.*

It was far more than a subtle difference; the primary lit up like a flare. But that was probably due more to the sensitivity of the Brenin scanners than any actual output differences. I opened a channel to Eraz. "This is our chance, Colonel. I'm sending you tracking coordinates on the ship now. If we can destroy it, the shield should drop long enough for you to get inside it.

*"Acknowledged."*

A curt reply followed by an immediate response.

I watched on the console display as the fleeing Udek and Obas ships spun around and swung in from every trajectory, reforming to focus all of their efforts on a single piece of the shield. But as they congregated closer, reassembling the allied fleet, they became easy targets, and the Brenin started mowing through their ranks again—just as before. The allies had intentionally placed themselves in a killing field, but there was no other way to concentrate the needed firepower. As Obas and Udek alike fell to the Brenin guns, other allied ships swooped in to take their places, working on the shield and outlying Brenin ships from the best possible firing solutions. Unfortunately, the primary was not on the perimeter, but the heavy assault launched by the allies viciously cut through the three ships standing between them and their goal. The shield fell back further each time one of the intermediate vessels exploded—finally retreating all the way back to the target.

They'd reached the primary.

And it was a big ship. A *very* big ship, only slightly smaller than the one I'd been on with Uli. But the entire allied force was pouring everything they had into its destruction. Other Brenin vessels moved in closer to defend it—drawing heavy fire down on themselves in the process—but the bulk of the allies ignored them and kept hitting at the primary. That effort paid off when the top of the gigantic ship exploded in a fireball—one that was quickly snuffed out in the vacuum of space. The large vessel then rocked to one side, falling over in relation to the rest of the Brenin fleet. But just before the hulking mass rotated enough to be completely 'upside down', its structural integrity failed and the ship broke apart into several large chunks, each spewing tons of debris as their atmospheres vented out. Floating among the growing clouds of detritus were many, many Brenin bodies.

But more importantly, the shield was *gone*.

Every allied ship that was capable flew or limped past the perimeter. Some were blown into atoms almost immediately, but others started pounding the Brenin ships with every weapon still functioning. Energy beams and projectile devices of every bent shot through space, looking for targets. And at every turn...*everywhere*, there was death—Brenin, Obas, and Udek, all perishing by the thousands.

Boe took us in closer and we watched the battle unfold directly through the scout ship's front window. We weren't exactly winning, but for the first time ever we were able to fight the Brenin ship to ship—on more or less even terms. And we were hurting them too...but not enough. Not *nearly* enough. Even without the shield they still held some huge tactical advantages, particularly their stronger hulls and advanced weaponry. And as a result of the way the battle had unfolded prior to the shield's collapse, the Brenin now had an immense numerical advantage as well.

I checked the scanner to confirm what my eyes were telling me; of the four hundred ships the Brenin arrived with, three hundred and sixty still remained. And the combined allied force that had numbered almost six hundred at the beginning of this battle, found itself with fewer than three hundred ships left. And of those, many were heavily damaged or adrift. Unsurprisingly, the largest portion of the destroyed and derelict belonged to the Obas.

*"Everybody back out Now!"* Eraz's voice blared over the speaker. *"The shield is going back up."*

I watched as the allied ships maneuvered away from the Brenin fleet, some providing cover fire for their damaged or defenseless brethren. Then the shield began to form again—perceptible as a slight shimmer of light reaching out through space to connect all of the Brenin ships together. Sixteen allied vessels hadn't gotten out fast enough, and were trapped inside when the shield went active; they were quickly cut to ribbons by Brenin guns. I scanned the enemy fleet and located the new primary, relaying its coordinates straight through to Eraz.

It only took a few moments for the Udek and Obas forces

to regroup and go after the new target. For a fleet that had never trained together—and one inherently distrustful of each other—they'd managed to coordinate their actions admirably. A testament to Eraz's leadership abilities, I reasoned.

She skillfully brought the allied attack fleet back around in a wide arc, diverting out away from the Brenin fleet and down the short side of their formation—maneuvering to the location the new primary while still avoiding their guns. It was a taxing approach, and some of the allied ships fell away, unable maintain the charge. I saw a wobbling Udek warship explode, taking out the Obas vessel next to it as well.

The allies then turned hard and dove back toward the enemy, and I watched them blow apart in the effort. The Brenin had anticipated the direction of their attack and pivoted most of their fleet to set up a kill zone. At least one hundred allied ships died in the charge...most of them Obas. A full one-third of the remaining allied fleet wiped out in an instant. I realized then that the Brenin were on to us—that they knew we'd found a weakness—and understood *exactly* what we had to do to exploit it. They'd prepared a defense against the tactic and we paid a heavy price.

*Damn it!*

I was so engrossed with the spectacle in front of me that I didn't follow my deduction through to its natural conclusion; I didn't anticipate the Brenin uncovering *our* role in the strategy, and then striking out at us in response. I figured *that* part out when the attack came and I was thrown facedown onto the console. Only our distance from the battle and the scout ship's reinforced hull kept us from being totally vaporized, but the Brenin assault was still strong enough to knock out the ship's power. Before we spun off, completely out of control, I saw more allied ships explode as they continued to press the charge to the primary. But there was something else as well; several large projectiles passed through the Brenin shield, diving down toward the planet's atmosphere.

I recognized them immediately.

*More poisoned missiles...*

But this time, no Obas ships chased after them. There simply weren't any capable of reaching the missiles in time. The allies were all out of position—away from the planet and engaging the Brenin fleet. And those that weren't were heavily damaged and in no shape to pursue.

*There would be no stopping them this time.*

The emergency thrusters arrested the ship's roll and we leveled out on the fringes of the upper atmosphere—giving us a front row seat for the destruction of the Obas ecosystem. We watched helplessly as the seven missiles began to glow red on entry, the aerodynamic heating marked their paths with long, white trails.

Boe smacked the controls in anger. "If this ship would move we could stop at least one of them! Save something..." The Obas gripped the console hard and stared out the front window, watching the missiles spread out on their divergent paths. As they dipped lower into the atmosphere, I saw his frustration turn into despair. "They are all going to die," he whispered.

Flashes of light shot through the blackness as the ship's emergency power fought its way to life—bathing the vessel's interior in a yellow glow, and illuminating a single emergency panel on the dash. Boe used it to run a ship wide diagnostic.

"The power loss is permanent," he announced. The Obas had regained his confident bearing—his instincts as a pilot taking hold despite what was about to befall his planet. "Both engines have been destroyed and we have limited battery power only." He checked the panel again and frowned. "*And* we are drifting into the atmosphere."

"How long?" I asked.

"Ten minutes before it becomes a real problem."

"Escape pod?"

"Intact, but I think it's showing a failure code. I'll go check it out." Boe took another look out the window before getting up—the missiles still visible as they continued on their deadly trajectories—then he turned his head away and raced to the back of the ship.

I tried to pull up the sensors and track the progress of the deadly projectiles, but the entire array was down. I did manage to locate one working exterior camera, and focused it in on the nearest missile—watching it sink down to the planet on the emergency panel's tiny display.

"It's just a power issue," Boe called out from behind me. "I can re-route everything from the battery and get it operational."

I was so engrossed in watching the destruction of an entire species that I didn't bother to reply.

Even though I could no longer see them, I knew that the missiles had already spread out—following pre-programed routes that would send them to carefully chosen impact sites, locations where the ocean currents would carry the toxin to every square inch of the planet. The original launch had been comprised of twenty missiles, and I had a feeling that these seven were hastily crafted replacements, but the information I'd stolen concluded that the Obas ecosystem could be completely killed off with as few as five properly placed strikes.

The Brenin had sent poison to spare.

I pulled the camera back to get a better view and a black flash zipped by, filling the screen as it flew past. It was a ship...a *very* fast ship. I struggled to zoom in on it as it blazed through the atmosphere, achieving speeds far above anything the Obas could manage, or even the Udek for that matter. As I worked to resolve the image, several more of the craft zoomed across the screen; they were small trapezoid-shaped ships with rounded edges, each one black with vibrant red markings. I *knew* those ships; I'd seen them before in intelligence reports and combat videos.

They were *Blenej.*

Small, but incredibly fast, Blenej fighters were notoriously difficult to hit in battle. Where the Obas had pushed weaponry at the expense of shielding, the Blenej had optimized their craft for speed. Their ships couldn't take a pounding like Udek vessels, but it really didn't matter—they were nearly impossible to target. The Blenej physical characteristics—four arms and superior dexterity—allowed them to operate at speeds other races envied, and ones automated systems couldn't match. It was a merging of reason and reflexes that no machine could ever hope to emulate. And unlike the Obas, *their* design gamble had paid off handsomely; the Blenej fighters were absolutely lethal.

*But where the hell did they come from?*

"Time to go," Boe said.

I turned around to find him standing next to a small, round door set into an interior wall—a hatch I'd not noticed before. "This conveyance is odd, but serviceable," he stated.

"Odd...odd how?"

"You will see, Udek. Let's go."

I stood up and watched him duck through the portal, and then I followed him in, taking a seat opposite the Obas on one of two, flat benches mounted to the round walls. The pod was roughly three meters in circumference, and as I gazed around at the sparse interior, I realized instantly what Boe had been referring to. The walls of the pod were completely transparent. In fact, the entire escape craft appeared to be made out of glass. But I knew that was impossible. It wouldn't be space worthy if it were.

The pod rotated a quarter turn and then an exterior hatch opened up, revealing the blackness of space. Before I had a chance to get my bearings, we were ejected with incredible force and sent hurtling away from the doomed ship. A patch of thrusters mounted on the outside of the pod kicked in, sending vibrations throughout the craft, and pushing us even further out from the planet. When their fuel was finally spent, the small engines detached and fell away, leaving us floating silently through space in a clear bubble. The view was incredible, if a little unnerving.

A large, translucent panel lit up across the glass-like surface next to me. At the bottom, left-hand corner of it, a red light flashed once brightly, and then started pulsating in a slow and steady cadence.

"Automated distress beacon," I guessed.

"Probably," Boe agreed.

"I can't explain it, but if I'm not mistaken, I saw several Blenej fighters tearing through the atmosphere, right before we ejected."

Boe's eyes widened and he started to stand, pointing straight behind me. "I'm looking at *a lot* of them right now," he said, clearly in shock.

I spun around to see that the battle still raged on, but now, there were *considerably* more ships in the fight. I saw Iriq, Volas, even a few Human ships.

*Humans? This far out?*

And yes, just as Boe had said, there were many Blenej as well. But how? And even more importantly, why? I watched in fascination as they all worked together, joining with the remnants of the allied forces to push hard at the shield.

They were really taking the fight to the Brenin.

The enemy understood the shield's vulnerability now, and the primary was now ensconced a little deeper within the Brenin fleet, but the allied forces were pounding their way through to it in quick order. I reached over to the wall panel and found the com system, turning it to an Udek battle frequency; I entered my clearance codes and opened a channel. Because of the Udek prohibition against receiving enemy transmissions during battle, I wasn't able to transmit—we *were* in a Brenin escape pod after all—but I could listen in on what was happening.

*"No. No. No!"* A voice blared, it was Eraz, and she was clearly agitated. *"Listen to me! Forget about the other ships; just keep hitting at the primary. When the shield drops we can all go in."*

As if on cue, the shield flickered then failed, and hundreds of allied ships poured in—attacking Brenin targets of opportunity with little rhyme or reason. It was obvious from the assault that this newly constituted fleet lacked a battle plan—or any proper command structure for that matter—but they were still doing some serious damage.

A lot of it.

I'd been in a few battles, and analyzed many more, but I'd never seen anything that matched the frenzy of this attack. Brenin ships began exploding at frequent intervals, some even diving into one another as they used unfamiliar and never before attempted escape maneuvers. The allied forces were relentlessly blasting their way through the hardened enemy hulls, destroying ship after ship. The Brenin had *never* suffered losses like this before, and I knew that they had to be unnerved by the quick turn of events. But they still had teeth, a lot of very large ones, and they were using them to chew through a fair number of allied ships as well. But despite these losses, the allies kept the pounding up, particularly what was left of the Obas fleet. They'd remained outside the perimeter, firing salvo after salvo at the newly exposed Brenin ships.

*"One minute until the shield goes back up!"* Eraz called out. *"Everyone start making your way out."*

Almost to the second, the shield flared back into existence. And with it, came the realization that we could no longer identify the primary. The scout ship was gone. There were still nearly three hundred Brenin ships in that fleet, and even though quite a few were heavily damaged, most were still fully operational. I watched as they continued to fire at the retreating allied vessels, damaging or destroying almost two dozen more as they fled.

*Now what do we do?*

The Brenin could go back to hiding behind their shield, attacking when and where they wished, while we struggled to take out a few of their ships on the outside perimeter. Without the scout's scanners—without knowing which Brenin ship started the shield—we were helpless...even *with* our curious new reinforcements. I prepared myself for a scene I'd witnessed far too many times before—the return of Brenin supremacy on the battlefield, and the complete destruction of hundreds of friendly ships.

I knew that this was the beginning of the end.

As before, the allied ships sped away from the Brenin fleet—out past the range of their guns where they could regroup safely and prepare for the final battle. But when I turned my attention back to the Brenin, I noticed something strange. They were condensing their vessels into a much closer formation than usual, and when the repositioning was complete, the entire armada slid into motion as a single unit—tightly maneuvering through a sharp turn...*away* from Obas.

The Brenin were leaving.

And then I understood the truth of it; they couldn't take the chance that we might still be able to locate the primary. That last charge by the allies had hurt them badly, and another, more coordinated assault, could cost them everything. They had no choice but to withdraw; the Brenin had never faced this type of opposition before, and they needed to repair their ships and reassess their strategy.

I had a hard time bringing myself to believe it, but we'd actually *won*.

As the Brenin fleet began to pick up speed, almost a hundred ships pulled away from the allied formation to pursue them. Most were Udek.

*"Get back here!"* Eraz barked over the open channel. *"Now!"*

Another voice rang out, one clearly lost in the lust for war. *"They are retreating, Colonel Eraz. This is our chance!"*

*"Get back in formation, Stantz, or I'll blow you apart myself. There are other things at play here you don't understand."*

*"Gah!"* the voice complained, but I saw the ships spin around and rejoin the allies.

Eraz's statement reminded me... I returned the communications channel to a Brenin frequency and reached down to turn off my translator. Boe looked at me strangely, trying to figure out what I was up to.

"Saba," I said in pure Brenin, "remember what happened here today. I am Yano. The trees are life..."

The reply was instantaneous.

*"And the ground is death. We will return for you, Yano, for all of you. And we will send every last one of your kind to the ground, no matter how long it takes. The Yano will pay for this treachery."*

For a brief moment, I worried that they would turn around—call my bluff, and bring a wave of destruction we couldn't stop. But they kept moving, ramping up to full speed on a course that would take them far away from both Obas and Bodhi Prime. I searched my memory, recalling the last status reports I'd read on Brenin fleet movements. The Saba were headed in the direction of the Yano detachment.

And they had revenge on their minds.

The ancient memories—the old hatred—had been rekindled. They no longer cared about us simple barbarians; the Saba had more important matters to deal with. Visceral concerns that trumped thoughts of conquest or territory—a primal impetus that drove everything else from their minds. They sought vengeance—for this defeat, for the marshal's death, and for the Yano's perceived treachery. And they were going to extract their revenge in blood.

Brenin blood.

# CHAPTER TWENTY-NINE

Our ejection sequence had propelled us toward the scene of the battle, and we soon found ourselves drifting through a sea of assorted wreckage. I was able to easily identify debris from ships on both sides of the conflict.

There were thousands of different sized pieces—some stationary, others zipping through space on varied trajectories—their course and speed determined by the manner of the ship's destruction. But despite our tenuous situation and the remarkable view outside, Boe remained silent—completely oblivious to the overwhelming scene that surrounded our clear bubble. I suspected that he was being haunted by thoughts of what had befallen Obas. Whatever occupied his mind, I left him to contemplate it as I continued to peer out through space.

Pieces of debris bounced harmlessly off our pod as we moved deeper into the battlefield, and although the clear walls *seemed* fragile, the craft was proving to be very resilient. The pod shuddered as we struck a large piece of some unfortunate ship's hull, scraping down the side of it before floating free again. The impact arrested our momentum and we coasted to a stop, next to a thick cluster of twisted metal. The color scheme told me that just a few short hours ago it had been an Obas warship. I wondered briefly if any of the crew had managed to escape before turning my attention back to the debris field.

It was hard to see them in the blackness of space, but I spotted other pods like ours among the wreckage—filled with Brenin prisoners waiting to be captured. Unsurprisingly, there were many allied emergency craft as well. Searchlights from rescue ships were slicing through the ebony wasteland—highlighting the larger pieces of broken vessels as they looked for sections that might still be pressurized. Their lights glinted brightly off floating pieces of polished metal, but disappeared almost entirely when they struck the deeply charred hull sections—swallowed up by a darkness that nearly matched the surrounding space.

Eventually, one of the search beams fell across our pod; the light flowing unimpeded through the clear walls to immerse us in blinding brightness. Moments later, an Udek light-warship pulled up alongside us, nudging wreckage out of the way as it oriented itself with our hatch. Boe looked over with interest, but I could see that he was still lost in his thoughts...morosely so.

We bumped into the ship and grappling arms shot out to capture us—pulling our craft up tightly against a mismatched, square hatch. Despite the different technologies, the Udek airlock was much larger that our pod's door, and the docking collar hyperextended itself to force a proper seal.

I looked over at Boe and found him staring through the clear wall at another Brenin escape pod—docked beside us at an adjacent airlock. There were three Brenin survivors inside it moving about excitedly, and I could just make out part of an Udek soldier, pointing a rifle at them through the docking collar. I watched as the Brenin skittered to the back of the pod, pushing their arms out in front of themselves defensively and trying to climb up the round walls. Then I saw a small ball fly through the air and land among them. The pod's hatch slammed shut as the grenade detonated, coating the interior of the clear bubble with bluish blood and chunks of Brenin flesh. Then the grapples released, withdrawing back into the ship as the lifeless pod drifted out to space.

"Why?" Boe asked. "I have no love for the Brenin, not after what they've done. But why kill them like *that*? What's the point now?"

But before I could answer, the air started to bleed out of *our* pod; it was being replaced with methane as the Udek prepared to come in. I felt around underneath the seat and found an oxygen mask; I saw Boe do the same. We'd just managed to pull them on when the hatch slid open, revealing two Udek standing behind it. One of them trained a rifle on us. The other was holding a grenade.

I knew what came next.

"An Obas?" one of them remarked. "What the fuck is he doing here?"

"I don't know, Reil," the other soldier answered. "Nor do I care. He's probably a spy working with the Brenin. Just toss the grenade in and get it over with."

"Hrelshhh! Lishnreee!" I yelled, and then quickly realized that I'd shut off the translator. The soldier with the rifle tightened his grip on the trigger.

"Wait," Boe pleaded. "I'm not the spy, he is. He's one of *yours*."

"We don't have time for this," Reil replied. He pulled his arm back to launch the grenade.

I hurriedly activated the translator. "Listen to him, soldier. Unless you are prepared to explain your actions to the Udek Special Corp."

"Special Corp?" he repeated. "Who...*what* are you? And how do you know about *them*?"

"I am Kiro Tien, of the Udek Defense Force. In disguise, obviously. I'm on a mission authorized by Colonel Eraz."

"Eraz?" Reil remarked, clearly surprised. "How could the Brenin already know about her new position?"

"Maybe that Obas spy told them," the other soldier answered, using his barrel to gesture at Boe.

Reil paused, and I could tell that he was thinking the situation over carefully. He shrugged and then disabled the grenade. "I don't need any trouble with Special Corp. Let's take them to Captain Queltz and let him sort it all out."

"Yeah, I agree. Better not take any chances."

*Queltz?* It wasn't a common name, but what were the odds of him being related to the general?

The soldiers motioned for us to come with them and we got up to leave. The pair backed out and stood in the ship's corridor, watching us closely as we exited the pod. "Special Corp or not," Reil laughed. "I'd hate to be you two. The captain's been a bigger bastard than usual since he found out his brother was killed on Bodhi Prime."

*What were the odds?*

Pretty good, apparently.

The two soldiers pushed us through the ship, never failing to kick at our backs when we didn't move fast enough, and not afraid to stab at us with the gun barrel even when we did. The other Udek were surprised to see an Obas onboard, and outright stunned to find a live Brenin in their midst. It soon became apparent that they'd taken no prisoners...at all. They were killing every Brenin they could find, helpless or not.

Between the hostile stares and constant prodding, I was glad when we finally reached our destination. Boe and I stepped up warily through the raised hatch leading to the bridge, and as the officers on deck slowly became aware of our presence, silence filled the room.

The captain, easily identified by his uniform and

resemblance to General Queltz, rose from his chair to meet us.

"And what do we have here?" he asked, giving our escorts a stern look. "An Obas refugee and a Brenin captive?"

"Refugee?" Boe repeated. "Then the missiles did strike planet? Obas has been poisoned?"

"I don't know," Queltz replied. "I've been too busy killing Brenin to notice." His eyes narrowed and he gave me a menacing glance—one designed to demonstrate *exactly* how he felt about them. Queltz then waved a hand at Boe, and two Udek soldiers stepped forward to grab his arms, dragging the Obas away and forcing him down into a nearby chair. He tried to get back up, but they shoved him down by his shoulders and held him there.

Reil spoke up, defending his decision to bring us to the bridge. He pointed an unsteady arm in my direction. "He says he's one of us, Captain. A Special Corp operative in disguise."

"Special Corp? Truly? In *there*?" Queltz stepped in closer to look at my face, as if trying to see the Udek hidden inside the Brenin body. "You spooks do get up to the most bizarre things. What is your name?" he demanded.

I had no choice but to tell him the truth. If I lied, he wouldn't be able to confirm my story and I'd die anyway. I had to trust that Special Corps' reputation for ruthlessly punishing anyone that interfered with their agents might offer me some protection.

"Kiro Tien."

"Tien!" he spat. "*You* are the spy that killed my brother!"

The other Udek witnessed their captain's rage and backed away, knowing better than to interfere; this was now a personal matter between the two of us. Before he had a chance to fully withdraw, Queltz grabbed the rifle from our guard and spun around to slam the butt of it into my chest. I fell back a few steps, gasping for air—the impact aggravating the lung injury I'd suffered on the Brenin ship.

"You son of a bitch," he yelled. "It's bad enough that you killed him, but somehow, you coaxed headquarters into erasing him completely—even got the *Bodhi* to back you. The Bodhi…of all people. Wait… Yes…yes, it all makes sense now. *They* put you in there, didn't they? You've made some sort of arrangement with the Bodhi."

Queltz walked around me in a tight circle, studying my form—like a predator searching for weakness in its prey. Without warning, he lunged behind me and drove the rifle butt into my left leg; I fell to the ground, landing hard on my side.

I rolled over onto my back, and looked up to find him staring at me through maniacal eyes. "Dead wasn't good enough for you, was it, Tien? No! You had to steal any chance for my brother's rebirth as well. But why? Your spook fraternity would protect you, even *if* the Bodhi brought him back. What do you fear, spy?"

"I fear nothing," I replied. "He died for what he did to my family."

Queltz stomped on my stomach—a quick, unexpected blow that left me coughing hard and unable to catch my breath.

"Family?" he scoffed. "Ha! What do *you* know about family? Nothing! But don't worry, spy, I'll teach you. And it'll be the last lesson you ever learn." He stepped back and glared down at me, and I looked at his face and knew that all reason had fled his mind. I was sure of it. "Eraz has been hounding us to take prisoners anyway—to use them to gather intelligence—and I'm starting to agree. I think we'll learn quite a bit from cutting you open."

He hit a release switch on the side of the rifle and a bayonet slid out from underneath the barrel. I saw the double-edged steel shine in the ambient light, and smelled the faint trace of oil on the blade—residual deposits left behind from its mechanical sheath. As far as I knew, the Udek were the only species whose military still used bladed weapons. A further testament to our famed barbarity, I supposed.

Queltz looked over at two of the officers watching us and motioned for them to approach. They knelt down beside me and grabbed my arms, pinning me to the deck, then Queltz stepped forward and pointed the bayonet at my torso.

The blade...Queltz's actions, all of it, made me think of the remorseless Brenin—how we'd condemned them for their actions. But how were *we* any better? Throwing grenades into sealed escape pods? And for what? Sport? I understood violence well, had practiced it my entire life, but always with reason—always with a purpose. The deaths I'd witnessed on this ship served no purpose whatsoever.

The Udek behavior didn't make sense from a military standpoint either. The enemy had been neutralized, and prisoners meant intelligence, of which we had precious little. Captives could be used as bargaining chips with the Brenin, or serve as experimental subjects for biological weapons—just as the Brenin were going to do with Boe. At least then their deaths would have *some* type of meaning. But to just kill them because we could... What does that say about us?

"What say we start with the chest?" Queltz said gleefully, placing the point of the bayonet on my sternum. He pressed the tip of it into my flesh, and a smile spread across his face as blood began to flow out, staining my tunic.

I ignored the pain, just as I'd been trained to do, and kept staring at Queltz. I watched his face contort through different emotions as he savored the damage he was causing—witnessed the sublime satisfaction that inflicting torture gave him. And I realized that I was no longer watching as an Udek operative; I was seeing Queltz as the Obas and Bodhi do...or even the Brenin. I was looking at him through a prism—colored by my experiences in this new body, and my time spent among the Obas. I saw Queltz the way the rest of the galaxy sees the Udek, and my mind struggled to reconcile my upbringing with the derision I now felt for my own people.

*Is this what we've become? Or who we've always been...*

Queltz continued to press the blade in slowly, savoring my discomfort; the oil on the cutting edges stung as it mixed with my blood. A few more centimeters and he would hit my damaged lung. But this time, without Uli to heal me, I would surely die. And *that* realization was even more sobering than my new outlook on the Udek.

*I was actually going to die.*

*Me.*

In that moment, I saw myself in Queltz's face. How many of my targets had looked up at me like this? *My* face the last thing they'd seen. A few, I remembered, but not many. Most never even knew what happened before they died...because I was good at what I did. I was a *very* proficient killer. And it didn't matter what body I inhabited, or what situation I found myself in, I'd always been good at one thing.

Killing.

The bledi emerged from my wrist and the universe slowed to a crawl. As the weapon sprang out, the soldier holding my arm released it in surprise—then froze for just a second, unsure of what was happening. But one second was all I needed. I kicked Queltz in the stomach with both legs, feeling immediate relief as he fell backward and the blade left my chest. Then I reached across my torso and drove the bledi straight through the face of the soldier holding my other arm. I withdrew it quickly, hopping to my feet as his body tipped over and fell to the floor.

I felt the bledi lock into a more rigid form, becoming a long serrated knife—a lethal extension of my own arm. Queltz swiftly regained his footing and lunged at me with the bayonet, but I dropped down low and swung the Brenin blade in a wide arc. With a single motion, I knocked the rifle from his hands, and disemboweled the other soldier that had restrained me.

The blow severed one of Queltz's hands, and sent him tumbling backward, landing hard between two seats mounted in front of an instrumentation panel. He was off-balance and unable to control the fall, and his head struck the panel hard before he slid to the ground. As I started to walk toward him something flashed across my peripheral vision.

I recognized the outline of a handgun.

I pushed off the ground and launched myself backward, sailing through the air in a tumbling roll as only a Brenin could—landing directly behind the armed, and very surprised, Udek. Before he could react, I pulled his head back and slit his throat with the bledi.

One of the other soldiers dove to the ground and grabbed Queltz's rifle, bringing it up to fire. But before he could pull the trigger, I tore the gun from the frozen grip of the Udek I'd just slain and shot my would-be assailant in the forehead. His brain sprayed out over the shoes of the soldiers behind him and they all stopped in their tracks, motionless. The remaining Udek looked at each other and all came to the same conclusion. They slowly held their hands up in the air, including the two restraining Boe.

This doesn't concern any of you," I said sternly. "Interfere, and die."

Boe stood up and walked over to pick up the rifle, pointing it at the collection of surviving Udek just in case any of them changed their minds and tried to stop us. Confident that everything was now under control, I headed back over to where Queltz had collapsed on the floor.

I felt the bledi slide back into my arm as I moved. Seeris had been right; there was no method to them. They just *worked.* Queltz was groggy, and slid back down the console repeatedly as he tried to stand. I grabbed his neck tightly with one hand and lifted him up, placing the gun at the side of his head.

"Let it go, Queltz. Your brother was a monster. And he paid for what he did to my wife. But there is no reason for you to die."

"Do it!" he yelled. He spat in my face and I felt the warm fluid run down my cheek. "Kill me, Tien. *Do it!* I swear...I will never rest until you're dead. *Really dead.* You and that bitch wife of yours. I will chase you across the galax—"

I pulled the trigger.

A muffled pop—an explosion of tissue and blood—and then his life was gone.

It's what I do.

But no longer who I *am*.

Queltz was dead. Not in furtherance of the greater Udek agenda, like all of my previous missions. No...he died because he was trying to kill me. *That's* why he lay quavering in my grasp—his residual nerve impulses flaring and subsiding as the last traces of life ebbed away. *He* did this. Not me. And I was no longer like him, or any other Udek for that matter. Nor would I ever be again.

I let his body drop and backed away.

One of the Udek officers behind me spoke up. "How the hell do you expect to get off this ship after killing the captain?"

I turned around to reply, but before I got the chance, a loud beeping sound filled the bridge. One of the officers pointed at a nearby console. "We are being hailed."

"Well, answer it," I replied brusquely.

The Udek hesitantly shuffled over to the com unit, keeping his eyes on me the entire time--as if expecting me to shoot him at any moment. He opened the channel and a familiar yet surprising voice rang out.

*"This is Brother Dyson of the Bodhi. I believe you have some of my property onboard. Colonel Eraz has given me leave to retrieve it."*

I used my tunic sleeve to wipe the spittle off my face, then tucked the gun into my waistband and smiled.

"It looks like my ride is here."

# CHAPTER THIRTY

Twenty minutes later, a transport docked with the Udek warship and Boe and I went aboard. It had been a long, tenuous wait—trapped on a hostile ship and surrounded by Udek, thirsty for revenge. But my gun, the dead bodies, and Eraz's orders, provided sufficient motivation for the crew to leave us alone. Nevertheless, the news of Queltz's death moved quickly through the ship, and the trip back to the docking area was even more uncomfortable than our first journey had been.

I looked back over my shoulder at the soldiers standing in the corridor; they were glaring at us as we exited through the airlock. Their anger was palpable, and I knew they were barely restraining themselves. These Udek had vengeance on their minds and I kept my gun conspicuous. But that was little comfort as they all had weapons of their own.

Those faces said it all, and I knew then that I could never go home again. After today, I would be marked for death on every Udek world and colony. Even if the Special Corp didn't remove me for *security reasons*, a reborn Captain Queltz or his extended family might. General Queltz's murder had provided me with plenty of other enemies in the military as well. No...there would never be peace for me among the Udek.

Never again.

Spending the rest of my life waiting for some unknown assailant to strike didn't appeal to me, and I didn't want that for Dasi either, but that was an issue for some other time—I already had my hands full thinking my way through *this* situation.

We cleared the airlock and were escorted aboard the small ship by two, heavily armed, Blenej Red. As was their custom, each held a rifle in their top pair of hands and a club in one of their bottom set—leaving one hand free to push us further into the vessel. These soldiers were equipped for any eventuality, from killing us outright, to simply beating us into submission. But I knew that neither would be necessary. They silently directed us where to stand, and then backed away to watch over us dispassionately as Boe and I removed our masks. The shuttle disconnected and we sped away from the Udek warship—the abrupt departure forcing all four of us to grab onto the flight straps hanging down from the ceiling.

"We will be there in fifteen minutes," one of the Blenej announced.

"Do you know what happened to Obas?" Boe asked, his voice tinged with desperation.

"You will be briefed on our carrier," the soldier answered brusquely, offering nothing more. His expression made it clear that further questioning was pointless.

"Does no one care?" Boe asked me, clearly exasperated.

"The fog of war being what it is," I replied, "it's more likely that they don't even know themselves. You should be able to contact the planet directly once we get onboard."

Boe fell into silence again as I looked past the Blenej and out one of the large portholes behind them. I saw dozens of ships moving through the debris field now, some looking for survivors, others no doubt transferring personnel and supplies for ongoing repair missions. I'd never seen the aftermath of so much destruction before.

There had been many prior encounters with the Brenin—by a few different races—and I'd read all of the after-action reports on the previous Udek engagements, but none of those battles had been on a scale of this magnitude. What I found even more remarkable was the amount of teal hull-pieces mixed throughout the debris...evidence of destroyed Brenin warships. No single species had ever enjoyed such success against the invaders, but working together, we'd been able to prove that they weren't invincible after all.

I lost the impressive view as we flew inside the huge carrier, setting down on the deck of an immense, well-lit hangar, bustling with activity. There were Blenej *everywhere*, and although the majority of the crew came from the red, warrior class, I saw representatives from all three segments of Blenej society.

Dozens of fighters were hovering into row after row of tightly spaced landing spots—hurrying to clear room for the tugs hauling in disabled and partially destroyed ships collected from the battlefield. One of the damaged fighters was towed past our window, and I saw what was left of the pilot, still inside it.

A loud, clanking sound, drew my eyes to the back of the shuttle as the entire section opened up, swinging down to transition into a lightly sloped ramp; we all stepped out together onto the flight deck.

"There you are," I heard. "I knew you'd find *some* way to survive."

It was Brother Dyson, standing next to Speaker Lews and Brother Kiva. Several Blenej were with them as well.

The old monk turned to his subordinate. "I told you he'd make it, Kiva. Queltz was right about him."

*Why does everyone keep saying that?*

"Speaker Lews!" Boe called out. He broke away from our

group and ran over to the Obas leader. "What happened to the planet?"

"Relax, Master Pilot," Lews replied. "Everything is fine. The Blenej saw the missile launch as soon as they entered the system and sent attack fighters to dispose of them. They destroyed the warheads in mid-air, then used wide-beam plasma fire to burn away any toxin before it could fall into the oceans. It was...quite remarkable."

One of the Blenej stepped forward. "If Colonel Eraz hadn't warned us about them when we offered to join the battle, we would have underestimated their potential. My name is Admiral Nezci, leader of the Blenej task force."

"You have my thanks," Boe said.

"I have already conveyed the gratitude of *all* Obas," Speaker Lews informed him.

"Speaking of which," I interrupted. "How exactly did this task force come to *be* at Obas?"

"You can thank Brother Dyson for that," Nezci replied. "He can be most persuasive."

"Oh, I am well aware of that," I replied.

The admiral took a look at my Brenin body and shook his head. "Yes...I can see that you are."

"I thought a coalition of races might be beneficial," Dyson explained. "Though I admit, my original thought was to simply protect Bodhi Prime from the looming Brenin attack. We detoured here when I got that most unexpected communication from Speaker Lews. After consulting with him and a few representatives from the other races, I became convinced that none of us could be protected from the Brenin, unless we *all* are. Despite our differences and frequently incongruent agendas, we *need* each other. Even working together, it will be difficult to defeat these invaders...if not impossible. But I believe we can do it. I have faith."

"Faith! Bah!" Colonel Eraz strode out from behind a large

fueling pod. "You monks and your ridiculous superstitions."

"Ah, my favorite non-believer," Dyson chided her.

She came to a sudden stop in front of me and then leaned in close, giving me a disapproving look. "You!" she exclaimed. "You have made my life very difficult. Must you kill *every* Queltz you run across?"

"He didn't give me much of a choice, Eraz."

"I see," she said, leaning back to her full height. "His entire crew would like nothing better than to see you dead. And I just got off the com with Special Corp; they want you as well. For reasons they *wouldn't* share with me. In fact, they want you returned to them as soon as possible."

"Yes...about that, Colonel," Dyson intervened. "Tien has Bodhi property inside of him. Or rather, *he* is inside of it."

"I know that, monk. That chamber's signal was the only way you found him in this mess."

"Well, we do like to keep an eye on things; it's why the soul chamber has a beacon in the first place, weak as it may be. We equip our cyborg bodies with a much more powerful transmitter." Dyson must have realized he was drifting off topic and returned to the issue at hand. "In any event, you can't have him until I get my chamber out, back on Prime."

"Now hold on!" Eraz snapped. "I still need to debrief him; we need the intelligence he's gathered."

"Of course, Colonel. Of course. By all means, acquire your information. But afterward," Dyson made a motion indicating Kiva and himself, "Tien comes with us. I'm sure that I don't need to remind you of the agreement between the Bodhi and Udek regarding transference rights and responsibilities—especially as they pertain to our unique intellectual property."

"Are you a monk, or a lawyer?"

"A monk. But one that knows his contract rights. And I also know with certainty that the Udek Confederation would mete out severe punishment to anyone jeopardizing their access to our cloning and transference facilities." Dyson stared her in the eyes, as if daring her to challenge him; his voice turned grave. "Get what you need from him, Colonel Eraz, but then Tien *is* coming back to Bodhi Prime with me."

Eraz scowled at the old monk, but it was clear she'd gotten the message. "Very well, Dyson. My ship is docked two hangars over. Let's go, spy."

She turned to walk away, but I grabbed her shoulder gently and pulled her back around. "Actually, Colonel Eraz, it might be better if I stayed off any Udek ships right now."

"You may be right," she admitted reluctantly, then looked over at Nezci. "Admiral, do you have a room I could use to speak with Tien, alone?"

"No. But I do have one that *we* can use to speak with him together," Nezci answered. "Brother Dyson, you and Speaker Lews are welcome to join us. I will be relaying anything we learn to the Humans, Iriq, and Volas as well."

"He is *our* asset!" Eraz yelled.

"Look around, Colonel," Nezci replied sternly. "It wasn't just the Udek that died here today. That information belongs to all of us now...we paid for it in blood." Several, armed Blenej stationed nearby heard Nezci's tone and walked over to stand behind their admiral. One of them loudly smacked his club against his own leg.

I saw anger flash across Eraz's face, and this time it settled in to stay. She was as mad as I'd ever seen her, but helpless as well. The Udek weren't used to being told what they could or couldn't do—it was a novel position for her to be in. First there was Dyson and his demands, and now Nezci was forcing her actions. It didn't matter that the Udek had the strongest fleet in the galaxy—excluding the Brenin of course—that fleet wasn't *here*. And even if it were, the Udek couldn't go to war with *everyone*.

Eraz had no choice but to concede.

"Very well," she said acidly. "Let's get this over with."

Admiral Nezci led us to a large conference room where we each took a seat around a long table. I watched as several recording devices were produced and placed on its surface, and when I was certain that everyone was ready, I began to speak.

I discussed what I'd learned about the Brenin ships, technology, and culture—described the fight with Marshal Toz and his Veilcat, and then detailed our escape from the armada. They all sat silently as I spoke and I anticipated most of their questions—answering them before they were even asked. I'd been on both sides of a debriefing before, and knew what I needed to say...and what they needed to hear.

They each knew part of the tale, either the beginning of it, like Eraz and Dyson, or the end of it, like Nezci—but none of them knew it all. I shared every detail of *every* action I'd taken since being reborn in the Brenin body, wrapping up with the events on Queltz's ship—looking at each of them in turn as I told about the use of grenades against trapped and unarmed Brenin. Eraz offered no apology or explanation for the Udek actions, but the others seemed just as disgusted as I was by the incident. I finished up my story with the death of Captain Queltz, and our timely pick up by the Blenej.

In the end, even Eraz seemed satisfied, particularly when it was decided that the Obas would share the decoded Brenin files with each race present at the battle.

And then it was done. I'd told them everything.

Well...*almost* everything.

Regardless, my mission was over.

I walked over to where Dyson sat and bent down to whisper in his ear. "Now for your part of our bargain, monk."

"Of course," he replied. "We will leave for Bodhi Prime immediately. But first, we have one other passenger to collect."

# CHAPTER THIRTY-ONE

I woke up on Bodhi Prime.

Not my personality, my *soul* as the monks believed—transferred into an electronic chamber and housed within a cyborg body. Nor as a reluctant prisoner, trapped inside a Brenin corpse.

No. This time, it was only me: Kiro Tien.

*'I'* woke up on Bodhi Prime.

And Dasi was there to greet me.

"Tien?" she asked hopefully. Her voice... It had been so long.

She hovered over the partially reclined chair where I lay, staring intently at my face. I saw the eyes behind the respirator and *knew* it was her. She was alive. We both were *alive.*

"Dasi," I muttered weakly, trying to sit up—my voice muffled by the mask over my own face. I tasted a familiar mixture of gasses—methane chief among them—confirming that I was back in my own body again.

"Relax," she said, pushing me back down in the chair. "Give yourself a moment to adjust. The monks have only just finished the transfer."

"Yes," I heard Dyson's voice call out from behind her, "one

moment."

I looked over to see him standing at a work console, adjusting the controls on its flat surface. On the wall in front of him, a small, black cylinder rested inside an elaborate cradle decorated with Buddhist symbols. Several multicolored cables stretched out from the bottom of the device, connecting it to back of the console.

*The soul chamber.*

I'd been *inside* that little ebony container.

"I can't believe you came for me," Dasi whispered in my ear. "You actually went to Nilot."

"Of course I did," I replied. "Did you really think I wouldn't come?"

"I'd hoped for rescue...dreamed of it even, but...*Nilot...*" She shook her head side-to-side slowly, and a sadness filled her eyes.

"It didn't matter where they'd taken you," I said angrily, and then calmed myself before speaking again. "I'm sorry I didn't protect you from them, Dasi."

"Sorry? Don't be ridiculous! *They* were supposed to be protecting me!"

"I was on my way to get you after I quit the mission," I explained, desperate to justify my actions. "I suspected they might do something. But I was too late."

She smiled widely and the expression pushed the respirator out from her face. A little wisp of colored gas escaped, dissipating quickly into the air. "That is all in the past, my love. Now, we need only concern ourselves with the future."

"It's an uncertain one," I admitted.

I was felt stronger now, and tried again to pull myself up with the armrests, this time managing to sit all the way forward. The back of the chair tilted upright in response, and the footrest dropped slightly before disappearing into the base.

I tried squinting to improve my vision, but soon realized that there was nothing wrong with my sight. I just no longer enjoyed the heightened Brenin senses I'd grown accustomed to. Compared to how I'd seen before, my normal vision was like looking through murky water.

And I was perfectly fine with that.

I noticed that I was in the same chair where I'd awoken after being transferred into Seeris' body, and then saw him lying dead still on a table next to me. Uli was standing beside her brother, meticulously inching a diagnostic scanner over his entire length. I watched as she reset the device and started scanning his head.

"Is he going to live?" I asked.

"Yes, but no thanks to these backward monks. If I hadn't been here when they removed that wretched machine of theirs he would have certainly died."

"That *is* why we brought you with us from Obas," Dyson replied, ignoring Uli's insults. He shut down the console and walked over to join us.

"I never did ask you how you managed that," I said to Dyson. "Certainly Eraz wanted to keep her for questioning...and study."

"Barbarians." Uli spat out the familiar refrain.

"Oh, they want her alright," Dyson said. "They want you as well. In fact, they want *all* of you. There is an Udek warship in low orbit now, waiting to take you all back to the Confederation."

"I'm not going back," I replied, then hopped off the chair to search the room for a suitable weapon and expedient exit.

Dyson read my intent and held his arms out straight in front of me. "Please...calm down, Tien. You're not going with the Udek. No one is. I keep my bargains." When he was confident that I'd relaxed somewhat, he strode over to the wall and hit a com switch. "Please locate Master Pilot Boe and send him to the lab."

*"At once, Brother Dyson,"* a voice replied.

*Boe?* He wasn't on the trip with us back to Bodhi Prime.

Seeris stirred next to me and started coughing, then he sat up and his eyes darted around the room. Uli helped him as he rose to stand next to the table. It was strange to watch that body move from the outside—see it become animate without my input or direction. It was almost as if the Brenin were still me, and now I was trapped inside *this* strange body.

After assessing his new environment and figuring out what had happened, his eyes came to rest on me. "I should kill you for what you've done to the Yano, Udek."

"You are welcome to try, Seeris," I answered defiantly, and then guided Dasi behind me to protect her.

But instead of attacking, the Brenin leaned back against the table to steady himself and looked at Uli. "You saved my sister, Tien. For that reason alone, I'll let you live."

I allowed his empty bravado to pass unchallenged. He was weak, and still injured. There was no doubt in my mind that I could kill him. But the ability to kill, and the desire to do so, must join together to take a life. And those two aspects of my nature resided far apart in me now.

I turned to Dyson. "I'm surprised to find myself in my own body, monk. I expected to wake up in some cyborg, preparing to make amends for all of my many sins."

"You have suffered enough, Tien." Dyson flashed a sympathetic smile and gestured at Dasi. "You both have."

The door opened and Boe walked into the laboratory. He looked at Seeris first, and then me. A confused expression spread across his face and he turned to Brother Dyson for help. The old monk smiled and pointed in my direction, and then the Obas approached us, acknowledging Dasi with a nod before speaking to me.

"Tien?"

"Yes, Boe. It's me." I noticed that he was trying very hard to ignore the pair of Brenin beside us. He was clearly uncomfortable with the transference process, and even though he *knew* I was an Udek, it still must have come as a shock to see me as one.

"How do you *feel*?"

"I'm fine," I replied. "What are you doing here?"

"I was sent by Speaker Lews with a proposition for you."

"A proposition? What *kind* of proposition?"

"One that we need to discuss in private." He tilted his head in the direction of Seeris and Uli.

"Like a frightened child," Seeris laughed. "You needn't worry about us, little Obas. I could care less about your secrets. Barring any treachery or broken promises from the Bodhi or this Udek, my sister and I are returning to Bren. Assuming we can find a ship, of course."

"We have one," Uli said. "Brother Dyson has agreed to provide us with a fast transport, as recompense for my help with the surgery to remove that chamber from your body. But I sense he also has another agenda, one that he *isn't* sharing."

"No doubt," Seeris agreed. "But as I said, Obas, we are leaving."

Boe seemed unsatisfied. "Why don't we step outside, Tien? As a precaution?"

"The Obas and their *precautions*," I replied. Then I glanced over at Seeris. "But in this case, I agree."

Dasi and I followed Boe out to the hallway and the Obas closed the door behind us. But instead of stopping there, he motioned for us to keep moving—until we passed through a pair of doors at the end of the long corridor and stepped outside the building. My eyes struggled to adapt to the bright sunlight as we walked away from the large structure and the shade it provided.

We finally came to a halt in an open courtyard and Boe

explained our curious exodus. “With their improved senses, I wanted to get *much* farther away.” He looked around to make sure we were alone before continuing. Apparently, he didn’t trust the Bodhi either.

“The Assembly would like to hire you as a military advisor, Tien. Not many of our ships remain, but we intend to rebuild the fleet—even larger and stronger this time. And we could use your expertise to do it. Although our engineers are excellent, and we have virtually unlimited resources, our experience with war has been limited to recent events. We would greatly value your input, on both ship design and military tactics.”

Boe glanced around the courtyard again and then looked down to avoid my eyes—unmistakably nervous about his next words. “To be honest, Tien, we know you have nowhere else to go.” He raised his head and I saw the determination on his face, a surety of strength that I’d never before associated with his race. “The Obas can protect you,” he said. “And you can help *us* be strong. We’ve learned our lesson; we *will* be participating in galactic affairs in the future. In fact, we intend to become a force in the galaxy...one to be reckoned with. We understand now that it’s the best way to protect ourselves. It will take time, and a great deal of adjustment, but we are ready to look beyond Obas.”

“What is he talking about, Tien.” Dasi was confused by Boe’s proposal, but I was merely surprised...and intrigued.

“He’s offering me a job, Dasi.” I pointed at my mask. “And what about this? We would have to spend the rest of our lives in respirators.”

“No! No,” Boe said excitedly. “We’ve already considered that. Our engineers are converting a large, private chamber into a methane-mixture environment on its own closed system—complete with a pool leading out to the ocean. We will arrange it however you like.”

“A beach around the pool would be nice,” I replied. “Along

with some Udek sized diving suits."

"Done. You will also have full access to our cities, of course. And the surface as well. Everything that Obas has to offer."

Dasi was even more bewildered now. "Tien. Will you *please* tell me what's going on?"

"We are going swimming," I said. Boe grinned at my reply and the answer it implied.

"Swimming?" she asked, now completely exasperated.

I smiled and took her hands in my own. "Don't worry, Dasi. I'm sure you will approve."

# CHAPTER THIRTY-TWO

The next day, I walked out onto the tarmac with Seeris and Uli. Dasi and Boe had remained behind to prepare for our departure, while Brother Dyson joined me in escorting the Brenin to their ship. I'd explained to everyone that I wanted a few words in private with the Brenin before they left. Thankfully, no one questioned why.

Because there was still one secret I needed to keep.

As we approached the vessel, Brother Dyson came to a halt, staying behind to afford me some privacy. Uli looked back at the monk curiously before walking up the short ramp to go inside the ship—leaving me alone on the landing pad with Seeris. He started to speak, but I cut him off before he got the chance. "Despite my current status—outside the Udek ranks as it were—I've managed to access a few classified intelligence reports. The Saba have attacked the Yano, and the other, smaller factions are already choosing sides for the coming clan war. The march against us continues, but there are now violent cracks in the Brenin unity."

Seeris took a few steps up the ramp, and then turned to me with an amused look on his face. "We will still prevail, Udek. Our fleet at its worse is still more than enough to dispose of whatever coalition you *children* manage to assemble. Our shielding—"

"Will prove useless, Seeris. The Obas collected an enormous amount of data during the battle, and have already developed a way to detect the primary...using their own technology." I shook my head and grinned. "You were right about my casual dismissal of them; I was being arrogant—but no longer. The Brenin will find out how wrong *they* were too, in underestimating all of us. I'll admit that the battles ahead will be difficult, but in time, between the Brenin infighting, our new alliances, and the ability to disrupt your shield, we will defeat you. And even if you do find a way to eliminate the shield's vulnerability, we will devise another way around it...again and again. We have no choice."

Seeris wasn't swayed by my predictions in the least. "You will *never* win. We will—"

"You will lose, Seeris," I stated flatly. "And one other thing, I *know* where Bren is. I saw it in the ancient dream. Your ancestor looked up at the sky several times, and I recognized the Mujen Nebulae and Kolis Expanse. I studied my view of them in-depth, gauging approximately where I'd have to be in the galaxy to observe them from that position. They filled the sky, so I knew that Bren was close. The Obas provided me with a dataslate, and I used a stellar cartography program from their library to determine which systems were proximate to that area. Then I searched for a planet that met the detailed description that *you* provided me with during our incarceration...and I found it."

"Impossible!" he snapped. "I don't remember that."

It was after your synapses had almost fully degraded—when you disappeared, and my mind was mine alone."

Seeris realized that I was telling the truth and his face blanked; his demeanor changing completely as the innate Brenin arrogance evaporated, replaced by unprecedented sensations of self-doubt and uncertainty.

"My people believe in vengeance," I told him. "They crave it, Seeris. And they will not stop until every last one of you are dead, even *after* this war is over."

"You told them where Bren is?" He breathed.

"No," I replied truthfully. "I told them everything else...but not that. You see, Seeris, we *will* win this war. And when it's over, there will be a reckoning. We are freeing you for a single reason—it's why Dyson gave you this ship in the first place. We want you to return to your planet and do everything you can to keep the Brenin from coming this way again. Because if they do, I will tell *every* race where your home system is."

He stared at my face as I spoke, his eyes glazed over in disbelief.

"Then we will invade *your* world, Seeris. And burn your trees to the ground."

For the first time, Seeris actually looked afraid. And it was clearly an emotion he had no familiarity with. He spun around without saying another word, walking the rest of the way up the ramp and into the ship. And as the door slid closed behind him, I heard the engines start to power up. But despite his hasty and silent departure, I knew he got the message.

I backed away from the vessel and rejoined Brother Dyson— still waiting patiently on the periphery of the landing pad— then we began our stroll back to the Bodhi complex. "A productive conversation?" he asked.

"I believe so. But I'm going to entrust you with some sensitive information as insurance—to use in the future if it becomes necessary."

"Ah... So you actually trust me now, Tien?"

"No, monk. But I trust myself even less."

We turned to watch as the ship rose into the air, hurriedly speeding off through the sunlit sky of Bodhi Prime. I knew that it would slip unnoticed past the waiting Udek warship, just as our departure would on the Boe's ship later that day. They weren't expecting us to flee, and there would be hell to pay when they found out. As the burst shuttle finally disappeared from view, Dyson and I resumed our walk to the building where Boe and Dasi waited.

"How will you explain our disappearance?" I asked the monk.

"I haven't decided yet. Transference mishap perhaps...it *was* a complicated procedure. But I've been dealing with the Udek for quite a while now, I'm sure I'll think of something."

"Oh, I'm sure you will," I replied. "You know, Brother Dyson, you are not at all what I expected a Bodhi Monk to be like."

"Truthfully, Tien, I never expected to walk this crooked path myself. But the ancient texts are sadly lacking in ways to deal with modern problems. I often find myself making some very difficult choices. At times, even desperate ones..."

There was a deep, melancholy timbre to his voice, revealing that I wasn't the only one haunted by my actions in the past. But something told me that Brother Dyson's ghosts would linger far longer than my own. The august monk was being forced to change—circumstances and situations beyond his control, conspiring to shape him into someone new.

*Very much like myself,* I realized.

As a result of this whole experience, I'd been changed as well. My drive for violence, that part of my psyche that made murder acceptable—commonplace even—that part of me was gone. I *was* someone new, and I would never kill again.

Not willingly anyway.

I stopped abruptly and turned to face Dyson, finding the old monk still struggling with his own thoughts. "At the beginning of this madness, you asked me why I let that boy live. Why I hadn't killed him like all of the others."

"I remember," he replied.

I sucked a deep breath in through my respirator and collected my thoughts, confirming my own understanding of what transpired that night before sharing it with the monk—reliving the memory as if it were only yesterday.

"I'd successfully infiltrated the compound," I began. "Easily making my way past the numerous guards undetected. I followed my pre-planned route precisely, evading the continuous patrols—dodging from structure to structure until I reached the boy's location at the main house. When it was safe, I climbed up the side of a building opposite his bedroom window and set up a killing perch on the roof. And then I waited...silent and still. Finally, two hours later, I watched through my rifle sight as he came out of the bathroom and pulled the covers back on his bed."

Dyson's eyes bade me to continue as I paused to remember the moment, recalling the thing I saw that night that changed the entire path of my life—the harmless little object that had brought down so much death and destruction, just by its presence in that room.

It was a small toy.

"When the boy pulled the sheet back," I continued, "a stuffed animal flew out and bounced across the floor, landing right in front of the window. He ran over to pick it up, then paused with his prize, looking through the glass at the courtyard below. As he stood there, I saw the toy clearly through the scope. It was a Kisiba, a blue one."

The monk's expression told me he had no idea what I was talking about so I explained. "It's a small creature from my home world, very dangerous actually, but toys in its likeness are popular with Udek children. I know this because I'd bought one just before leaving on that last mission; it was blue as well. A present, for my unborn son."

Dyson seemed unfazed by the revelation, but what are children to a monk? Did they mean anything to the Bodhi beyond the life force they represented?

*Probably not.*

"Dasi didn't know that she was pregnant," I told him. "But we Udek males can tell. We are always the first to know. I was going to surprise her with the good news and the Kisiba when I returned home."

"I understand what happened to you now," the old monk said knowingly. "You saw your own son in that child at the window."

"Yes," I hissed, angry that my weakness had been revealed. *No...* Not weakness. I was convinced that my newfound morality might one day prove to be my greatest strength. But right now, it felt like a badge of abject failure. There was still a large part of me that defined itself by my successes as an assassin.

"I had the shot, monk...more than once. But I let each opportunity pass. Instead of pulling the trigger, I watched the child get into bed and pull the covers up to his chin, then I turned off the scope and lowered my rifle. I just couldn't do it...not anymore. I imagined another Special Corp assassin, like myself, waiting outside *my* son's window in the future—a soulless murderer, sent to kill my child for something *I'd* done."

The memories came even faster now as I detailed my next actions. "I quickly packed up everything and rappelled down the side of the building—retracing my steps back out of the compound and abandoning the mission. I headed straight for the starport, then left the planet to make my way home.

But Special Corp found out about my betrayal almost as soon as I'd committed it. I should have known; gathering information is what we...what *they* do. The Corp had already taken Dasi away by the time I got there, and then killed them both on Nilot. My wife and my son."

I started walking again to break the growing melancholy,

and Dyson fell into step beside me. "At least I have Dasi back."

He reached up and placed his hand on my shoulder and I resisted the urge to pull away. "You have more than that, Tien. The records they sent from Nilot were quite complete," he said approvingly. "And *surprisingly* complex."

"What are you saying, monk?"

"That your son is *alive*, Tien. Restored...inside Dasi, just as he was."

"What?" I exclaimed. "But how?"

"Well, our reputation *is* justified," he smiled.

*My son...is alive.*

"I...I don't know how to thank you, Brother Dyson."

"There is no need to thank me, Tien. Life is its own reward. Besides, you are no longer the man you were; you will be an excellent father. A man your son can be proud of."

Yes. *I will.*

This whole experience *had* changed me. Being in Seeris' body and living among aliens, even for such a short time, had fundamentally altered the way I viewed other races. And the events aboard Captain Queltz's ship *forever* changed how I saw the Udek.

And my former self.

I couldn't help but smile. The Bodhi had managed to impose their will on me whether they'd intended to or not; I *did* regret my sins. And General Queltz *had* been right about that, there were many to atone for. But now, as unlikely as it was, I'd found some measure of redemption, and I was enjoying the growing solace it provided.

On the horizon, I saw Boe's ship perched atop a small landing pad, the vehicle that would take me to my new life. Soon, Dasi and I would leave for that tranquil sanctuary, a place where I would teach the Obas how to thrive in this violent galaxy—even as I myself withdrew from it. On Obas, we would build a peaceful life together for our son. The three of us would be happy, and I would never look back.

Unless they came for me.

I knew that Special Corp would be preoccupied with the war now, but later, they might send someone to tie up loose ends—to remove me as a potential threat...and to protect their secrets.

In which case they would find me ready: A seasoned killer, ever training, never letting my skills wane. An accomplished assassin with no compulsion to kill, but every ability to do so if it became necessary.

An instrument of death...best left alone.

In peace.

# ABOUT THE AUTHOR

Gregg Vann is a writer, teacher, polyglot, and perennial student. He has a ME.d in Teaching English as a Second Language, and a BA in Asian Studies. When not writing, he can usually be found on the sunny beaches of Florida.

Please visit Greggvann.com to discover other books and sign up for the author's mailing list.

Printed in Great Britain
by Amazon.co.uk, Ltd.,
Marston Gate.